HE/

*Forever Yours*

# HEARTBEAT
## *Forever Yours*

## David Martin

This first hardcover edition published in Great Britain 1996 by
SEVERN HOUSE PUBLISHERS LTD of
9-15 High Street, Sutton, Surrey SM1 1DF.
by arrangement with Reed Consumer Books Ltd.

British Library Cataloguing in Publication Data

Martin, David
    Forever yours. – (Heartbeat)
    1. English fiction – 20th century
    I. Title
    823.9'14 [F]

    ISBN 0-7278-4947-6

All the characters and events described in this story are entirely
imaginary: any resemblance to real people, living or dead, or
happenings present or past is coincidental.

Typeset by Hewer Text Composition Services, Edinburgh.
Printed and bound in Great Britain by
Hartnolls Ltd, Bodmin, Cornwall.

# One

Nick took Kate's breakfast carefully up the narrow stairs of Aidensfield Police House. When the baby came, and started to crawl round their small grey-stone cottage, he'd have to put one of those little wooden gates top and bottom. It was amazing, he reflected, how many things, big and small, were going to have to change.

Reminding himself to look out for some suitable wood, planed and even-grained, he paused on the landing and glanced through the small square panes into the garden, wondering whether there would be enough room for one of those new whirly aluminium clothes driers.

The pale winter sun had carved a line across the frost so that half the small patch was dark green and glistening while the rest was still a whitened mass, with the stiff hoar-frosted snowdrop leaves sticking up here and there in the borders like miniature explosions.

Daffodils, he thought, a couple of vases of daffodils would be nice, one upstairs, one down; give Kate something to look at, remind her that spring was on the way. Spring, and a new baby. Neither could be that far off. A day, a week, a couple of weeks at most. He found himself smiling idiotically to himself, and wondered if all prospective fathers went a little bit

1

soft in the head. It had certainly affected his concentration – not when he was on the job, dealing with people face to face, but when he was on the bike or making out report-sheets, he'd suddenly find himself miles away, thinking about all sorts of things: prams, babies' names, what he or she would look like, how Kate would be.

He made a mental note to have a scout round Ashfordly Market and see what flowers were about. Even chrysanths, russet and lemon and gold, would brighten the place up.

Holding on to the blue-and-white striped eggcup to stop it wobbling, Nick shoved the bedroom door open with his elbow.

Kate was lying on her side, pale and tired, her blonde hair lank. Automatically, he brightened his grin. 'Here we are, love. Four triangles of Hovis, one four-and-a-half-minute egg, one mug of steaming hot tea, half Earl Grey, half Typhoo – just what the doctor ordered.'

'Rub my back, would you, Nick?' Her voice sounded flat and irritable.

'Certainly, madam.' Nick set the tray down on the bedside table and gently coshed the top of the egg with the teaspoon to stop it hardening. 'Nothing I'd like more.'

'Do you have to be so damn cheerful?'

'Why not? It's a nice morning – '

'Only stupid people are cheerful in the morning.'

'Can't all be the brains of the family, can we?' Nick drew the curtains open. 'You sleep all right?'

'No, since you ask,' said Kate, relenting. 'You did, though. Like a log.'

'The sleep of the just, love.' He sat on the edge of the bed and slid his hand gently up Kate's morning-warm flank and into the small of her back. 'There?'

'Mmm.' Nick moved his hand in small circular motions over her smooth skin, feeling the muscles grow warm and relaxed under his fingers. He watched the steam rising from the blue and white mug into the cold morning air.

'Ohh, that's better,' said Kate. 'I must have got stuck in one position.'

'I reckon I'm getting quite good at this,' said Nick. He bent over and kissed the damp tendrils of hair at the back of her neck. 'It must be love.'

Kate smiled sleepily, took hold of his other hand and cupped it round her breast. 'I know exactly what it is.' She turned her face up to his. 'And if that's all you ever think about – '

'You're a fine one to talk, Kate Rowan.'

'You'll have to wait – '

Their lips met, kissed softly and parted. 'I love you, Kate.'

'I love you, Nick.'

He stretched out along the edge of the bed. They gazed at each other and warm, calm love flowed between them. 'Don't tell anybody,' he whispered against her throat, 'but I never thought it was this easy – '

'What?' said Kate. 'What's easy?'

'To be with somebody. Be happy with somebody.'

'All right for some,' said Kate, pulling a face. 'You're quite soft really, aren't you? For a copper.'

He grinned back at her. 'I can't be hard all the time.'

She raised her eyebrows, sighed, and rolled over on to her stomach. 'Now do my buttocks.'

'My pleasure, ma'am.' He sat up and lifted the covers back. 'You sure you're not squashing it, lying like that?'

'It's not an it,' said Kate. 'It's a her.'

'Or a him.'

'A her,' said Kate firmly. 'We mothers know such things. Now do my buttocks. Please – '

He saw it as soon as he pulled her nightie up to her waist. 'What the hell's this, Kate?'

'It's a bottom.'

'No, no, no. You've got a bloody great bruise here – '

'Where?'

'Here.' He circled the edge of a livid green and purple circle on the upper part of her right buttock. 'It's huge. Looks as if you've been kicked by a donkey. You haven't fallen out of bed or anything, done something stupid and not told me?'

Kate did not reply at first. He watched her lying there, face moving into the pillow away from him, her gaze turning inward.

'I'm sorry love,' he said. 'I wasn't getting at you – just worried, that's all.'

She turned to face him again, fixing a smile on her face. 'It's all right, love, it's nothing – '

'It doesn't look like nothing, Kate.'

'It's the injection, that's all.'

'What injection?'

'The one Maggie gave me – '

'What did she use? A pneumatic drill?'

'It doesn't hurt, love,' said Kate. 'It's just that some

4

of us are tender little flowers, and bruise more easily than others.'

Nick cocked his head on one side. 'And that's it, is it? That's all there is to it?'

'It's once a copper, always a copper with you, isn't it?'

'I'm only asking, love.'

'Nick, I am a doctor – '

'Yeah,' said Nick, 'and nurses make the worst patients.'

Kate ignored him. 'All sorts of things happen in pregnancy besides getting bigger and bigger and bigger. There are all sorts of whole-body changes. It's not just eating coal and having backache and going into hospital. Some women get swollen ankles, some get a touch of anaemia, some bruise more easily . . .' Kate paused to get her breath. 'And some women get depressed when their husbands start treating them like suspects.'

'But you have had a touch of anaemia, Kate,' insisted Nick.

'And I've had iron injections for it,' said Kate. 'I might have to have more, I don't know.' She pulled herself up in bed. 'There's nothing to worry about, love.'

Nick passed her the tray. 'Honest?'

'Honest.' Kate cut the top off the egg and dipped a triangle of toast in it.

'How is it?'

'Perfect,' she said.

Nick took the Francis-Barnett up over the moor. There were still pockets of snow among the shaggy

5

russet bracken, and the air was as keen as a knife. But the sun was shining, the sky was a hard pale blue, and Nick, thinking of the commuters coughing their way into Waterloo, felt glad to be alive.

Five years now he'd been the local bobby in Aidensfield, and on mornings like this, swooping along the narrow empty moorland roads with nothing but the hills and crags and the occasional hooded crow for company, he knew he'd made the best decision of his life when he and Kate decided to leave London and head north.

Well, the second-best decision: the first had been marrying Kate. Not that it had been easy, but then, nothing worthwhile ever was. There were the hours they both worked for a start, with Kate in big London teaching hospitals and him on various beats and divisions north and south of the river. Often for days on end they only met in the hall, one coming in as the other went out, and Kate complaining they had slept together more often before they married than they had since. Some nights the only conversation they had was 'Can't stop, I've left a note.' Kate was a great one for leaving notes in those days – still was, in fact.

But the really big problem was the fact that as a junior doctor she earned a lot more than he did as a copper on the beat. A hell of a lot more. She still did, come to that. But up here, in the North Yorks moors, it didn't seem to matter so much: both had roughly similar positions in the community, and both had found it equally difficult being accepted, Nick because he was what the locals tended to call 'a bloody Southerner' and Kate because she was 'a lady doctor'.

Nick reflected that even after five years they still hadn't quite cracked that one. Maybe they never would – the locals were certainly a dour lot, some of them, especially the old hill farmers who regarded the moors and dales as theirs to do what they liked with and even a copper was just another trespasser. But by and large, it was working out pretty well . . .

Come off it, Nick Rowan, he told himself. You and Kate both know the money thing is still there, baby or no baby. And it's going to stay there, no matter how many children you have, unless you do something about it. Such as getting your finger out and going in for some serious promotion –

The problem was, promotion meant cities, not quiet rural backwaters like Aidensfield. And cities meant Kate would almost certainly go back into hospital work, and then where would they be? Back where they started.

His mind drifted back to the day of their arrival. Kate's Triumph Herald, laden to the roofrack, rolling down into the peaceful greystone village of Aidensfield – and immediately being buzzed by a couple of local bikers. He smiled to himself, remembering the look on their faces when he got out of the car in civvies, produced his warrant card and told them he was the new copper on the beat.

Yes, well, he thought, there would always be bikers and tearaways. He'd been a bit of a tearaway himself before he joined the Met. Now look at you, Rowan – a respectable member of the community, married and about to become a father . . .

What was it Sergeant Blaketon had said when Nick had told him the good news? 'The pram in the hall, Rowan. That's when you know you're married. You can forget the confetti and the cuddles. It's the pram in the hall that counts.'

There was a flurry in the moorland off to his left and a crow and a harrier rose screeching and fluttering out of the ground. Nick slowed, glanced at his watch. Ten-past eight. He was due in at Ashfordly station at half-past.

He propped the bike and crashed his way through the wind-flattened bracken. The two birds screeched and cawed above him, wheeling in circles, determined not to leave the spot.

Then he saw the reason. One of the moorland ewes had died in the night, and the birds had found it.

Nick turned back to his bike. He'd ring Ron Laidlaw, the farmer who ran his sheep on this part of the moor, and that would be that. There was nothing else to do but let nature finish it off; up here, on the open moor, life and death were never more than a heartbeat away from each other. He drove slowly down through the dark and still frosted pine plantations of the Whitly estate and arrived at Ashfordly station in a sober and reflective frame of mind.

'What's all this, Rowan?' Sergeant Oscar Blaketon, an immaculately uniformed man in his fifties with a lined and serious face, stood in the doorway of his office watching Nick take off his black leather gauntlets and hang up his greatcoat.

'What's all what, sarge?'

'You're early, that's what,' said Blaketon, eyeing

8

Nick suspiciously. 'It's a departure from the norm. Departures from the norm are significant and warrant investigation.'

'Sorry, sarge,' grinned Nick. 'It won't happen again.'

Blaketon's pale grey eyes narrowed. 'You're not getting keen, are you, Rowan?' He paced self-importantly forward to the edge of Nick's desk. 'Not getting keen after all these years, are we? Not thinking of getting our finger out at last and chasing up a bit of promotion now we've got a nipper on the way? Well, are we, Rowan?'

Underneath the bluster, thought Nick, old Blaketon was as sharp as a tack. He looked up at Blaketon with his guileless little-boy smile. 'I don't know what you mean, sergeant.'

'No need to look like that, Rowan. It might work on old ladies, but not on me. Understand?'

'Yes, sarge.'

Blaketon strode round to the other side of Nick's desk without taking his eyes off him. 'Dr Rowan all right, is she?'

'Fine, thanks, yes.'

'No . . . complications?'

Nick bent down to open a drawer and take out a file. 'Not really, no, not so far.'

'I see,' said Blaketon, sensing that Nick did not want to pursue the matter. 'Well, that's all to the good. And do we have any clear idea of when this young Rowan is about to make his or her entry into this world of ours?'

'Any day now, sarge. But it could be any time during the next two weeks.'

9

'Splendid.' Blaketon placed his big hands firmly on Nick's desk and leaned forward, his voice serious. 'You do realise, I hope, that if it is a boy, he'll be qualified to play for Yorkshire?'

'I thought of putting him down for West Ham, sarge.'

'West Ham?' exploded Blaketon. 'West Ham!'

'It's a football team, sergeant – '

'Apology for one, more like,' said Blaketon, drawing himself up to his full height. 'Now then, why the early bird?'

Nick picked up the file. 'It's this hop at Aidensfield village hall. I thought I'd get the paperwork cleared up before I started the rest of the day – '

'Highly commendable,' said Blaketon sourly. 'Who've you got down for it?'

'Just me and Bellamy, Sergeant. There shouldn't be any trouble this time of year. It's only the locals – they're mostly skint – and there's no drinks licence involved.'

'I see. Dansette and records job is it?'

'Well, not exactly,' said Nick. 'The Ashfordly Rebels are playing.'

'And who are the Ashfordly Rebels when they're about?'

'They're a Who-type group, sarge.'

Blaketon nodded and sucked his teeth. 'It may surprise you to know, Rowan, that I have heard of the Who. I have even seen them on my television.'

'I didn't know you watched *Top of the Pops*, sergeant.'

'Not from choice,' said Blaketon. 'Not from choice. They're the young maniacs who go round

10

smashing up valuable musical instruments, are they not?'

'They have been known to, sergeant, yes – '

'I don't want to hear of anything being smashed up in Aidensfield, Who or no Who.'

'Don't worry, sarge. We'll be there.'

'You'd better be.' Blaketon shook his head sorrowfully. 'Modern youth. I don't understand it and I don't much like it.' He turned round in the doorway of his office. 'On your head be it, Rowan. Any trouble, and on your head be it.'

# Two

Although it was only just after nine the centre of the floor was packed with young Mods bopping away to the Rebels' frantic assault on 'My Generation'. One or two older couples were attempting a more sedate fifties-style jive around the edges. Nick stood at the back of the hall with Kate and Bellamy, watching the Mods: the boys in their boxy suits with their stiff little arm movements trying to look cool, the girls with their noses in the air, twisting and spinning, their short skirts flying.

He leaned close to Kate's ear. 'Fancy a quick bop then, love?'

'Not unless you want me to give birth on the floor,' said Kate.

'You were the one who wanted to come, Kate.'

'I can't sit at home every night,' said Kate. 'I'm not a seed pod waiting to pop. Besides, I thought this might wake things up a bit.'

'It's certainly loud enough,' said Nick. 'You sure you're all right?'

Kate patted her stomach. 'We're quite happy just listening, thank you.'

'I'll have a stroll round then.'

'Fine,' said Kate. 'Oh, you couldn't get me a packet of crisps and a Vimto, could you?'

'Crisps and a Vimto?' echoed Nick.

'We do have these occasional cravings, you know.'

'Right,' said Nick. 'Phil – '

'What?' Bellamy, a boyishly good-looking, auburn-haired lad in his twenties, was leaning forward like a pointer, his eyes moving hungrily from one mini-skirted figure to another.

'I know you're off-duty but if you can bear to take your eyes off the talent for a minute – '

'What? Oh right,' said Bellamy, coming out of his trance.

'I'm going to take a stroll,' said Nick. 'Keep an eye on Kate for me, will you? I don't want anybody barging into her.'

'Fine,' said Bellamy, eyes straight back on the mini-skirts.

Nick moved into the lobby. The admission table was manned by two older teenagers, Julie Stanton and Ollie Renshaw. Julie was the only daughter of Walter Stanton, a well-to-do jeweller and chairman of the parish council, and Ollie was her not-so-well-to-do boyfriend.

Just in front of them was a refreshment stall, presided over by the lumbering figure of Greengrass in his army greatcoat, battered trilby and red neckerchief. As Nick strolled over to look at the assortment of crisps, Wagon Wheels and dusty-looking bottles of soft drinks, Gina Ward, the pretty, eye-linered Liverpool barmaid from the Aidensfield Arms, came bouncing up to him in a tight white sweater and check miniskirt.

'Thanks, Mr Rowan,' she said, her skin glowing from her exertions on the dance floor.

'What for, Gina?'

'Oh, come on,' she replied. 'I don't think the parish council would have let kids like us have the hall if you hadn't put a good word in for us.'

'Well,' said Nick, 'it all looks to be going well so far.'

'Wheels on fire,' said Gina.

'That's what worries me,' grinned Nick, taking her arm and moving her away from the others. 'Look, Gina, you work in the pub – '

'I know I do – '

'So if you see anybody who you think might have had one or two, or who's bringing bottles in, just tip me the wink, will you?'

'Right, Mr Rowan,' said Gina.

'Because if there's any trouble,' said Nick, 'I'm the one that gets it in the neck.'

'Don't worry,' said Gina, 'there won't be.'

A couple of miles away in the upstairs main bedroom of the Sutcliffes' isolated cottage on the outskirts of Aidensfield, District Nurse Maggie Bolton had just finished weighing the latest addition to the Sutcliffe family. Maggie, an attractive woman in her mid-thirties with clear grey eyes and a determined chin, entered the birth weight on her chart, slipped off her apron, smoothed down her blue uniform, and set her cap straight on her light brown hair. The mother, Mary Sutcliffe, lay back pale and exhausted on the pillows, watching Maggie briskly soothe and clothe the naked squalling boy.

'I don't know how you keep going, Maggie, I really don't.'

'You did all the work, Mary,' said Maggie. 'But I

know what you mean. We shall both sleep well tonight.' It had been a long labour for a third child, sixteen hours in all, and not without its difficulties.

'Maggie,' said Mary. 'I'm sorry I said what I did.' During the final agonising moments, with Maggie encouraging her to push and push and push again, Mary had cried out in pain that it was all right for Maggie, she'd never had a child.

'Don't worry, Mary.' Maggie wrapped the baby boy in his flannelette sheet and crocheted shawl. 'People shout out all sorts of things. I've had a lot worse than that said to me, I can tell you.'

'I didn't mean it, Maggie.'

'I know you didn't, love,' said Maggie with a smile. 'Anyway, you know what they say, marry in haste, repent at leisure.' During intervals in the long labour, the two women had talked to one another, and exchanged confidences. Both had married young, but Maggie, who had a strong independent streak in her character, had decided, after a few months of sitting at home, to go back to her career in nursing. After that, as she told Mary, she and her husband had just drifted apart. 'He was my first boyfriend, you see, Mary. We were too young, that's all.' Then she had added with a grin and a toss of her head. 'Mind you, I've made up for it since!'

As she passed the newborn child into his mother's arms, Maggie caught sight of the bedroom door opening, and two small faces appearing: Mary's other two sons, for once strangely quiet and overawed. 'Here you are, Mary. Weighed in at nine pound seven ounces. Built like a truck, he is.' She smiled at the boys standing uncertainly in the doorway. 'Took his time, didn't he? Your chubby little brother. Come on then, come and say hallo to him, and I'll tell your dad he can come up – '

A few minutes later Maggie was driving her Land Rover through freezing drizzle back to Aidensfield. As usual after a birth, she felt a light, heady mixture of exhaustion and elation. Now that Mary Sutcliffe was safely delivered, Kate Rowan was next on the list.

She fell to thinking about Kate, how she would probably react. It was always difficult to tell with a first pregnancy, even though Kate was a doctor and had delivered children herself. Things had proceeded more or less according to plan so far – but only more or less . . .

Maggie went over the indications. Kate's blood pressure was fine; the anaemia seemed to be coming under control, although it looked as if the iron injections would have to continue until she had another blood test; Kate's end-of-pregnancy exhaustion, back pain and swollen ankles were normal enough – but there was something else, some other cause for concern Maggie couldn't quite put her finger on. Maybe it was because Kate was a doctor: like all the doctors Maggie had ever worked with, there was still an edge of 'Doctor Knows Best' with Kate. Perhaps that was all it was, thought Maggie, a touch of professional rivalry, Kate keeping things back, doing a bit of self-diagnosis. Some first mothers were like that, part apprehension, part possessiveness – a whose-baby-is-it-anyway sort of thing . . .

Twin headlamps blazed up in her rear-view mirrors, dazzling her. For a second she thought some

16

lunatic in a car was bearing down on her, about to crash into her –

She braked and pulled over, nearside wheels thudding into the verge; then, miraculously, the headlamps separated and swerved round her. With a prolonged and terrifying roar, a dozen or so motorbikes slammed past. She caught a glimpse of pale faces and black leather, and a girl pillion-rider holding up two fingers at her and laughing –

'You bloody lunatics!' screamed Maggie, fighting to get the Land Rover back on to the crown of the narrow slippery road. 'You stupid bloody fools!

Roger Wellins sat astride his BSA Gold Star outside Aidensfield village hall, waiting for the rest of the gang to catch up. A pale, greasy-haired youth in his early twenties, Roger had already had three or four pints in Whitby, and as soon he and his Rocker mates had shown these poncy little Mods what for, he fully intended to have three or four more. Yeah, he thought, hauling his bike back on to its stand, let's make a night of it –

The other bikes drew up round him, throttles blipping and revving. He swaggered over to where a clutch of Vespa and Lambretta scooters were parked next to Greengrass's dark red truck.

'Hey up!' he shouted to the others, swinging his leg back and viciously putting his steel-shod boot into a Vespa engine cover. 'The Noddy mob's here – toy bikes, an' all!'

Maggie could hear the music halfway down the street. As she drew up by the village hall, she saw the posse of motorbikes and heard the Rockers

17

shouting and jeering. She parked well away from them, jumped out, checked all the locks on her car, and hurried into the hall.

The pretty blonde girl singer was belting out 'You Keep Me Hanging On' and the Rebels were backing her at full volume. It was impossible to hear yourself speak. Nick tapped Kate on the shoulder, passed her a packet of Greengrass's crisps and opened one himself. The crisps had a stale musty odour.

'What d'you think, Kate?'

'They taste a bit damp – there's a sort of smoky smell to them,' said Kate.

'I'll be back in a minute,' said Nick.

Greengrass had his back to him. Good. Nick liked to catch the cunning old blighter off guard, and watch his eyes blinking furiously as he wondered what he been caught out at this time.

'Hey up, Claude.'

'What the – ' Greengrass turned round, hastily stuffing a hip-flask into his pocket. 'Oh, it's you Mr Ronan.'

'Rowan,' said Nick automatically.

'Aye, aye, well, I'm no good on names, but I never forget a face, me.'

'What'd you do, go down the fire sale?'

Greengrass's eyes twitched again. 'What you talking about? What fire sale?'

'These crisps,' said Nick.

'You what?'

Nick held out the opened bag. 'These crisps I bought off your stall.'

He watched Greengrass start to bluster. 'Them

crisps – them crisps were fresh made the day I bought them!'

Nick pulled a soggy crisp out of the packet. 'They're uneatable.'

'You must have spilled summat on 'em.'

'Get rid of them, Claude.'

'Nick!' It was Maggie, hurrying through the entrance door. 'A gang of Rockers have just arrived. They practically ran me off the road. They look like trouble – '

'Right, I'll have a word.' Nick moved to Julie and Ollie at the admission table. 'Were you expecting anyone?'

Julie and Ollie looked at each other and shook their heads. There was something furtive about the look Ollie gave her, Nick decided; he went on staring at them.

'They could be from Whitby,' said Ollie at last.

Nick gave him an old-fashioned look. 'Thanks for the warning.' He moved out into the entrance lobby.

Kate and Maggie met in the doorway to the hall. 'Maggie!' said Kate. 'How did you get on with Mrs Sutcliffe?'

'It's a boy. Sixteen hours' labour, what do you expect?'

'Her last one took even longer.'

'How about you?' said Maggie. 'Any sign of action?'

'A bit of a twinge climbing the stairs last night.'

'You have more false alarms than Alfred has fleas.'

Greengrass lurched past. 'Spotlessly clean is Alfred.'

Nick waited inside the lobby. He could hear the

drunken shouts, the shrieks of one or two girls, and the clatter of steel-shod boots approaching. Any second now –

Roger teased his hair into a Tony Curtis peak, kicked the door open – and found himself face to face with Nick in his blue police shirt and sweater. Behind him, the other Rockers and their girls fell silent.

Nick's gaze moved from Roger to the rest of the gang, deliberately making them think he was memorising their faces. He could see that they were looking to Roger to make the first move. He spoke quietly, direct to Roger. 'From Whitby, right?'

Roger did his best to look and sound truculent. 'What about it?'

'Nothing,' said Nick evenly. 'Not so long as you get back on your bikes and go back there.'

'Get lost,' said one Rocker.

'Tell him, Rog.'

'Coppers,' muttered a scrawny blonde girl.

Within seconds Greengrass had appeared, with Alfred at his heels, and Julie Stanton and Ollie Renshaw beside him. Mods from the dance started to gather. Everybody, Nick knew, was waiting for the trouble to start. So was Roger. He stuck his face closer to Nick.

'Who are you to tell us what to do?'

Roger was close enough for Nick to smell his breath. 'You've been boozing,' he said. 'That bars you for a start.'

Roger hunched his shoulders, did his best to curl his lip in imitation of Elvis. 'Think we're scared of you?'

20

It was patently clear to Nick that Roger was scared, knowing that if anything happened, he'd be the first to get his collar felt. The trouble was, kids who were scared often lashed out without thinking, to try and look brave in front of their mates. Best to try and defuse the situation, give Roger the chance to back down. Nick shrugged, making it sound as if he had all the time in the world. 'You heard,' he said.

Roger decided to shift the target. He tilted his head and sneered at Ollie, standing behind Nick. 'Your Mod nancy boys not up to handling us?'

Ollie tried to push forward. 'You greasy git!'

Julie held on to him. 'Leave it, Ollie!'

Roger gave Julie the once-over. 'Drop him darling. You're wasting your time. You could do a lot better, you know that?'

His mates laughed. Roger grinned back at him. It was the moment Nick was waiting for. 'Are you leaving,' said Nick, 'or do I have to make you?'

Roger held Nick's stare for a moment, then shrugged and turned away. 'Forget it,' he said. 'Don't want the little Mods wetting themselves, do we?'

As Nick turned round, he came face to face with Greengrass. 'Flaming kids,' said Greengrass. 'All the charm of an open grave.' He shook his head sorrowfully and took out his hip-flask. 'Youth today, I don't know. They don't know the meaning of self-restraint, do they, Alfred?'

Nick stood with Gina, watching Maggie put Bellamy through his paces on the dance floor.

'She's quite a goer, isn't she?' said Gina.

'Too much for our Phil, by the look,' said Nick. 'You haven't seen Kate, have you?'

'I think she's in the cloakroom,' said Gina.

'You couldn't have a look, could you Gina? See how she is.'

'Yeah, course,' said Gina.

Maggie came off the floor with an exhausted Bellamy. 'I was doing all-nighters when you were still playing with your train set, my lad.' She saw Nick looking towards the cloakroom. 'What's up Nick? You seem worried.'

'He's expecting,' said Bellamy.

'It's not exactly the ideal environment, is it, Maggie?' said Nick. 'All this smoke and noise and people pushing and shoving all over the place – '

'It is if it gets things started, Nick,' said Maggie. 'We're all keeping an eye on her, you know. You're not the only one.'

'Yeah. Sorry, Maggie.'

Kate made her way through the teenage girls talking excitedly about who said what to whom and who they thought they might get off with, and looked in the cloakroom mirror to see if her mascara had run.

Actually, she thought, you don't look that bad for a nine-month-pregnant mother-to-be. Going out has done you a power of good. Then she leaned closer, and the harsh light above the wall-mirror showed up the shadows under her eyes and the lines of exhaustion across her brow. Oh well, she thought, Max Factor can't cover up everything –

Another face, hot and shiny, joined hers at the mirror. 'Oh my God!' wailed Gina. 'Look at me! I'm a total wreck!'

'You look great, Gina.'

Gina reapplied her thick black eyeliner and violet

22

eyeshadow. 'I don't feel it,' she said. 'Anyway, it serves me right, putting my neck on the line for this lot.'

'It's going brilliantly,' said Kate. 'It's a great success.'

Gina frowned at her reflection, realised that Kate obviously knew nothing about the Rockers, and busied herself with her lip-gloss until she could think of something to say. 'You know we almost didn't get the hall, Dr Rowan?'

'No,' said Kate.

'Yeah,' said Gina. 'It was your Nick who swung it for us.'

'Better not waste it, then,' said Kate on her way out. 'I only hope there's room enough on the dance floor for me.'

Nick was waiting for her, looking anxious. 'Come on, Nick,' she said. 'I'm fine, let's dance.'

'You sure, Kate?'

'I certainly am, it might be the last chance I get for months.'

They moved out on to the floor. She could feel the tension in his back as he tried to keep her out of the crush. 'Oh come on, Nick, you're not going to let a little thing like this come between us, are you?' He held her closer, and she felt him start to relax. As they got into the rhythm of the music, his face came closer, and his lips brushed her neck.

'Just like the old days, love.'

'Nearly,' smiled Kate, feeling the baby move.

Some of the Rockers were already mounted up,

circling the car park and revving up to drown the sound of the Rebels booming out of the hall.

'Come on, Rog!'

'Where to now, Rog?'

Roger strode through the circling bikes with a set expression on his face. Bloody Mods. He'd show them. With one shove of his boot he kicked a Lambretta off its stand flat on to the ground, buckling the wing-mirror double. 'Come on then!' he shouted. 'Let's show 'em!' He took a flying leap at Greengrass's truck and put a double dent in the door.

Within seconds the scooters were toppling like dominoes. Roger wrenched open the truck door, ripped his knife through the brown Rexine upholstery, and started strewing the contents of the cab across the car park.

Councillor Walter Stanton, in his business suit and Morland's sheepskin jacket, was on his way back from chairing a parish council meeting. The racket from the village hall grew louder with every step. He began composing his complaint about the noise level: 'An insane row, Constable Rowan, which can be heard from one end of Aidensfield to the other – '

Then he saw the Rockers. Scooters lay everywhere, front wheels spinning round as they rode their bikes in and out of the wreckage. There were three or four of them climbing all over Greengrass's truck.

'Hey you!' he shouted, as Greengrass's front seat squab hit the ground in front of him, 'What the hell do you think you're playing at?'

Seeing him, the mounted Rockers turned and began to circle and taunt the bulky grey-haired councillor.

24

'What are you doing here, Grandad?'

'Looking for totty?'

'Ya dirty old man!'

A bike drove straight at him and chased him round in tighter and tighter circles. Abandoning his dignity, Councillor Walter Stanton leaped out of the way, stumbled, half fell – and scrambled his way into the safety of the village hall.

He burst into the dance, ashen-faced. 'Constable Rowan!' he shouted over Chubby Checker's 'Twist and Shout': 'You guaranteed, you personally guaranteed, there'd be no trouble – '

'There weren't any till you arrived,' Greengrass shouted back. 'Kids have been as good as gold – '

The councillor swung round on Greengrass. 'Think so, do you? Wait till you see what they're doing to your truck!'

'My truck?' Greengrass, looking stricken, flailed out into the night.

'I'll check it out,' said Bellamy.

As Bellamy hurried after Greengrass, Stanton started to rant at Nick. 'I have nothing against young people enjoying themselves – absolutely nothing at all – but once it starts encouraging hooliganism, then that is enough and more than enough. I was all but run down out there – I want this event stopped, Constable Rowan.'

'Dad,' pleaded Julie.

'You stay out of this, young woman!' Stanton glared at his daughter. 'I knew this would happen, knew it!'

'If there is trouble, Councillor Stanton,' said Nick,

25

trying to move past Stanton, 'it's outside, not in here.'

Stanton was still not satisfied. 'Inside, outside is neither here nor there! It's this event, this damn diabolical row, that's caused the trouble, and as chair of the parish council, I insist it is stopped now!'

Having thoroughly vandalised the cab, Roger and some of his mates were chucking junk off the back of the truck while the other Rockers circled the sprawling scooters.

Greengrass stared at the flat tyres and the wrecked cab of his beloved truck. 'You young hooligans!' he bellowed, wrestling his jacket off and waving his arms about. 'Come on! One at a time! Let's have you!'

The Rockers grinned at each other and raced their bikes towards Greengrass. The ever-faithful Alfred took one look and bolted into the driver's cab.

'Come on then!' Greengrass lumbered round, slinging punches at the air. Bellamy, running towards him, was knocked sideways by a passing bike.

'Show 'em!' yelled Roger from the back of the truck. He bent down and picked up a flat bar of metal from the truck cab. His mates looked for things to throw on the bed of the truck. A rain of wood, rock and bits of metal hurtled towards the village hall.

Glass shattered inwards, showering the dancers. Girls screamed. The band trailed off in mid-number. Nick, followed by Stanton, leaped on to the stage and grabbed the mike, shouting over the chaos to make himself heard. 'Ladies and gentlemen! Ladies and gentlemen! The trouble is outside! Stay where

26

you are, keep calm – and bear with us while we sort it out!'

Face set hard, Nick ran past Kate and Maggie in the lobby. 'You're needed in there!' he shouted.

By the time Nick got to Bellamy, Roger, V-signing away, was leading the Rockers off into the night. Nick and Bellamy watched their red tail-lights recede. 'Great!' said Bellamy, brushing the dirt and grit off his black leather jacket. 'This'll go down a treat with Blaketon, won't it?'

'You all right, Phil?' said Nick.

Bellamy looked after the vanishing bikes. 'I'm going to have that one,' he said.

Greengrass was laboriously pumping up a flat tyre on his truck. 'Where the flaming hell were you when you were needed?'

'What's the damage?' asked Nick.

Greengrass straightened his back, puffing and blowing. 'Upholstery ripped out, tyres let down, God knows what else. I'll be here all night sorting it out. Times like this I wish I had some insurance.'

'Make a list,' said Nick. 'I'll be back when I've checked out who's been hurt – '

Greengrass started pumping again. 'Aye, you go back in there where it's warm. Flamin' coppers,' he grumbled to himself, 'never there when you want 'em, and always there when you don't.' A movement inside the cab caught his eye. It was Alfred timorously lifting his shaggy muzzle into view. 'A fat lot of help you were,' said Greengrass.

Alfred cowered down out of sight.

Most of the teenagers, bundled up in their duffel

coats and parkas, were drifting disconsolately out of the hall. Quarter to ten and the dance was over. Nick hurried over to Kate who was dabbing at a cut on a fair-haired girl's forehead.

'Anyone hurt?' said Nick.

'Just one or two minor cuts from flying glass,' said Kate. 'Nothing serious.'

'Thank God,' said Maggie, giving Nick a meaningful look. He glanced at Kate. After the shock and the sudden flurry of action that followed, Kate looked white with exhaustion.

'Look,' he said, 'it's going to take us some time here. Is there any chance you could drop Kate off, Maggie?'

'Sure,' said Maggie. 'I'd be glad to.'

'Thanks.' He kissed Kate on the cheek. 'You've had enough for one day, love. I'll be home as soon as I can.'

Kate nodded, too exhausted to speak, let alone argue.

Gina, Julie Stanton and Ollie Renshaw had stayed behind along with a few other Aidensfield kids to sweep and tidy up. Bellamy was fitting pieces of cardboard in the broken windows. Nick took a look round the hall and went straight over to Ollie and Julie.

'The mob who did this, do you know them?'

Ollie hunched his shoulders. As before, he seemed reluctant to answer. 'Like I said, Whitby.'

'Whitby, right,' said Nick patiently. 'And who's the big-mouth who did all the talking?'

Another shrug. 'Not sure,' said Ollie, scuffling his feet and looking at the floor.

'You don't owe him any favours,' said Nick.

28

Ollie looked up, aggressive and sullen at the same time. 'I said I don't know, all right?'

'Fair enough,' said Nick. 'Just asking. You two had better go now, we'll finish off here. We don't want your father more upset than he already is, do we, Julie?'

'I shall get a right earful when I get home,' said Julie.

'You take it from me, Julie,' said Nick. 'The longer you leave it, the worse it'll be.'

Nick watched them leave. There was no doubt Ollie knew more than he was willing to admit, but with some kids there was no use pushing: they just clammed up. Ollie would probably see things differently in the light of day – and even if he didn't, there was always Julie. Girls were generally more forthcoming about this kind of thing; Nick was pretty sure he'd get more out of her when he saw her on her own. Her father, Councillor Walter Stanton, was another matter altogether.

Phil was right, he thought. Wait till Blaketon gets to hear about it. Especially from Stanton. 'Any trouble, and on your head be it, Rowan.' And then there was Kate to worry about.

Nick sighed with exasperation and kicked a paper cup across the floor. 'Cheer up, Nick,' said Bellamy, 'it might never happen.'

'I hope it does, Phil. And soon.'

Outside the hall, Ollie and the others were picking up their scooters, examining them for damage. Ollie wrenched his wing-mirror straight. 'We'll let them think they've got away with it for now. Then we'll do 'em. On their patch.'

Maggie's Land Rover pulled up by the Police House and Kate heaved herself awkwardly out of the passenger seat. 'Thanks, Maggie. You want to come in for a minute, cup of cocoa or something?'

'No thanks, love. I'm done in and so are you. I'll call by tomorrow, though, and put you through your paces.'

Kate summoned up a smile. 'You're a hard woman, Maggie.'

'Get on with you!' She watched Kate trudge head-down through the cold, slanting rain towards the front door, pressing one hand against the small of her back as she fumbled for the key with the other. 'Goodnight, love,' she called out to Kate. 'See you tomorrow.'


By ten o'clock everybody else had gone and Nick was making his last round of the hall, looking for the odd cigarette end, broken bits of glass, anything that could give Councillor Walter Stanton the chance to have another go at him. He was bound to be on the blower to Blaketon first thing tomorrow –

Something caught his eye underneath the wooden drinks trolley. He bent down and picked up a flat bar of lead in a rusty angle-iron frame. He turned it over. There was a vague outline of what looked like the figure of a woman on the reverse. The angle-iron frame came away in his hands. Nick pressed it back round the bar of lead, and popped it into a bag. It could be evidence; on the other hand it could be some bit of old rubbish, some doorstop or something, that had been around the hall for years.

Footsteps sounded in the empty hall behind him. It was Julie Stanton.

'Hello, Julie. Looking for something, or just don't fancy going home to face the music?'

Julie shook her head. Nick could see she wanted to tell him something, but couldn't work out where to start.

'What is it, Julie?'

'Mr Rowan – ' Again she hesitated, then plucked up her courage and came out with it. 'The lad you want – his name's Roger Wellins.'

'Any idea where I could find him?' said Nick.

'Not where he lives,' said Julie, 'but he hangs out at the Rocker caff near the front in Whitby.'

'Thanks for letting me know, Julie.'

'Better you sort him out before anybody else does,' she replied.

'Such as who?' said Nick. 'Ollie?'

Julie shook her head. 'I don't know, I think he thinks that Rocker fancies me or something. I don't know. But after what they've done to the lads' scooters and the hall here – well, work it out for yourself, Mr Rowan.'

Nick watched her go. He weighed the lead in his hand. With that, and what Julie had just told him, at least he'd got the start of a case to put to Blaketon in the morning – whatever Councillor Walter Stanton might have to say.

# Three

Half-past eight in the morning, and Kate was lying on her back, mouth slightly open, fast asleep. She had been in much the same position when Nick came back last night. He laid the tray of tea and toast – three slices, this time, in one of the four chrome toast racks they had been given for a wedding present – on the bedside table, and moved the small vase of anemones to where Kate would see it.

'Room service,' he said, kissing her on the cheek. Her eyes opened, blinked, and then her arms reached out for his neck and drew him down close to her warmth.

'Mmm, love,' she said sleepily, and then, wrinkling her nose, 'You stink of paint.'

'I've got something to show you.'

Kate pulled herself up. 'Oh, Nick. Anemones – '

'No, love. Something else.'

'What?'

'Have a look in the nursery when you get up.' Nick kissed her again, removed her arms from his neck and stood up. 'It's half-eight, love – '

'Already?'

'I've got to put my report in on last night's shenanigans.'

'Best of luck.'

'I'll need it,' said Nick. 'You take it easy today. No more rocking and rolling, OK?'

'You worry about you. Leave me to worry about us.'

Kate lay in bed listening to Nick's Francis-Barnett retreating down the village street.

You're a lucky woman, she told herself, to have such a lovely, loving husband. She moved her hands down over her stomach and patted the baby inside her. And you're a lucky girl to have such a kind and nice-looking father.

For the umpteenth time, she fell to wondering whether the baby would be dark like Nick or fair like her. There was no question that it was going to be a girl, no question at all. As a mother, she just knew it, that's all, no matter what the doctor side of her said.

She had wondered about the new sonic scans the Health Service had introduced, but boy or girl, she and Nick wanted it to be a surprise – except that it was going to be a girl.

So much for medical advances, she thought, all that interest you used to take in new developments, new treatments, new technology. 'I want to be in on the cutting edge of medical science,' she remembered telling Nick just after they met. It had sounded rather pretentious even then; now, lying in bed in Aidensfield, it seemed part of another world.

She'd been wrong about the direction of her career as she had been wrong about so many things. At the start, she thought it would be just a quick fling with Nick. They met, over her lost cat, instantly fancied each other, and fell into bed on the second date.

33

That was what you did in those days, when London was just beginning to swing. Even months later, she was still convinced it was desire, simple sexual attraction, that kept them together; long, lazy Sunday mornings in bed, lunch at a pub, then back to bed in the afternoon. And much the same thing at night. Both of them, because of their jobs, trying to pack a whole weekend into twenty-four hours.

Then, after a few more months, when Nick had to go away on a three-way course, she had realised how utterly dependent she had become on him, how much she needed that calm strength of his. Nothing seemed to faze him: not drunks, not fights, not even what he called 'domestics'. Kate, left on her own, missed him desperately. She forgot to feed the cat or put the rubbish out, she missed the tube, arrived late and frazzled, got ratty with her colleagues and patients . . .

When he came back, he took one look round her grotty Camden bedsit, lifted her into bed and proposed. 'I don't know what it is, Kate, but I don't seem to be very good at living without you around, and since you don't seem to be making too good a job of it either, what do you say to getting married?

Three months later, they were. Smiling at the memory, Kate finished off all three slices of toast and turned the eggshell upside down in the blue and white eggcup.

It was something she had done ever since she was a child; even after her parents had been killed when their car hit a fallen tree, and she had moved down from Yorkshire to London at the age of eight to live with Aunty Eileen and Uncle Robert, she still

34

remembered playing the 'egg-trick'. Uncle Robert fell for it every time, or at least he pretended to. Nice, pipe-smoking Uncle Robert. At least Aunty Eileen was still around . . .

Kate levered herself out of bed and into the bathroom. The pallor was still there, and the dark rings under her eyes. If only she didn't feel so tired all the time.

She cleaned her teeth and began to feel better. Anaemia or no anaemia, she hadn't lost her appetite. What you need to do, my girl, is stop thinking so much about yourself, and start thinking about somebody else for a change.

She glanced out of the bathroom window. Damp, cold, misty. Not the best of days, but at least there wouldn't be four feet of snow between her and the hospital. Maybe she ought to go and see how Netty Pickard was; she wasn't too far away, and she was a cheerful, shrewd old soul, living on her own, but not one to moan about it. Yes, she could see how Netty's arthritis was, take her a few pills so she wouldn't run out, have a cup of tea and a chat; cheer each other up on a dark, rainy day.

A gleam of pale sunlight ran across the moor through a rent in the streaming clouds, and the sodden bracken turned golden-brown for a moment. Seconds later, a squall of sleety rain rattled against the glass like a handful of gravel. 'Typical North Yorks winter weather,' her father used to say. 'It gets bad, stays bad, and then gets worse.'

Even after she and Nick got married, she had been opposed to coming back. That was another thing she'd been wrong about, but Nick, who often seemed

35

to be able to sense her moods before she knew them herself, patiently went on waiting until she realised that her reluctance to return was nothing to do with the place, or the people: it was to do with facing up to the fact of her parents' deaths. Put like that, it was a test, and Kate was enough of a Yorkshire lass never to turn her back on a challenge.

The difference in what they earned was another source of conflict; she had thought it wouldn't matter. But it had. Male pride was involved, and male pride was something else she had to learn to deal with. Not just Nick with the money, but Alex Ferrenby, the long-standing local GP, his friends and colleagues – not to mention the bloody-minded old hill farmers who wouldn't take their shirts off in front of a woman, let alone their trousers.

Poor Alex – she still missed him and his old-fashioned common sense, despite his stubborn, cantankerous ways.

At least she and Nick had learned to talk over their differences, and had come to agree on one thing: never let the sun go down on a quarrel. But then, of course, she had run off to Whitby, to work in James Radcliffe's practice, so what was all that about, Kate Rowan? When it came down to it, she was just as stubborn and headstrong as anybody else, and it had taken James and Nick, as well as the fact she was pregnant, to make her change her mind and get herself back to Aidensfield.

She hauled on her dressing gown, and walked across the landing into the nursery. It was a thing she did every morning, picturing to herself how it would be when the baby came. But this time, for some reason, she lost her balance, swayed and banged her arm hard against the door frame.

'Ow!' She leaned against the door, rubbing her upper arm. Surely she wasn't getting too big to get through the door? She couldn't even remember swaying: one second she was walking through the door, the next she was walking into it. Surely she wasn't going to start passing out?

Then she saw it: in the middle of the brightly decorated blue and yellow nursery, a gleaming, freshly painted, hand-carved dapple-grey Victorian rocking-horse. Smiling, the pain in her arm forgotten, she walked up to it and gave it a push. Lo and behold, it actually rocked. Disregarding the smudges of pale grey paint on her fingers, she stood there watching it, entranced as any child.

So what if she had been wrong all along the line – it had all turned out right in the end, hadn't it? Touch wood . . .

Love for Nick and the baby flooded through her. No doubt about it, she thought, you are a lucky, lucky woman, Kate Rowan.

Abruptly, her unsentimental Yorkshire streak surfaced: 'Stop being so bloody smug and get yourself dressed.'

Blaketon paced up and down the duty room, watched by Phil Bellamy and Alf Ventress, a stocky, greying man in his forties with a baggy, lived-in-face. Nick kept his eyes on the evidence bag on his desk. 'I warned you it would end in tears, Rowan,' said Blaketon, squaring his shoulders and rocking on his heels. 'Hooliganism, masquerading as youth activity.'

'It wasn't the village kids, sarge. It was that Whitby lot,' said Nick.

'That's right, sarge,' said Bellamy.

Blaketon tapped the end of his nose. 'See this, Bellamy? Keep it out.'

'Yes, sarge.'

'You guaranteed no trouble, Rowan. Made yourself a hostage to fortune.' Blaketon jabbed a forefinger at Nick. 'You, constable, represent the law in Aidensfield.'

Nick considered it was time to stick up for himself. 'Helping kids to help themselves can prevent crime, sarge. It's good policing.'

'Not if it brings the wrath of influential businessmen like Walter Stanton down on our heads,' said Blaketon sharply.

So that was it, thought Nick. Blaketon was looking to avoid what he called 'interference from on high'. He exchanged a glance with Ventress. Here we go again . . . Obligingly, Alf Ventress took the half-smoked cigarette out of his mouth, and tried to take the flak off Nick.

'Walter Stanton also happens to be an influential member of the council, sarge. The chairman, no less – '

Blaketon lowered his head, and swung a pained look at Ventress. 'The expert on the blindingly obvious has spoken. Thank you, Ventress.'

'Just thought I'd mention it, sergeant,' said Alf, looking at the end of his cigarette and wondering whether there was another drag left in it.

'Mend fences with Stanton, Rowan,' said Blaketon. 'He's worried about his precious daughter Julie hanging round with these long-haired louts – '

'Mods have short hair, sarge – '

'Look, Rowan. Just find out who's responsible for the criminal damage and arrest them. That's what you're paid for, so get on with it.' Blaketon opened a filing cabinet, slammed it shut, and opened another. 'You hear me?'

'Yes, sarge.'

Nick tipped the slab of metal out of the evidence bag. The angle-iron frame came completely away. The mood Blaketon was in, he'd have Nick for 'wantonly tampering with the evidence'. Nick tried to slot the angle-iron back round the metal while Blaketon's back was turned. The edge of the slab was a different colour, paler, as if someone had painted it. Why would anyone want to paint a lump of lead?

Nick scratched away at the slab with the pointed end of the angle-iron. Paint came away in thick flakes revealing a set of stamped markings. As he gouged the point into the hollowed-out markings, the metal gleamed yellow.

'Sarge!'

'What is it now?'

'Have a look at this,' said Nick. 'It's one of the things they smashed the windows with last night.'

Blaketon closed the filing cabinet and joined Nick. 'And?'

'I thought it was lead,' said Nick, handing Blaketon the slab of metal. 'But it's hallmarked, look. It's solid gold.'

Blaketon hefted the slab in his hand, and looked

suspiciously at Nick. 'Why should a hooligan chuck a gold bar through a window?'

'He wouldn't have known,' said Nick. 'It was framed and painted to look like lead.'

Nick, Bellamy and Ventress waited for the pronouncement they knew was coming. 'If it is gold,' said Blaketon, drawing the words out slowly, 'then it's almost certainly nicked.' He drummed his fingers on the edge of the desk. 'Get the car round, Ventress.'

'Yes, sarge.'

'We shall need some proper identification of these markings,' said Blaketon. A wintry smile creased his face. 'And who better to ask than Councillor Walter Stanton?'

Stanton was standing over one of his employees, watching him remove the balance wheel of an old gold hunter when Blaketon and Nick entered.

It was a large, prosperous, Edwardian-style establishment, with polished mahogany showcases of gold rings and watches, and displays of silver cutlery and plate. Stanton looked up sharply: clearly not liking the presence of coppers in his showroom, he immediately took them through into the workshop.

He screwed his eyeglass self-importantly in place then held out a hand for the heavy gold plaque. Stripped of its grey paint, it shone seductively under Stanton's desk-lamp. He turned it over lovingly in his thick white hands. Nick could have sworn the jeweller's mouth was watering. The engraved figure on the reverse was still ingrained with paint but it was obviously female, and crudely enough done to be either very old, or faked to look like it.

40

Stanton laid the gold on a piece of chamois. 'Good-quality gold bullion,' he announced, reaching for a thick leatherbound book of marks. 'The type used by wholesale jewellers like ourselves.'

'Does the bullion mark identify where it came from?' asked Nick.

Stanton pulled the book of marks towards him. 'Oh yes, it will do, it'll all be in here. Source, serial number, year, mint. I'll draw up a report for you.'

'Most kind, Councillor Stanton,' said Blaketon.

Stanton removed his watchmaker's glass. 'May I ask where it came from?'

'Constable Rowan here found it in your village hall last night, councillor.'

Stanton looked up at Nick. 'You found . . . this . . . in Aidensfield?'

'It was used to smash one of the windows,' said Nick.

'A valuable object like this?' There was more than surprise on Stanton's face, thought Nick; it was the baffled look of a man trying to put two and two together.

'Whoever did it, Mr Stanton, obviously didn't know it was gold.'

Stanton picked the plaque up again and turned it over. 'Obviously.'

'That figure on it,' said Blaketon, 'do you have any idea as to what it might represent, councillor?'

Stanton hesitated before he spoke. 'Well, from the look of it . . . just off the top of my head, you understand . . . it seems to be intended to be some sort of goddess figure – '

Nick interrupted him. 'Does it mean anything to you, Mr Stanton?'

Stanton leaned back in his chair. 'It's far too crudely executed to identify with any certainty,' he said easily. 'Not at this stage, anyway. It could be Celtic, it could be Romano-British, it could have been done last week, or whenever.' He smiled briefly, then changed his tone. 'Does this mean it was thrown by one of those youths?'

'Yes, Mr Stanton, it does,' said Nick.

'In that case, Constable Rowan, the sooner you do something about those hooligans, the better.'

Kate saw the bikers as she drove up to Holywell Cottage. Four or five of them, using a hillocky patch of ground opposite the cottage as a scramble track. As Kate parked the Triumph Herald, they swerved out into the road and roared off.

She found Netty Pickard in the rambling garden, secateurs in hand, snipping away at an overgrown forsythia and trying not to look frightened.

'Hello, Netty!' called Kate as she approached.

'Oh! Dr Rowan!'

Kate reached her; she looked closely at her bright, perky little face, now lined with age. Netty was smiling in welcome, but the veined hand holding the secateurs was trembling.

'Are you all right, Netty?'

'Oh, those boys, they are a nuisance. Up and down, up and down, all the time.'

'I'll mention it to Nick, shall I?'

'Oh yes, if you would,' said Netty. 'Well, doctor, I never expected you to come today!'

42

'I've brought your pills,' said Kate. 'I didn't want you to run out.'

'I thought you'd have given up attending to folk for now,' said Netty. 'You must be due any minute.'

'Still looking out for my special people,' smiled Kate.

'Well since you're here,' said Netty, pocketing the secateurs, 'you'll have time for a cup of tea, won't you?'

Kate could see the loneliness behind the quivery little smile. 'If the kettle's on the go, I will.'

'It will be,' said Netty, brushing the cuttings off the weed-grown path, 'soon as I've tidied up here.'

'Right.' Kate took a couple of steps along the path. Behind the wall of shrubbery, the path curved round to a paved area and a large, set-back stone circular well with a gabled wooden well-head and bucket. 'D'you know Netty, this is the first time I've had a good look at your wishing well.'

'Oh, I know, everything's run a bit wild this winter,' said Netty, joining her. 'But there hasn't been the weather, and what with that and this arthritis, I've just had to let it go. But I hate to see it neglected. Arthur used to attend to it regular, you see.'

Kate walked up to the stone perimeter. 'Is it a real wishing well?'

Netty smiled. 'Aye, perhaps it was. I know folk used to come miles for the water. Why it's called Holywell Cottage, I suppose.'

'Oh yes, of course,' said Kate.

'Arthur used to say that long ago pilgrims used to come, and offer money and valuables and such. You know, for the relief of ailments, thanksgiving and that.'

'It must have been very special,' said Kate.

'Oh yes,' said Netty firmly, 'it's always brought good luck.'

'We could all do with some of that,' said Kate. 'What do you do to make a wish?'

'Just make an offering,' said Netty. 'Anything valuable, and think what you'd best want to happen.'

'Sounds like a good deal to me.' Kate opened her purse, fished out a half-crown, and tossed it into the water. Netty, watching, smiled as Kate placed her hands across her abdomen and closed her eyes in concentration.

An hour or so later, Kate found herself wishing she had stayed at home. She was lying on the floor in the living room, going through her ante-natal breathing exercises watched by a critical Maggie Bolton.

'Now how do you feel?' asked Maggie when Kate had finished.

'Since you ask,' said Kate, heaving and gulping for breath, 'pretty jiggered.'

Maggie cocked her head on one side. 'Not overdoing the active pregnancy bit, I hope?'

'Not really.' Kate decided to keep quiet about her visit to Netty. 'I've practically cut out anything to do with real work.'

Maggie looked long and hard and Kate's pallid complexion. 'I thought we'd dealt with your anaemia,' she said finally.

'So did I.'

Maggie sighed. There was a problem with Kate's

44

condition, and both of them knew it. The anaemia should have responded by now; in fact for a time it had, but now Kate looked no better than before. There was another problem, too: that of Kate being a doctor... Maggie opted for the diplomatic approach. 'Why don't we try boosting your iron intake, just in case?'

Kate groaned and looked away. 'No more pills, please, Maggie.'

'No,' said Maggie decisively. 'Starting now, a course of injections.'

Kate's distress, and her unwillingness to face the implications, were only too visible. 'But I'm almost there, Maggie. Is it worth it?'

'Don't worry,' said Maggie, deliberately making light of it. 'By the time I'm finished with you, you'll feel like jumping the garden gate.'

They looked at each other, smiling, neither of them believing a word of it.

It was lunchtime when Nick and Bellamy walked into the caff overlooking Whitby pier. The place was a real Greasy Spoon, with the pinball machine flashing, the jukebox thudding and the smoke hanging in thick horizontal layers. A group of heavily built Rockers looked up as Nick and Bellamy advanced through the smoke. The proprietor reached for a switch under the counter and both machines went quiet.

'Well, Phil,' said Nick quietly, 'here we go.'

'I don't fancy our chances much against this lot,' said Bellamy.

'If you recognise him, just nod,' said Nick. 'I'll do the same.'

Without another word, fully aware of the atmosphere thickening round them with every step they took, Nick and Bellamy walked slowly round the caff, scrutinising each face in turn. They were a hard-looking bunch, but Roger Wellins was not among them. He was too young for a start: this lot looked more like the annual outing of a chapter of Hell's Angels than the young kids Bellamy had seen outside the village hall. He glanced over at Nick and gave a slight shake of his head.

'Ey,' said a voice softly, close behind him. Bellamy turned to see a hulking great brute about seventeen stone with a battered face under a blue fisherman's woolly staring down at him. Slowly, a long stream of beer-laden smoke was blown straight into Bellamy's face. 'Now blow, copper.'

Taking his time, Bellamy walked to Nick who was gazing out of the window at the pier down below.

'He's not here, is he?' said Nick.

'No, thank goodness,' muttered Bellamy. 'Let's get out of here.'

'Hang on,' said Nick peering through the steamed-up window. 'That looks like Julie Stanton.' Down below, a slight figure was standing by a parked scooter surrounded by Rockers.

As they moved out of the caff, they saw Julie run from her scooter to an anti-traffic bollard at the entrance of the pier. A motorcycle wheelied out of the pack and began chasing her in tighter and tighter circles.

'That's him, Nick!'

Nick drove the pale green minivan through the jeers of the Rockers and parked it to one side of the bollard, blocking off half the exit from the pier. As Bellamy leaped out to take care of Julie, Roger Wellins gunned his engine and roared down to the end of the pier, skid-turned, and wheelied back down the pier, aiming straight at Nick.

'Chicken! Chicken! Chicken!' chanted the Rockers in unison.

Nick, swallowing hard, stood his ground as Roger bore down on him. With barely a couple of yards to go, Roger laid his bike into a flat skid and rolled off. The bike spun off the harbour wall and crashed into the hard-packed sand below.

Roger ended up in a tangle of arms and legs at Nick's feet. He looked up, wild-eyed, shaking his head, unable to believe that Nick hadn't moved.

'I want a word with you,' said Nick, trying to keep his voice calm.

On the way back to Ashfordly, with Roger slumped in the back of the minivan, Bellamy told Nick that Julie had been delivering some watch repairs to a Whitby gift shop for her father.

'Pretty stupid thing to do,' commented Nick.

'Some girls are like that,' said Bellamy. 'They like to stir up trouble, get blokes thumping each other over them.'

'Yeah,' said Nick, 'you could be right. I wouldn't have thought that about Julie, though.'

Bellamy glanced back to check on Roger, and then grinned at Nick. 'Anyway, she thinks you're wonderful.'

'All I need,' said Nick.

Blaketon was standing to attention phone in hand when Nick and Bellamy came in with Roger. He gestured peremptorily to Nick and dismissed Bellamy and Roger to the interview room. 'Yes sir,' he smarmed into the phone, 'I appreciate the urgency. And of course the need for discretion. You can rely on us, sir. Yes, you'll be the first to know . . . Goodbye, sir.'

Blaketon replaced the phone with the utmost care. 'Division,' he said with the air of a man who had just received a direct communication from the Almighty. 'Assistant Chief Constable himself, Rowan.'

It transpired that the report Nick had sent to Division on the gold matched up with records of a shipment of bullion stolen in a security van hold-up in Leeds seven years ago. The villains had intended to smuggle the gold out through Whitby, but the CID had intercepted them, and after a high-speed chase across the moors, they picked up the whole gang.

'What happened to the gold?' asked Nick.

'Stashed during the chase,' said Ventress. 'When our lads were taken to where the villains said they'd buried it, it was gone.'

'All of it?' said Nick.

'The lot,' said Blaketon. 'That gold bar is the first of the consignment to show up, Rowan.'

On the way to the interview room, Blaketon laid a hand on Nick's shoulder. 'You play your cards right, Rowan, and I can smell promotion in this. Mebbe not this year, nor the next, but I shan't be here for ever you know, and Ventress isn't interested, so think on, lad. You'll need the money with that pram in the hall.'

'Haven't bought one yet, sarge.'

'Time you did, then.'

Roger Wellins slumped in the interview room chair, toying with his white silk miner's scarf. 'There were others there too, you know,' he said truculently. 'Why pick on me?'

Nick leaned on the interview table and stared hard at Roger. 'You broke the window. You were seen by a police witness.'

'Everybody was chucking stuff,' said Roger. 'Do what you like. I've said all I've got to say.'

Nick laid a rectangular lump of lead on the table. 'You were seen with a piece of metal like this in your hand. I picked it up inside the hall. Where did you get it?'

Roger looked from Nick to Blaketon, saying nothing.

'You don't want to do time, do you?' said Nick.

'We could charge you with assaulting a police officer,' said Blaketon. 'Twice. You could be looking at six months, lad.'

Roger thought it over. 'All right,' he said at last. 'I just picked it up.'

'Now pull the other one,' said Blaketon.

'It's true – '

'Picked it up where?' said Nick.

'It was part of the junk we turfed out of that old truck – '

'The one parked near the village hall?' said Nick.

'Aye,' said Roger, relieved now it looked as if they were starting to believe him. 'Belonged to some old bloke with an army greatcoat and a lurcher dog.'

Blaketon reacted as if he had just been told he'd won first dividend. 'Greengrass!'

Nick grinned back at him. 'Yes, sarge.'

49

# Four

Nick and Blaketon picked their way through mud, tyres, tea chests and car bodies. Greengrass was rooting about in the straw outside his ramshackle shed. Blaketon cursed under his breath. 'Quarter-past nine in the morning and shoes already thick with muck and chickenshit – '

Greengrass shooed a dozen or so scrawny brown pullets back towards the shed. They ran squawking all over the yard. 'If you've come for my eggs,' he called out, 'you're just in time. So fresh they don't know they've been laid. Here, look at these.' He held out three of the smallest, filthiest eggs Blaketon had ever seen.

'The idea is to stay alive, Greengrass,' he said sombrely, 'not die of food poisoning.'

'No pleasing some people,' muttered Greengrass, putting the pullets' eggs in his battered brown trilby. 'What d'you want, anyway?'

'Did anything go missing from your truck the night before last, Claude?' asked Nick.

'Not after I'd spent most of the night picking it all up, no. Nothing of value, that is.' He hunched his shoulders up and down, squinting sideways at Nick. 'Just an old lucky piece of mine.'

Nick held out the rectangular block of lead he had shown Roger Wellins. 'Something like this?'

'Aye, something like it,' said Greengrass, 'but mine had the figure of a lady on it. Summat I keep hanging in the back of the cab, for luck.'

'Something you've just run out of, Greengrass.' Blaketon took him by the arm and steered him back towards the black Ford Anglia. Alfred loped along behind. 'Into the car,' ordered Blaketon.

'Me?' said Greengrass indignantly. 'What for? What am I supposed to have done now?'

'We're taking you in for questioning,' said Blaketon. 'Now get in the car – '

'But what about Alfred?' said Greengrass. 'I can't leave me dog running loose – it's – it's wilful neglect – it's against the law – he's a valuable animal is Alfred.'

Blaketon sighed, picked the dog up and tried to shove him into the back of the car. Alfred, assuming this was some new sort of game, swivelled his hairy muzzle round and licked Blaketon's neck. He held the dog out disgustedly at arms' length. 'For God's sake, Rowan, take that grin off your face, and look after this damned animal!'

Greengrass was still chuntering away as they marched him through the station into the interview room. 'Treating innocent people like this! Worse than Russia, if you ask me – '

'Nobody's asking you,' said Blaketon shortly. 'And tell Ventress to put that damned animal in the yard, and get the inside of my car cleaned out!'

'Yes, sarge.'

'No explanation, no charge, just dragged out me 'ome without so much as a word – I'm the flaming victim, Blaketon!'

Nick closed the interview room door. 'We just want to know how you came by your lucky piece, Claude.'

Greengrass seated himself heavily. 'In the course of my commercial activities. How d'you think?'

'We need to know a bit more than that, Claude,' said Nick.

'Way I've been treated, me, a respectable citizen – why should I tell you lot anything? Eh?' He looked up challengingly. 'Go on then, go on. Give me one good reason!'

'All right, I will,' said Blaketon. 'You're in serious trouble, Greengrass.'

'Oh, aye,' he said sarcastically. 'I'm all of a tremble, aren't I? And for why? All because of a piece of lead not big enough to roof a flaming sparrer's nest!'

'No,' said Blaketon, leaning over him. 'Not lead, Greengrass. Gold!'

Greengrass's eyes narrowed and flicked from Nick to Blaketon and back. 'Gold, did you say?'

Nick nodded. 'Stolen gold bullion. Which you admit to having in your possession.'

Greengrass's eyes started to twitch. He opened his mouth to start blustering away as usual, but nothing came out.

'What's the matter, Greengrass?' Blaketon drew back and eyed him with a smile of grim satisfaction. 'Lost your sense of humour?'

'I'm saying nowt till I see my lawyer,' said Greengrass.

'You haven't got a lawyer,' said Blaketon. 'There's not a solicitor round here would touch you with a bargepole. In addition to which you haven't been charged, yet.'

'It's known as helping with inquiries, Claude,' said Nick.

'In that case,' said Greengrass, sitting back and folding his arms, 'I'm still saying nowt.'

Ten minutes later, with tempers fraying and Alfred whining pitifully in the yard outside, Greengrass muttered something about an old car.

'What was that?' said Nick. 'Are you saying you found it in an old car?'

'I'm saying I might have done. Three years is a long time,' said Greengrass, shifting his weight in the chair. 'I'm an old age pensioner, and my memory's not what it was, without all this aggravation – '

Blaketon exploded. 'We're the ones with the aggravation, Greengrass!'

'All right, Claude,' said Nick patiently, 'you're saying now you might have found it in an old car about three years ago?'

'How many more times do I have to tell you?'

'Whose old car?' asked Blaketon in exasperation. 'Where did this old car come from?'

Greengrass's eyes blinked as if they were staring into a very bright light. 'What? Eh? How d'you mean?'

'You heard!' Blaketon was at the end of his tether, and Greengrass knew it.

'It were a cash transaction,' he said. 'Buy and sell old cars all the time, don't I?'

'I don't believe you,' said Blaketon, glaring at him.

'Look,' said Nick, 'just tell us where it came from.'

Greengrass shook his head. 'I've told you all I

53

know, Constable Ronan. I can't say fairer than that, can I?'

Blaketon glowered at Greengrass. 'You don't know the meaning of the word.'

Outside, Alfred began to howl. Defeated, Blaketon gave Nick a nod.

Nick pushed a ballpoint pen and a form across the table. 'All right, Claude. Sign the statement.'

Greengrass licked the end of the ballpoint and laboriously signed his name.

'Now get out of here,' said Blaketon.

Greengrass stood, and hesitated. 'Don't I even get the chance to hold this gold in my own hand, then? I mean, some folk might think it rightfully mine – '

'Out!' shouted Blaketon.

They watched him shuffle, muttering, towards the door.

'Greengrass!'

'Yes, Sergeant Blaketon?'

'Don't stray too far.'

The door closed on Greengrass's back. Blaketon exhaled slowly. 'He's lying, Rowan.'

'I'll work on him,' said Nick.

'Do that,' said Blaketon. 'Preferably with a cudgel.'

Greengrass and Alfred stayed on the dilapidated smallholding all day. 'At the first sign of bother, Alfred, best thing is to get your head down and keep it down.' Alfred cocked his head on one side and waited for the next pearl of wisdom. 'Trouble is,' Greengrass continued, brow furrowed in concentration, 'bother's one thing, and gold's another.' Alfred lay down, put his head on his crossed paws, and watched his master gnawing his lip, muttering, and generally worrying away at the problem like an old dog with a marrow-bone.

As night fell, Greengrass loaded a dozen pullets' eggs into a tray and drove his truck over to Holywell Cottage. There was no sense in putting on the lights. After sixty-odd years roaming and skulking and poaching around Aidensfield, he knew his way around blindfold. Besides, it only wore out the battery and the bulbs, and there were more than enough busybodies poking their noses out of their net curtains without going round in a blaze of light.

He pulled in off the road between Netty's back door and poor old Arthur Pickard's workshop, and let Alfred out for a wander. The late Arthur had got a lot of decent stuff in that workshop, he reflected, welding gear and oxy bottles, a forge and bellows, a potter's kiln, tools and all sorts. City folk were starting to pay decent prices for old farm implements; they hung them on the wall for decoration, or something equally bloody daft. Maybe he ought to offer to help old Netty out by taking them off her hands . . .

He shambled across the back yard and balanced the tray of pullets' eggs on one hand to reach for the door knob. In the shrubbery off to his right he heard a twig crack. He swung round, almost losing the eggs, and peered into the darkness. Alfred came up, wagging his tail. 'You'll be the flaming death of me, Alfred. Now stay here and watch that truck, I've had enough trouble for one day.'

Netty was ironing as Greengrass poked his head in the back door. 'Now then, Netty. Hard at it as usual?'

Netty smiled to herself without bothering to lift her head from the ironing. 'You, is it, Claude? I thought I recognised your truck.'

Greengrass scraped his boots, walked in and shut the door. 'I had a few pullets' eggs left over. Surplus to requirements, like.'

'Very generous of you, Claude,' said Netty.

Damn, he thought, setting the eggs down on the scrubbed kitchen table: he'd reckoned on getting a couple of bob out of her but she'd outwitted him again. She was a shrewd old bird all right; you'd have to get up early to put one over on Netty Pickard, for all her sweet-little-old-lady ways.

'What neighbours are for, in't it?' he said, trying to make the best of it.

She laid the old-fashioned flat-iron down; it was the sort folk used to put hot cast-iron ingots inside in the old days, pointed at both ends, with a thick, polished steel shoe. They were getting valuable now, and Netty had a good collection of them, all ranged round the hearth.

'Do you have time for a cup of tea, Claude?'

Greengrass grinned and rubbed his hands together. 'I thought you'd never ask, Netty.' He sat himself down at the table. 'Anyway, I was hoping to have a word with you, bit of a chinwag like, so it'll kill two birds with one stone, won't it?'

'How'd you get on today?' said Nick, over supper.

'Oh, Maggie came round,' said Kate, just a little too casually.

'And?' prompted Nick. Usually, Kate was only too

keen to tell him the day's events, particularly where Maggie and the baby were concerned.

'I've started another series of injections,' she said flatly.

'What for, anaemia?'

'Yes,' said Kate. 'Maggie says it's not responding as well as she thinks it should.'

'And you?' asked Nick.

'I feel fine,' she said with a smile, 'but then, I'm only the doctor.'

'I hope you told her about that bruise on your backside.'

'I certainly did,' said Kate.

'And what did she say?'

'Well,' said Kate, 'first of all she wondered how you came to be looking at it – '

'Then what?'

'What d'you think?' said Kate. 'She told me to turn the other cheek.'

'Anything else?'

'Well, we both agreed the baby's the right way up and the head's engaged, so really it's just a matter of time until she decides to put in an appearance.'

'I hope she's not going to be too much like her mum,' said Nick.

'And what d'you mean by that, Nick Rowan? I hope you're not implying I'm always late – '

'I wouldn't dare,' said Nick.

They were ready for bed by half-past ten. Nick came out of the bathroom in his pyjamas to find Kate sitting at the dressing-table with her head tilted back and a wad of tissue held to her nose.

'You all right, Kate?'

She nodded, and then took the tissue away. It was blotched bright scarlet. 'Just a nosebleed, that's all.' She tossed the tissue into the basket by the dressing-table.

'Is that normal?' asked Nick.

'Please don't fuss, Nick. I'm fine.' Nick, detecting the edge to her voice, moved to the dressing-table and put his arms round her from behind. In the mirror, the reflection of her face looked up at him, pale and vulnerable. She leaned her head back against him. 'I wish the baby would come, Nick.'

It was the first time in days she had admitted to feelings of anxiety, of helplessness. Nick's heart went out to her. 'Don't worry, love,' he said, 'we're almost there.'

In the mirror their reflections stared back at them. The feeling of waiting, of strain, was only too palpable. He bent down and kissed the top of her head. 'I bet you a pound it comes tomorrow.'

'Right,' said Kate, 'you're on.'

Sharp on the dot of twelve noon, Greengrass's truck drew up outside the Aidensfield Arms. Nick, who had deliberately deployed his morning rounds to be in the village near Kate, decided it would be a good moment to have another word with Greengrass: like most folk, old Claude was a lot more talkative when he'd had one or two.

'Large brandy, please George.' The other early regulars, nursing their solitary half-pints and manifold disappointments, glanced up dully at Greengrass.

'Not suffering from shock are we, I hope?' said George Ward, the landlord.

'Just a little heart-starter, George.' Greengrass passed over a handful of coins. 'Here y'are, lad. Keep the change.'

George pushed the coins about in his palm. 'What you talking about, change? This is the right money, exactly what you owe me.'

'Joke, George, joke.' He downed the brandy and pushed his glass forward towards Gina. She was wearing a leopardskin chiffon blouse, and Greengrass was too busy ogling her to notice Nick move up behind him. 'I had spots like that, I'd be straight down the quack's – '

'Full of jokes today then, Claude,' said Nick, moving to the bar. 'I like your jokes. The one about the car had Blaketon rolling about the office carpet.'

'Hellfire!' said Greengrass. 'Not again!'

'Pork pie please, Gina,' said Nick.

'Coming up, Mr Rowan.'

'We need to know about that car, Claude,' said Nick.

Behind the bar, George's ears pricked up. 'What car's that?'

'Some old banger he sold three years ago,' said Nick.

'Old banger!' blustered Greengrass. 'What you talking about, old banger? Think I'd pay good money to advertise summat like that?'

Nick took a thoughtful bite out of his pork pie: if the car had been advertised, it was traceable.

'I tell you what, Claude,' said George, leaning over the bar. 'You could buy two of your old wrecks for the price of a newspaper ad, and still have change left over.'

'You hear that remark, Alfred?' said Greengrass. 'That's a slur on my commercial reputation that is. Note it down for future reference.' Alfred went on looking hungrily at Nick's pork pie.

'So,' said Nick, 'you advertised the car in the local paper?'

Greengrass, trapped, looked from Nick to George to Alfred. 'And take his name, an' all!' He downed his second large brandy, and scowled at Nick. 'Just in case we decide to sue a certain copper for downright persecution!' He slammed his glass down and stomped off, dragging Alfred with him and muttering darkly about 'justice' and 'victimisation'.

'Funny thing, that, George,' said Nick, finishing his pork pie. 'You can have somebody in the interview room as long you like and they won't say a blind word. Ten minutes in the pub and they're telling everybody.'

'Aye,' said George, 'you hear all sorts over the bar.'

Just in case Nick was right and Rowan junior did decide to come today, Kate was sorting out sets of baby clothes and nappies in the nursery.

Downstairs, the front door clicked open. 'Kate? You there?'

'Up here, Maggie!' called Kate, placing a pile of bibs on top of the chest of drawers. 'Come on up!' She heard Maggie run lightly up the stairs, and cast her mind back to the last time she had been able to do that. Certainly not for the last three months. 'In here, Maggie, in the nursery!'

As Maggie came bustling in, Kate turned to meet

60

her and caught her elbow on the open top drawer. 'Ow!'

'You all right, love?' asked Maggie.

'I'm fine,' said Kate. 'Just getting clumsier and clumsier.'

'It won't be long now, then,' said Maggie briskly, 'that's always a good sign.' She looked Kate up and down. 'For once I thought I might find you resting in bed.'

Kate piled the clothes and nappies back in the chest of drawers. 'Just trying to bribe the little beggar into showing her face.'

'Or his,' said Maggie.

'No way.'

'You'll be doing the wedding ring on a piece of thread next.'

'I did that months ago,' smiled Kate.

'Let's get a bit more scientific, then,' said Maggie, moving to the door. 'Time to start work on our breathing exercises.'

Kate sighed, feeling her energy draining away. 'Must we?'

'You'll be glad you did when the contractions start, I can tell you.' Maggie waited at the top of the stairs, and held an arm out to steady Kate. 'Are you feeling the benefit of the iron shots yet?'

'I'm not sure. I think so,' said Kate.

'That's what I like,' said Maggie. 'Positive thinking.'

Netty Pickard came back from Ashford market on the one o'clock bus to find her cottage vandalised.

There was glass in the garden where one of her

61

flat-irons had been thrown through the window; inside, the neat and cosy little sitting-room looked as if a bomb has hit it. The carpet was rucked up in a great heap, curtains had been ripped down, furniture tipped over, and the contents of every single drawer lay strewn all over the floor.

Netty wandered through the wreckage of her home dazed, still carrying the flat-iron and her shopping, unable to take it in. Floorboards had been wrenched up at the foot of the narrow staircase; even the bricks in the hearth and the fireplace had been crowbarred up and scattered about.

Moving as if in a dream, she placed the flat-iron back in the hearth with the rest of the collection. The ironing she had done the night before was thrown and trampled all over the place; pictures had been smashed, and on the walls in dribbly red paint someone had daubed 'ROCKERS RULE' and 'ELVIS IS KING'.

Netty stood by the wrecked fireplace. Everywhere she looked things had been ripped, torn up and smashed. It was only when her eye fell on a tiny pottery vase labelled 'Cornish Violets', and saw that it, too, had been boot-heeled into the debris, that the shock hit her. Everything she had lived with and loved for years, gone in a morning. Her home, her life, desecrated and in ruins.

She felt herself swaying, going, clinging on to the mantelpiece for support, her fingers slipping . . .

By the time the ambulance arrived half an hour later, both Kate and Nick were already there. Nick had managed to organise Netty a cup of tea in the wreckage of the kitchen, and Kate had examined her for shock; now she waited with her, holding her hand in silent consolation. Dry-eyed, Netty stared into the remains of the fireplace and said that she was glad Arthur hadn't been there to see it.

Kate led the frail old lady gently out of the front door to the ambulance. Netty took a last look back into the devastated cottage. 'I don't like staying away from home, Dr Rowan.'

'It's just for a while,' Kate reassured her, knowing the fear old folk had of being taken out of their homes into hospital. 'Mostly for observation, Netty.' She handed Netty over to the burly ambulanceman. 'I'll come in to see you later this afternoon.'

'On no,' said Netty, 'you shouldn't, you really shouldn't, not with the baby so close – '

Tears sprang to Kate's eyes. She blinked them away. 'Now then, Netty, no more arguments,' she said lightly. 'And by the time you come back they'll have all the mess cleared up, you'll see.'

Netty turned her head slowly to look at Kate. She didn't say anything; she just shook her head.

Nick found Ventress in Arthur Pickard's workshop, examining a green-painted ex-W.D. mine detector. 'This is what old Arthur used to use for his metal-detecting. Used to come across him in all sorts of out of the way places.' Ventress ran the mine detector over an iron ingot on the flagstone floor. It emitted a faint pinging noise. 'Last time I saw him was just before he died. Nice old bloke, he was, twenty-four-hour smile and never a bad word to say about anybody. What a lot of folk round here would call barmy.'

★

'Alf, poor old Netty's had her house turned over – '

Ventress went on imperturbably waving the old mine detector over the paved floor. 'There was this family, not far from here, got themselves into a lot of money trouble. I was sent in with the bailiffs. Anyway, this well-wisher, that was what he called himself, paid off their debts – '

'Yeah, well, it's all very interesting, Alf, but I can't see what it's got to do with Netty – '

'I heard later it was old Arthur Pickard.' Ventress played the mine detector over the toecaps of Nick's boots. There was a faint 'ping'. Satisfied, Ventress switched the machine off.

'Very generous,' said Nick, 'but that must have been years ago.'

'So was this.' Ventress picked up one of the set of hardbacked exercise books lying on the workbench. 'He was a very meticulous man, was Arthur. Kept logs of all the years he spent metal-detecting – '

'Never mind metal-detecting, Alf – '

'Hold your hosses, Nick, just bear with me for a minute.' Ventress flicked through the pages of the exercise book. 'Here we are, the last entry poor old Arthur made. Dated August the fourth, seven years ago.'

'So?'

'The day before the gold went missing,' said Ventress. 'It's funny old Arthur didn't bother to write anything after that.'

Nick went back to check the house. If Ventress was right, he thought, looking through the wreckage and wondering whether Forensics would be able to make anything of it, it would certainly explain why somebody had turned the place over. He frowned at the red paint on the walls. But how would a bunch of bikers know about old Arthur's metal-detecting? Come to that, why daub slogans all over the wall?

He felt something crunch under his boot. Looking down, he saw he had trodden a mass of pills into the floor. He was kneeling down to scoop up the rest when Kate came in.

'How is she?' he asked Kate.

'Have to wait and see,' said Kate.

'You're not looking too good yourself, love.'

Kate looked round the room, and shook her head. 'How could anyone do this to her, Nick?'

'At this point, it's not about how – it's who.'

'Kids?' said Kate, looking at the red paint. 'Local kids? I just can't see them doing this. Not to Netty Pickard. Everybody loves Netty – '

Nick was looking at a scrunched-up ticket he had picked up with the pills.

'What's that?' asked Kate.

'Something I found on the floor, looking for poor old Netty's pills.'

'Oh, don't worry about them, they'll give her some more at the hospital.'

Nick smoothed the ticket out flat and passed it to Kate. 'It's a ticket for the rock and roll do the other night.'

Kate looked up sharply at Nick. 'I saw some bikers here the other day.'

'Well, that's a start,' said Nick. 'We can't do much here until the Forensic lads have had a look at it.'

The local Mods were clustered round the petrol

65

pumps, taking it in turn to fill up their Vespas and Lambrettas. As Nick approached, he could see Julie Stanton and Ollie Renshaw standing apart from the others, arguing heatedly. The other Mods, seeing Nick slow down and turn towards them, drifted away, shoving spanners and jack handles into their parkas and saddlebags.

Julie and Ollie fell silent as Nick pulled in next to them. 'I've just come from Mrs Pickard's,' he said bluntly. 'You know what happened, don't you?'

'We heard, yeah,' said Ollie.

Nick held the admission ticket out. 'I found this there.'

'It wasn't any of us, Mr Rowan,' said Julie.

'I don't see one of Mrs Pickard's pensioner mates doing it, do you, Julie?'

Ollie kick-started his scooter. 'The Whitby greasers bought tickets too, you know.' He blipped the throttle, revving the engine unnecessarily.

Nick waited for the racket to die down. 'I know,' he said. 'Now listen to me, Ollie Renshaw. I don't want any trouble from you, or any of this lot. Any sorting out to do, I'll do it.'

Ollie watched Nick drive off, and took his fist out of his pocket. On it was a metal knuckleduster. 'Yeah,' he said, turning it this way and that, admiring it, grinning at his mates. 'Well, great minds think alike, don't they?' He let the clutch out and left Julie standing.

'Ollie!' she shouted after him, but her voice was drowned by the rest of the Mods accelerating away from the pumps. She jumped on her own scooter and took off after Nick, beeping her squawky little horn.

Nick pulled in and waited for her to catch up. 'What's going on, Julie?'

'It's Ollie being stupid, isn't it?' she said angrily. 'I told him I'm not interested in that Roger Wellins bloke – he just keeps following me around.'

'And what's Ollie up to, then?'

'He said Roger had asked for it, and he was going to get it, said Julie. 'They're all tooled up, Mr Rowan, chains and everything. They're going to see to the Whitby Rockers, aren't they?'

Nick picked up his radio-telephone. 'Right, thanks Julie.'

With the Francis-Barnett's top speed nearer fifty than fifty-five, Nick knew he had no chance of catching them; all he could hope to do was get there before any real trouble started.

Half an hour later Ollie and his Mods were driving in a solid phalanx through the back streets of Whitby, the noise of their motors rebounding off the walls, forcing pedestrians to flatten themselves back in shop doorways. One or two pensioners shook their fists and shouted; Ollie and his mates gave them the V-sign and rode on regardless.

Roger Wellins and his mob had already gathered at the pier. He wrapped a length of motorcycle chain round his fist and watched the Mods come streaming along the seafront. 'Here we go then, lads.'

One or two dog-walkers and mothers with prams, taking the spring air, saw the spanners, tyre irons and chains being produced, and scurried for shelter.

Ollie and the rest of the Mods parked some distance away and, brandishing a selection of hammers, wrenches and chains, strode along the front, brushing people aside and chucking deckchairs over the sea wall.

By the time the two groups met, every other pedestrian had fled. Nick saw them as soon as he turned on to the deserted seafront. With a sinking heart, he realised the back-ups he had radioed for hadn't arrived. There was just one solitary scooter approaching from the opposite direction.

Julie Stanton –

Nick accelerated past the anxious faces watching from the shelter of shops and doorways.

Roger stepped forward to confront Ollie. 'Brought your buckets and spades, have you?'

Ollie brought out his knuckleduster. 'I'm going to have you, Wellins!'

'Come on then!' taunted Roger. 'I'm waiting!'

'Ollie!' screamed Julie, running from her scooter.

'Hallo, darling,' grinned Roger, moving towards her. 'Come to see the fun?'

Ollie lunged forward. 'You leave her alone!'

Nick drove his motorbike straight between the two youths. He dismounted slowly, and faced Roger Wellins. 'Glutton for punishment, aren't you?'

'This is nowt to do with you, copper!'

Nick ignored him, and spoke to Ollie. 'You and your mates – out of here before I book the lot of you.'

'Greasy Rockers owe us for Aidensfield!' said Ollie.

Roger went for him, swinging his chain up and then down towards Ollie's head. Nick shouldered Ollie aside, and caught the downward swing of the

68

chain round the cuff of his gauntlet. As the chain wound itself round Nick's arm, he pulled Roger forward, off balance, and twisted his chain arm up hard behind his back.

'Ow!' yelled Roger. 'Breaking me arm!'

'Drop the chain!' ordered Nick. 'Or I will!' Any second now, he reckoned, he'd be down on the floor under a mass of kicking, punching Rockers –

With a screech of tyres, Bellamy's minivan pulled up with the Black Maria of the Whitby police close behind. Doors banged, whistles shrieked, and the Mods and Rockers took off in all directions, throwing their chains and weapons away as they went, with most of the Whitby force in hot pursuit.

'You all right, Nick?' said Bellamy.

'Fine.' Nick unwound the chain from his arm and shoved Roger into the arms of a couple of Whitby constables. 'Charge him with assault.'

It was just after three when Kate came down the steps of Ashfordly Hospital. Councillor Walter Stanton was extricating his bulky form and a vast bouquet of flowers from his black Rover saloon. For a moment, he seemed surprised to see Kate. Then, recovering, he doffed his hat. 'Hello Dr Rowan. I've just come to see Netty Pickard.' He adopted an expression of grave concern. 'How is she? Can you tell me?'

'She's pretty shaken,' replied Kate. 'It'll take her some time to get over it.'

Stanton nodded. 'Yes, of course.' Then, his voice hardening, 'Young hooligans, I hear. No respect for age or anything else. Is she up to a visit?'

'Well actually Mr Stanton, she's resting at the moment.'

Stanton frowned briefly, and then held out the bouquet of flowers for Kate to admire. 'From the council,' he said. 'They're very concerned, as of course we all are. They've asked me to let her know that they'll do everything they possibly can to help.'

'She'll appreciate that, Mr Stanton,' said Kate, unsure whether Stanton was being kind or self-important. Probably a bit of both, she decided.

Stanton took a step towards the hospital entrance. 'Well, I'll drop these off and see her another time. Goodbye, Dr Rowan.'

Kate watched him hurrying into the hospital, determination in his every step.

Nick stood uncomfortably in Blaketon's office, watching him go through a pile of thirty or so statements from the Whitby incident. Nick hoped Blaketon wasn't going to read every one: it was already half-past five and he wanted to get back to Kate.

' "Praise for the bravery of the young officer",' Blaketon read out from one statement, then, picking up another, ' "Courage beyond the call of duty" . . .' He looked up over his glasses. 'I hope you're not letting your quest for promotion cloud your judgement, Rowan.'

'I'm not looking for promotion, sarge.'

'Well, you should be, Rowan,' said Blaketon, tersely. 'But I don't want my officers playing the hero unnecessarily, is that clear?'

'Yes, sarge.'

'You should have waited for PC Bellamy and the other officers.'

'If I had, we'd still be picking up bits of Mods and Rockers off the beach,' said Nick.

Blaketon, sighed. 'I thought you had the Aidensfield lot under some sort of control, Rowan.'

'So did I, sarge.'

'I've already had another earful from Stanton.' Blaketon picked up a complaint report between two fingers and shook it disdainfully. 'Council representation to Division about this is all we need, isn't it?'

Ventress knocked and stuck his head round the door. 'Some good news and some bad news, sarge.'

'Get on with it, Ventress.'

Ventress entered, scratched his ear, and flipped over the pages of his notebook. 'The bad news is that all the kids' alibis stand up. Neither the Aidensfield lot nor the Whitby mob could have been at Netty's when it was vandalised.'

'Thank you,' Ventress,' said Blaketon wearily. 'And the good news?'

Ventress flipped over a few more pages. 'I've been phoning round the local classifieds, and that car Greengrass claims he found the gold bar in . . .' He paused, and grinned at Nick, 'I think we've traced it, sarge.'

# Five

Another night passed, and still no sign of the baby. The only good thing, as far as Nick could see, was that Kate's concern for Netty had taken her mind off her own problems. In fact, everybody in the village seemed shaken by what had happened at Holywell Cottage; when he walked into the pub at half-past twelve, even Greengrass was staring morosely into his brandy glass.

'Rotten thing to happen,' Gina was saying as Nick entered.

'Aye,' agreed Greengrass, 'them as did it want thumping, if you ask me.'

'We'll find out who it was, Claude,' said Nick. 'Never fear.'

'For once I hope you do,' muttered Greengrass. 'And you do, don't you, Alfred?'

'How is she, Mr Rowan?' asked Gina. 'Have you heard?'

'Kate and I are going in to see her this afternoon.'

'I were thinking of going in some time,' said Greengrass.

'They'd never let you through the door,' said George. 'Not dressed like that.'

'What you talking about?' said Greengrass. 'I got me best jumper on.' He plucked at a moth-eaten canary yellow pullover underneath his greatcoat.

'I'll send her your best wishes, Claude,' said Nick.

'Aye, do that, you'll save me the petrol.'

'Oh, by the way,' said Nick, 'we've traced that car of yours.'

Greengrass glanced up warily. 'What are you on about now?'

'That car you couldn't recall for Sergeant Blaketon the other day,' said Nick. 'You know, the one that came with that lucky piece.'

'Somebody must have crossed you with a lurcher,' said Greengrass. 'You never give up, do you?'

Nick took out a faded copy of the *North Yorks Gazette*. ' "For sale – a One Owner Only 1948 Austin 10 in perfect condition, regularly serviced – " '

'Rubbish!'

'You can say that again,' said George.

'No, Mr Ronan, you don't understand – I mean I advertise all the time, don't I?' Greengrass's eyes started to twitch. 'You have to, don't you?'

'That's not what the newspaper office say,' said Nick. 'Once in three years, and then they had to threaten to take you to court to get you to pay up – '

'Austin?' said George. 'Not the Austin you offered me three years ago was it, Claude?'

Nick grinned. 'Well, was it, Claude?'

'Arthur had just died,' said George, 'and you told me Netty had need of the cash.'

Greengrass drained his glass. 'Right, that's it! I can't stand here chewing the fat all day with you lot, some of us have got a business to run, haven't we, Alfred?'

Nick stopped him at the door. 'Just a minute, Claude.'

'Hellfire. What is it now?'

'This car,' said Nick patiently. 'This car with the gold bar, your lucky piece you call it. It came from Arthur Pickard, didn't it?'

'What d'you mean?' Greengrass's blink went into overdrive.

'Why didn't you tell us, Claude?' said Nick. 'You've had plenty of opportunities. You know what that's called, don't you?'

'What what's called?'

'Deliberately withholding information about a serious crime,' said Nick. 'Which is a serious crime in itself. I think you'd better come in again, Claude.'

Greengrass's eyes were still blinking half an hour later when Nick and Blaketon led him into the interview room.

'You don't deny you sold the car for Mrs Pickard?' said Blaketon.

'Aye – '

Blaketon breathed out heavily. 'You mean you do deny it, or you don't deny it?'

'No,' said Greengrass.

'Give me strength,' sighed Blaketon.

'No, I mean, aye, I did sell the car, but, no, not for me own benefit. I were doing Netty a favour, weren't I?'

'So how did you come by the gold piece?' asked Nick.

'Arthur kept it in the car. You know, as a lucky token – '

'And you nicked it, I suppose,' said Blaketon.

'Oh no, not me, Mr Blaketon. Netty gave it me for helping her out. It were precious to her, you see, on account of it were Arthur's, not because it were gold, Netty didn't know it were gold, any more than I did – '

'That being the case,' said Nick, 'why didn't you tell us where you got it the first time we asked you?'

'Ah, well, you see, Mr Ronan, when you said the gold were nicked, like, I thought to meself I don't want to get Netty mixed up in owt like that.'

'How very noble of you,' said Blaketon.

'You can think what you like, Mr Blaketon, but what you don't know, you see, because coppers don't know everything, even though they think they do – '

'Get on with it,' said Blaketon.

'Arthur helped me out once, when I was skint. Give me a bit of money to tide me over, like.'

' "Gave"?' said Nick.

'Aye.'

'You as well?'

'He were like that, were Arthur,' said Greengrass. 'Very generous man.'

'Are you sure Netty didn't know it was gold?' said Nick.

'How could she?' said Greengrass. 'Arthur never used to tell her owt about nowt. Not what he found, nor where he found it. He showed me some Roman coins he dug up once, but he wouldn't say where – '

'All right, Greengrass,' said Blaketon, rising. 'That's enough.'

'What?' Greengrass was so taken aback he forgot to blink. 'You mean I can go?'

'Yes,' snapped Blaketon. 'Now get out before I change my mind!'

They watched Greengrass scuttle out of the station, stoop to untie Alfred from the Belisha beacon, glance round suspiciously to see if he was being followed, and shamble down the road into the four-ale bar of the Bull Hotel.

Ventress and Bellamy had their heads together over a preliminary report from Forensics as Blaketon and Nick came through into the duty room.

'Right,' said Blaketon to Nick. 'You'd better find out what else Arthur's left lying around. And just what Mrs Pickard knows about it.'

'And who else is on the same track,' said Nick.

'Sarge – ' interrupted Ventress.

'Wait a minute,' said Blaketon. 'How d'you mean, Rowan?'

'Carpets ripped up, fireplaces dug out, floorboards smashed – it's more than just bloody-minded vandalism, sarge,' said Nick. 'Job like that needs tools, planning. I'd say it was a search.'

Blaketon paced up and down considering the matter. 'If you're right, Rowan, it's attempted robbery.'

'Sarge – '

'Yes, Ventress?'

'We've just been going through this prelim from Forensics,' said Ventress. 'It says they found fifteen pound in an old tea caddy on the mantelpiece.'

'Mrs Pickard mention that to you, Rowan?'

'No, sarge.'

'If it had been kids,' said Ventress, 'and they'd found that much cash, they'd have scarpered with it.'

'You're probably right there, Ventress,' said Blaketon, thinking hard. 'So whatever whoever was after, it wasn't just money. Which leaves only one thing.'

'Looks like it,' said Nick.

Blaketon came to a decision. 'You'll have to sign that gold out of the safe, Rowan, and take it in and show it to her.'

'Right, sarge.'

'When you see her, take it easy. There's no point in upsetting her more than she is already,' said Blaketon. 'But try and find out exactly how much Netty Pickard does know.'

'Greengrass said Arthur Pickard never told her anything,' said Nick.

Blaketon nodded. ' "Owt about nowt" were his words. Let's hope Greengrass is right for once.'

'I can't see Netty being mixed up in it,' said Nick. 'I mean, if she had all that money, why stay on here after Arthur died?'

'All I know, Rowan,' said Blaketon with an air of finality, 'is that you're going to guard that gold with your life.'

'Yes, sarge.'

Nick and Kate got to Ashfordly Hospital about three o'clock. He moved round to the passenger door of the Triumph Herald to help Kate out. 'At least we're in the right place if anything happens, love.'

'I wish it would,' said Kate, heaving herself up on Nick's arm.

As they walked slowly to the hospital entrance, a black Rover saloon pulled away sharply in front of them.

'Good Lord,' said Kate, 'that's the second visit in two days.'

'What's that, love?'

'Councillor Stanton,' said Kate. 'He was here yesterday with a big bunch of flowers for Netty.'

'I didn't know he was a particular friend of hers,' said Nick.

'He said they were from the Council,' said Kate. 'But why come back again today?'

'Perhaps he forgot the grapes, love.'

Netty was out of bed, sitting in a chair. The room was full of flowers, cards, baskets of fruit, sweets, tins of biscuits and bottles of Lucozade.

'People have been very kind,' said Netty, 'and it's very nice here, but one more night will be enough for me, Dr Rowan. I shall be glad to be back in my own bed again.'

'The whole village has rallied round,' said Kate. 'Your sitting-room's been repainted, the floor and the fireplace have been done. You won't recognise the place.'

'That's what I'm worried about,' smiled Netty.

Nick brought out the heavy gold bar. 'Do you recognise this, Mrs Pickard?' He waited, notebook at the ready.

'Well, it's been polished up, but I can see it's Arthur's lucky piece,' said Netty. 'He carried it about in his car. You got it from Claude, I expect.'

'That's right,' said Nick.

'I gave it to him,' Netty smiled faintly. 'I thought he could do with a bit of good luck.'

'Did you know it was made of gold?'

'Not until Claude told me a few days back.'

'I'm sorry to have to tell you it's stolen gold, Mrs Pickard,' said Nick. 'Part of a large quantity that went missing seven years ago.'

'Do you know where your husband got it, Netty?' said Kate.

Netty shook her head, the same vague, faint smile on her face. 'I'm afraid I've no idea.'

Nick looked up from his notebook. 'Did he ever tell you about the things he found with his metal detector?'

'Oh no!' Netty's smile broadened. 'It would have spoiled his luck to talk about it.'

'How do you mean?' asked Kate.

'Arthur always said that good luck goes the minute you make mention about it. He was funny like that.'

Nick tried to break it to her as gently as he could. 'We've reason to believe he knew it was stolen.'

Netty fell silent. Hurt by the accusation, she reached a pocket handkerchief from her sleeve and wiped her eyes. Then, lifting her head up proudly, 'Arthur wouldn't harm anyone. He liked to make people happy.'

Kate took her hand. 'A lot of people were given money by your husband, Netty. Have you any idea where it might have come from?'

'No. But if he had money beyond our needs, it's how he'd use it.'

Nick wrote down her exact words, and considered his next question. 'Let's say your husband found that gold. What do you think he'd have done with it?'

'He'd have shared it,' said Netty firmly.

'D'you mean he'd have given it away to people?' asked Kate, looking puzzled.

'Oh no,' Netty smiled as if explaining something to a child. 'He would have had to keep it, to keep his luck strong. I mean, you can't help people unless you're lucky, can you?'

'How do you mean, exactly?' Nick tried to work out what the old lady was getting at. 'You mean he'd have kept the gold and given people money?'

Netty paused to reflect. 'What I mean is that Arthur thought you had to put back what you take, in the way of luck. And if you put back what you take, you're not taking anything really, are you? You're just sharing it.' She fingered the small gold charm on the chain around her neck. 'Well, that's what Arthur thought anyway.'

'I see,' said Nick, closing his notebook. Netty had virtually told him all he needed to know. Whatever the late Arthur had got up to, Netty had kept well out of it. Ask no questions and you'll hear no lies, was what it amounted to; just about enough to give Netty the benefit of the doubt – unless of course, she knew what had happened to the rest of the gold . . .

He watched her fingering the small gold charm. 'Can I ask you what that is on your chain?'

'Oh,' said Netty, holding it out for them to look at, 'it's a good luck token Arthur gave me, when we moved into Holywell Cottage.'

'Did he make it for you?'

'Oh no, he had it made special, by Stantons.'

Nick leaned forward for a closer look; the figure engraved on the charm was a copy of the goddess inlaid on the gold bar. 'D'you have any idea of who the figure is supposed to represent, Mrs Pickard?'

'That's Lady Fortuna, Mr Rowan,' smiled Netty.

80

'The patron of the wishing well. Arthur always said she brought him luck, so it was only fair to share it with her.'

After dropping Kate in Aidensfield, Nick hurried back to the station. Blaketon and Bellamy had bank statements and papers strewn all over the duty room. 'Sarge,' he said, striding in. 'We've struck gold!'

Blaketon straightened up, and tapped a finger on the bank statements. 'So have we. Arthur Pickard's bank statements: £15,000, deposited a few weeks after the bullion raid.'

'Some people are born lucky,' said Nick. 'I reckon Arthur Pickard believed you had to buy it – '

'What's that supposed to mean, Rowan?' frowned Blaketon. 'He nicked that gold from the villains who nicked it in the first place – '

'But he nicked it to give the proceeds away,' said Nick. 'He believed that was the price he had to pay – '

'I thought you said you'd struck gold, Rowan,' said Blaketon. 'I hope you've brought that bar back safe and sound.'

Nick laid it on the desk, the figure of Lady Fortuna uppermost. 'There we are, sarge. She's called Lady Fortuna, and she's the patron of the old wishing well in Pickard's back garden. According to Netty, Arthur reckoned he had to share it with her.'

Blaketon looked blank for a moment, then the penny dropped. 'It's in the well?'

'I'd lay odds on it,' said Nick. 'What he kept back, he flogged and used the money to play Robin Hood in Aidensfield – ' A sudden thought occurred to Nick. 'Is Alf still out at the cottage?'

'He's on his way back with the logbooks Arthur kept,' said Bellamy.

'I think we ought to get out there, sarge.'

'Why's that, Rowan?'

'If you knew Arthur had the gold, and you'd turned the house over and found nothing – where else would you look?'

Blaketon reached for his cap. 'Radio Ventress and tell him we're on our way.'

It was almost dark when Maggie parked her Land Rover outside the Aidensfield Police House. Five o'clock, she thought, and still another three weeks before they put the clocks forward.

Kate was lying on the bed, looking worn-out. Maggie put her bag down, and bustled about drawing the curtains.

'So how are we?'

Kate reached for a box of tissues. 'I think I might be coming down with a cold, Maggie. All I need – '

'Let's have a look at you.' Maggie put her hand to Kate's forehead. It was definitely feverish. 'Hot and sticky,' she said brightly. 'Exactly how I like my blokes.'

Kate smiled wanly. 'Don't make me laugh.'

Maggie took hold of Kate's wrist and glanced at her watch. 'Fun is essential to my bedside manner.' Kate's pulse was in the low eighties: not serious, but high for someone lying down.

'You should have been a doctor,' said Kate.

'No chance.' Maggie opened her bag and shook down the thermometer. 'When it was an option, I was addicted to enjoying life, not saving it.'

'And now?'

'Lucky in life, absolute disaster in love,' said Maggie briskly. 'Say cheese!'

With the thermometer in place, Maggie rolled up Kate's sleeve to take her blood pressure. The place where Kate had caught her arm against the chest of drawers was a mass of yellow and purple bruising. Seeing Maggie's frown, Kate removed the thermometer from her mouth. 'I told you I bruised easily.'

'And in Technicolor,' said Maggie. Then, more seriously, 'You're not responding to those iron injections, Kate.'

'Anaemia often drags on, Maggie. You know that as well as I do.'

'Maybe, but persistent anaemia needs treating,' said Maggie. 'We're going to need another blood sample, Kate.'

Kate was silent.

'There's no problem, Kate.' Maggie looked in her bag. 'We can do it now – '

'No,' said Kate. 'I'd rather wait until I've delivered.'

Maggie took in Kate's set, stubborn expression. 'What's wrong now? I have taken blood samples before, you know.'

Kate turned her face to the pillow. 'It's not that, Maggie.'

'What is it then, Kate? Not Doctor Knows Best, I hope – '

'No, of course not. It's just – oh, you know – tests and all that. I've had enough, Maggie. All that's behind me now. I'm looking forward, not back.'

'Kate, I'm not telling you anything you don't know.'

'No,' said Kate reluctantly, 'just what I don't want to hear.'

Maggie took a syringe from the metal steriliser tray in her bag, and waited.

'OK,' sighed Kate. 'If you insist.'

Maggie pumped up the rubber armband. 'I'll drop it in at the hospital first thing tomorrow.'

'No need,' said Kate quickly. 'I'll take it straight round to the lab.'

Nick and Blaketon found Ventress's Prefect parked halfway up the track leading to the cottage. Of Ventress there was no sign. They snicked the Anglia's doors closed, and listened. Apart from the drip of rain through the leafless shrubbery, not a sound.

Nick led the way to the wicket gate in the back garden fence.

'Psst!' Ventress emerged from the bushes, rain dripping off his helmet. 'He's in there!'

'Who is?' whispered Blaketon.

'I don't know,' replied Ventress. 'I was on my way back when I got Bellamy's call, turned round, and when I got back here, I heard this clinking and scraping. Like a spade or something – '

'Shh!' said Nick.

The three of them crouched down, listening. At first, all they could hear was the soft hush of rain falling. Then – a distinct metallic clink. 'Coming from the well,' hissed Ventress.

'Right,' said Blaketon. 'Open the gate.'

Ventress nodded, reached forward, lifted the catch,

and pushed. Ting! A small bell rang on the end of a rusty iron spring. Nick put out a hand, silenced it, and held the gate open for the others.

'You shouldn't be let out, Ventress!' growled Blaketon.

'How did I know there'd be a bell on it?' muttered Ventress.

They inched forward through the darkness of the dripping shrubbery until they had a good view of the old wishing well. At first there was nothing, then, as they watched, a bulky grey-haired figure in a yellow pullover rose up in the middle of the well, breathed heavily, and then sank down out of sight again.

'He must be up to his waist in there,' whispered Ventress.

They listened to the bulky figure sploshing about, bent double and grunting with the effort of dredging through the thick slime of mud and leaves. There was another metallic clink, and the yellow-pullovered figure rose up at the edge of the parapet and dropped two heavy metal objects into a Gladstone bag.

The grey head dipped out of sight again. 'Now!' whispered Blaketon. Nick and Ventress crept forward out of the cover of the shrubbery. With his last step before he reached the open, Ventress trod straight on the pile of twigs Netty had swept off the path.

Up came the grey head, jerking round towards Nick and Ventress. The next second, Nick was up and running, with Ventress lumbering along behind him. Before they could reach the well, the bulky figure had clambered out, seized the bag and was off down the curving path through the shrubbery.

Nick gained on him at every step; Ventress, blowing like a walrus, lagged a couple of yards behind. Weighted down by the bag, their quarry turned and flung it at them. It caught Ventress smack in the midriff, and sent him down, winded.

Nick launched himself forward in a flying tackle and brought his man face down on the sodden earth, knocking the breath right out of him. Nick grabbed him by his collar and kept him face down until Ventress and Blaketon came up with their flashlamps.

'Who is it?' puffed Ventress.

Nick swung the mud-stained face into the torchlight.

'Well, well, well,' said Blaketon. 'Councillor Stanton, as I live and breathe.'

'Come on. On your feet.' Nick dragged Stanton up by his collar.

By the time they had marched him back to the car, Nick had worked out the sequence of events. 'He lied when we first showed him the gold, sarge. He recognised the figure. Then today I found out that he'd made one for Netty Pickard.'

'So it was you bought the gold off Pickard,' said Blaketon.

'I only did it as a favour,' said Stanton, wiping the mud off his face. 'Look, I'm a respectable businessman – '

Blaketon's jabbing finger stopped him dead. 'You were his fence!'

'No, no,' said Stanton desperately, 'it was just the once. He said it was all he had – '

'Until that piece we showed you turned up,' put

in Nick. 'And you did recognise the figure on it, didn't you?'

'Well, yes,' admitted Stanton, 'I did.'

'And after that,' continued Nick, 'it was easy for you to check out where it came from, and find out how much more was on offer.'

'No, I swear – '

'He visited Netty in hospital,' said Nick. 'Twice.'

'Wormed it out of her, I expect, sarge,' said Ventress.

Stanton's eyes darted from one to the other, guilt written all over him.

'But he didn't know about the well the first time he came,' said Nick, 'so he took the house apart.'

'Made it look like kids were responsible,' added Ventress.

It was enough for Blaketon. He held out his hand for Nick's handcuffs. Seeing then, Stanton started to smile and bluster. 'Look, we're all professional men here, I'm sure we can sort this out to everyone's satisfaction – '

'Cuff him,' said Blaketon shortly. Stanton's attempt at a smile faded to nothing. 'I won't express a personal opinion on your conduct,' said Blaketon. 'It wouldn't be professional.' Then, unable to resist the temptation, Blaketon put his face close to Stanton's. 'Greed . . . hypocrisy . . . theft . . . a canker in the body of the parish council!' Blaketon drew back, restraining himself. 'All right Ventress.'

Ventress held the door open for the handcuffed councillor. 'In we go, councillor. We'll have a nice comfortable cell all ready for you.'

As Ventress stooped to enter the car after Stanton,

Blaketon detained him. 'You keep an eye on the well, Ventress. We'll send someone out to relieve you later.'

By eleven o'clock next morning, Holywell Cottage was swarming with police and security men from the insurance company. Nick and Ventress watched two of the men, black from head to foot in mud and leaf mould, clamber awkwardly out of the well and load the last of the gold bars, still covered in slime, into the back of a security truck.

'At least we were spared that, Alf,' said Nick.

'I was beginning to wonder,' replied Ventress. 'It was half ten before I got home – I was that wringing wet, the missus made me change in the outhouse.'

Netty, not long out of hospital, came up with a yard broom to sweep round the well. 'How much longer will you be, Mr Rowan?' she said anxiously.

'Not long now,' Nick reassured her. 'They've almost finished.'

'I don't know,' said Netty, pottering back towards the cottage. 'If it's not one mess, it's another.'

'I think she's seen enough of us,' said Ventress.

'Yeah,' said Nick reflectively. 'I wonder why?'

Blaketon touched the peak of his cap to the over-coated supervisor from the insurance company and marched over to Nick and Ventress. 'Right,' he said. 'That's it. They've scoured every inch of the premises, and beyond.'

'How much is still missing?' asked Nick.

'Four ingots,' said Blaketon.

Ventress scratched his chin, puzzled. 'Stanton said he only bought two off Arthur Pickard.'

88

'Not thinking of prospecting for them, are you, Ventress?'

'No, sarge.'

'Anyhow,' said Blaketon, leading them back to the Anglia, 'the insurance company aren't complaining. So, apart from the paperwork, which you two will now be completing, the case is as good as closed.'

Nick climbed into the car. 'Isn't there a reward, sarge?'

'I don't know at present,' said Blaketon. 'The insurance supervisor's looking into it. As it stands at the moment, the only potential claimant is Mrs Pickard. And we can hardly reward the wife of a thief, can we?'

Netty waited until three o'clock to make sure nobody was coming back. Then she went over to Arthur's workshop, carefully selected a stout, short-bladed screwdriver, and put it the pocket of her pinafore.

Twenty minutes later, she was on her knees by the newly restored fireplace taking the baseplate off the last of her four double-ended flat-irons.

A gleam of golden light caught her face as she removed the fourth small gold ingot and laid it beside the other three.

Her mind went back to the day, not long before Arthur died, when he had brought the four flat-irons back from his workshop, and laid them in the hearth. 'Well, there we are, Netty. If owt happens, I've melted down two ingots' worth there. I know you've never wanted to know about this business, so just call it our nest-egg, eh, love?'

Netty gave the four lumps of gold a final polish

with her duster. 'Sorry, Arthur,' she said softly, 'I'm going to have to take our nest-egg for a walk.'

Netty gamely pushed the heavy old wooden wheelbarrow to the edge of the wishing well, and set it down to get her breath. Then, one by one, she tossed in the four lumps of gold. 'There we are, Arthur. You always did say what you give, you get back.' She peered over the edge, waiting for her reflection to re-form. 'Didn't he, old girl?'

The Rebels had agreed to come back to finish off their cancelled gig and were blasting their way through a strobe-lit '5–4–3–2–1'. Nick, Kate and Maggie stood near the entrance watching Julie and Ollie and the rest of the Mods bopping away in the crowded hall.

There was a draught of cold night air, and Greengrass stuck his head through the entrance door. 'Mr Rowan! Have you got a minute? I don't want to come in in me gumboots, but it's urgent!'

Nick stepped outside to join Greengrass and Alfred. 'What's urgent, Claude?'

'I read that report in the paper,' said Greengrass, eagerly, his eyes glinting. 'You know, about recovering the gold and such – '

'Yes,' said Nick, 'it weighed in at over two hundred grands' worth.'

Greengrass drew Nick closer. 'It's the reward I'm on about. You know, for information leading to recovery.'

'I thought you might be,' said Nick. 'What about it?'

'Well it can't go to Netty, can it?' said Greengrass.

'And the way I see it, I'm the next in line – it were my piece from old Arthur that put you on the trail.'

'You're absolutely right, Claude,' said Nick. 'If anybody deserves the reward, you do.'

Greengrass's face beamed in triumph. 'I always said you were a good man, Mr Rowan – '

'The trouble is, Claude, the newspaper report got it wrong,' said Nick. 'There was a reward, but it was withdrawn five years ago – '

'What?'

'Nobody came up with any information, so they cancelled it. Sorry, Claude.' Nick moved back into the hall.

Greengrass followed, plucking at him, trying to stop him.

'No! They can't! They're depriving me of my due! It's diabolical! I'm an old age pensioner – you can't muck about with an old age pensioner – '

Nick turned to face him, firmly removing Greengrass's mittened hands from his leather jacket. 'Look, Claude. I've told you what I know, and that's it. Now, are you staying?'

'Why,' muttered Greengrass, wiping the dewdrops off his nose, 'what's it to you? It's a cold night out there, and I've just had a serious shock,'

Greengrass's hand reached for his pocket; Nick beat him to it, and pulled out the battered hip-flask. 'In the first place you haven't paid,' said Nick. 'And in the second, no alcohol allowed. Have to set the younger generation a good example – '

Greengrass snatched the flask back. 'Give it here!' He shambled back out to the waiting Alfred. 'They can't muck about with an old age pensioner!' he shouted, 'We'll show 'em, won't we, Alfred?'

The number came to an end. Kate, dazzled by the strobe lights, put her hand in Nick's. 'Let's go home, love.'

'Right,' said Nick. 'Maggie – '

'Yes, Nick?'

'Keep an eye on things for me.'

Maggie arched her eyebrows. 'And who keeps an eye on me?'

'Goodnight, Maggie.' Kate kissed her. 'See you tomorrow.'

'You bet.'

Nick and Kate strolled arm in arm away from the village hall, the music pounding out behind them, and the strobe lights flashing through the curtained windows.

Kate breathed in the cold night air. 'Bet you the baby comes tomorrow?'

'You haven't paid me for the last bet you lost, let alone today's,' said Nick.

'Hang on a minute,' said Kate. 'You were betting me – ' She saw Nick grinning. 'You tightfist! All right, double or quits, OK?'

'You're on,' said Nick, putting his arm round her.

# Six

Wednesday morning dawned bright and sunny, so Joe Norton and his two mates decided to bunk off school.

Joe was a big lad for his age. Apart from the spots round his mouth and chin where he had just started to shave, he looked nearer eighteen than fifteen. As a result, going to school bored him; living at home on the farm bored him; in fact, any sort of discipline bored him. Oddly enough, given his distaste for discipline, all Joe Norton lived for was the idea of joining the Army and getting into the Paras.

He was handy with his fists – too handy for his short and vicious temper – and saw himself one day boxing for the regiment. That was as far as his ambition went. Until he was sixteen, Joe had nothing to do with his life except hang around Aidensfield and cause trouble. The day his birthday came Joe was determined to enlist. Then he'd get the respect he deserved. Then he'd show his hard-faced Scots father who was the real 'maggot' of the family . . .

By half-past nine Joe and his mates were hanging over the stone wall, looking into Nick and Kate's back garden.

Frank was another big lad for his age, and a natural hanger-on: what Joe said went, as far as Frank was concerned. Dave was the weed of the trio: he seemed to think that by hanging round with the two big lads, some of their tough bully-boy reputation would rub off on him.

'I thought we were going to Whitby,' said Dave. 'Go down the arcade, have a bit of fun.'

'Well, we ain't,' said Joe.

'Ain't got no money, have we?' said Frank.

'I wouldn't have bunked off if I knew we were just going to hang round this dump all day,' said Dave. 'And I don't see why we got to do the copper's house anyway.'

'Because we have,' said Joe shortly, 'so shut it.'

'I don't want to,' said Dave.

'It'll be a laugh,' said Frank.

'No – '

Joe grabbed Dave by the lapels and banged him hard against the wall. 'Want me to tell everybody you're chicken?'


Kate was lying on the bed fully clothed, looking at the sun streaming through the window. At least the weather had improved in the last couple of days. She could smell the sun warming the earth outside, the moist, musky smell of returning life. It won't be long now, she thought.

She stretched and relaxed in the warmth, listening to Nick singing along to Herman's Hermits on the transistor in the nursery. The spring sunshine had driven her anxieties away for the moment; the only faint cloud on the horizon was the result of the blood test, and that should be coming through soon –

'Joshua!' shouted Nick from the nursery.

'Jehoshaphat!' she called back.

'Jeremiah!'

'I'm not calling any child of mine after Greengrass, even if it is a boy!'

Nick slipped the last hook into a blue and yellow curtain and clipped it on its slider. He climbed off the stepladder and swished the curtains satisfactorily to and fro. Perfect.

He had a sudden inspiration. 'Geronimo!' he called through to Kate, and listened, smiling, to her delighted laughter.

'Geronimo Rowan! I love it – '

Crash! The dustbin lid banged against the garden wall and clanged down the stone path. Nick went to the landing window. Three lads were emptying the dustbin all over the garden. Joe Norton, his sidekick Frank Sewell, and that little kid they dragged round with them, David Edgeley.

He pulled the window down. 'Hey! What the hell d'you think you're doing?'

'Bob-a-job week!' shouted Frank. 'We're emptying your dustbins!'

'You pick that lot up! Now!' Nick headed for the stairs.

'Hey up! He's coming,' said Frank, seeing Nick's head disappear from the window. 'Scram!'

He and Dave ran for the wall. Joe leaped after them, grabbed the back of Dave's donkey jacket and shoved him down in the border, using him as a stepping stone to leap for the top of the wall.

When Nick came out of the back door, he saw Joe Norton standing on top of the wall with a ten-inch flowerpot in his hands. He deliberately let it smash on the paving below.

'Sorry – it just slipped out me hand!' Joe leaped down from the wall and ran off after the others.

'I'll be seeing you later, Joe Norton!' shouted Nick. 'And you other two!'

He was clearing up the rubbish, earth and pot-shards when Kate appeared at the back door. 'What a mess,' he said. 'Then he had the brass nerve to stand there – '

'Who?' asked Kate.

'Joe Norton, who else?' said Nick, slamming the lid back on the dustbin. 'I know I was no saint, love, but I didn't go round asking for it. I'd have soon got a thick ear – from my mum as well as the bloke on the beat.'

Kate sighed. 'He must be a terrible worry to his parents.'

'There's got to be something wrong with a kid like that,' said Nick. He put his arm round Kate and patted her gently on the stomach. 'What if this one turns out to be a little monster?'

'No chance,' smiled Kate. 'Our baby will have the best of both of us.'

'What,' said Nick: 'your looks and my brains?'

Kate gave him a shove into the kitchen. 'Time you got to work, Constable Rowan.'


The old Romany caravan had seen better days; so, for that matter had Peg, the old bay mare pulling it, and Flo Briggs, the owner. Nevertheless, the caravan was newly painted in dark red and decorated with traditional Romany designs in golden yellow, and as they clopped slowly along the empty moorland road, they made a picturesque if somewhat dilapidated sight.

Flo was an old lady with a lined but lively face, sharp grey eyes, and a complexion weatherbeaten to the colour and texture of creased old leather. She sat high on the driver's seat in a small mountain of clothes, a balaclava under an old fur hat with a sprig of white heather in it, a couple of woollen scarves round her neck, and a long, tatty, pre-war motorcycle coat encasing layer upon layer of skirts and cardigans.

Although Flo was a shrewd and indomitable old bird, well used to the rigours of life on the road, there was a definite wariness about her. It was the look of a woman who'd had more kicks than ha'pence in life, and underneath the banter and the cajoling that made up her daily round, the bitterness was still there, sewn into the lines around her mouth.

Now, however, as she came over the brow of the hill above Greengrass's ramshackle smallholding, her eyes lit up. Now *there* was a place with possibilities . . .

'Come on, Peg,' she said in her cheery crackle of a voice, 'I smell breakfast.'

Greengrass was about to sit down to a huge fry-up of eggs, bacon, sausages, tinned tomatoes, beans and black pudding, when Alfred set up a furious racket in the yard outside, barking, yelping and snarling as if he'd cornered a rat or fox in the chicken run. Cursing, Greengrass shambled out at top speed, leaving his breakfast untouched in his anxiety to save his pullets.

There in the yard stood Flo, Peg and the caravan.

'What the flaming hell . . .' said Greengrass.

'That dog's a menace,' said Flo. 'Call it orf.'

'He's a guard dog,' said Greengrass over Alfred's excited yelps.

Flo looked dismissively round at the old piles of old tyres and rusting machinery. 'What's he supposed to be guarding?'

'Me, for a start,' said Greengrass.

'Why?' asked Flo, eyeing Greengrass's solid, unshaven bulk. 'Have you got a nervous disposition?'

'Course not,' said Greengrass. 'Shut it, Alfred.'

Alfred lowered his head and, still growling, skulked back into the house. Flo waited, as was her habit, and then got down from the caravan with a basket of white heather in her hand. She picked up a sprig, its stem covered in a bit of paper doily, and proffered it to Greengrass with a crooked, toothy smile. 'You could buy a sprig of lucky heather.'

'Summat up with your eyes?'

'I'm sorry?' said Flo.

'Heather?' said Greengrass, flinging an arm out at the purple-swathed moor. 'Have a look up there. We're falling down under the stuff here.'

'Ah,' said Flo mysteriously, screwing up her eyes into a squint, 'but not this kind.'

'Only type of heather that's lucky round here is full of dead pheasants waiting to be plucked.'

'So you won't spare a few coppers for an old woman and her 'orse?'

'You mean folk are daft enough to buy that?' said Greengrass.

Flo smiled, unnervingly. 'Some folk reckon they'd be daft not to.'

Greengrass wondered why he'd never thought of it before. 'It's quite lucrative like, this luck business?'

Flo's smile went out like a light. 'Look, mister,' she said, 'if you've got any ideas about muscling in on my territory, forget it.'

'Why?' said Greengrass, 'what's to stop me?'

'I am.'

Greengrass looked at the diminutive little figure bundled up in her old leather motorcycle coat. 'That right?' he challenged. 'How?'

Stung by his fat, red-faced grin, Flo cast about for a suitable reply. It came to her out of the blue. 'I'll hex yer!' she said vehemently.

Greengrass laughed in her face. 'Hex me? It takes more than some potty female to frighten Claude Greengrass. Nerves of steel, me – '

'You'll need them,' said Flo. She twirled her mittened hands round each other, muttering to herself, and flashed them open in front of Greengrass's startled face. 'Consider yourself well and truly hexed.'

Greengrass decided he'd had enough of the old bat. Besides, his breakfast was going cold. 'Stick your hexing up your jumper!'

Tilting her chin, Flo turned Peg round. 'Come on, Peg. This is no place for ladies.'

'Load of flaming mumbo-jumbo!' shouted Greengrass after the retreating caravan.

He walked into the kitchen to see Alfred standing on his chair, front paws on the table, wolfing down the last of the fry-up. Stricken, he glared at Alfred. 'One more trick like that, and you're asking to be taken to the vet!' he roared. Alfred looked up, licking his lips and wagged his tail.

As Greengrass fried up his last piece of stale bread in the beans and tomatoes Alfred had left, Flo's words ran through his mind: 'Consider yourself well and truly hexed.'

Telling himself not to be so flaming daft, he tipped the mixture of bread and smoking grease on to the plate Alfred had licked. It was not until he sat down, knife and fork in hand, that he realised he had lost his appetite.

'Do they always get as bad as this?' asked Nick, massaging Kate's swollen ankles.

'It'll be worth it when the baby arrives,' said Kate patiently. 'Honestly, Nick, you're getting worse that I am. You'll be having twinges next.'

'I already have,' grinned Nick, pulling his uniform jacket on. 'But I'm not telling you where.'

'Oh, you poor thing.'

'What I'm more worried about is the pram.'

'I've told you,' smiled Kate, 'it's tempting fate to get one too soon. You don't go walking babies about from day one, you know.'

'The rate we're going we'll be pushing it round in the wheelbarrow,' said Nick. He gave her a kiss on the cheek. 'Bye, love. Don't forget, ring the station if anything happens.'

'I will,' said Kate.

Her smile faded as soon as she heard him close the front door. It was always harder just after Nick had gone. The small house seemed to close round her, silent and oppressive, shutting her off from everything but her fears and anxieties.

She got off the bed and walked around, trying to pull herself together. 'Do something, Kate Rowan, find something, anything to be getting on with – put a bit of make-up on for a start.' Her pale face stared back at her, hollow-eyed. Sometimes, she reflected, it was no great shakes being a doctor: the more you knew, the worse you imagined.

She brushed her hair vigorously; as she applied her foundation, eyeshadow and lipstick, she began to feel better.

Flo decided to try her luck on the redbrick cottage on the outskirts of Aidensfield. If the first knock went well, the rest of them usually did. She walked up the path, basket of heather over her arm and peered through the window before she knocked. You could tell a lot about people from their front rooms. This one, dark and polished with an aspidistra on a lace mat, bolt-upright furniture, and an embroidered text on the wall, had the look of a religious house.

As soon as Mrs Hardaker came to the door, Flo knew she was right. Mrs Hardaker was a tall, raw-boned lady not much younger than Flo herself. Her expression, when she saw Flo standing on her front doorstep, changed from suspicion to disapproval in a flash.

'Yes?'

Flo held out her basket. 'A sprig of lucky heather, lady?'

'I let the Lord take care of that side of things,' said Mrs Hardaker, drawing back through the door.

'From what I heard, we're all God's creatures.' Flo indicated Peg standing patiently on the other side of the hedge. 'I'm sure He wouldn't object to a small contribution for me and my 'orse.'

Flo waited, watching Mrs Hardaker hesitate. Mentioning animals nearly always worked, even if it hadn't with that miserly old blighter, what was his name, Greengrass.

Mrs Hardaker's charitable instincts got the better of her. 'Just stay there then. No need for you to come in.'

Flo turned and winked at Peg. Mrs Hardaker came back clutching her old black purse. A threepenny bit and four pennies dropped into Flo's grimy palm.

'Thank you,' said Flo, picking out a sprig of heather and offering it to Mrs Hardaker. 'Here y'are, lady.'

'Oh no,' said Mrs Hardaker, closing the door, 'you're all right.'

'Take it please,' said Flo, pushing it through the gap. 'We're not a charity. May it bring you all you wish.'

'I doubt it,' said Mrs Hardaker, gazing abstractedly over Flo's shoulder into the road.

Maggie's Land Rover pulled in behind the caravan. She and Flo crossed on the path.

'Morning!' said Maggie cheerfully.

Flo took one look at Maggie's dark blue uniform. 'Morning,' she muttered, scurrying off down the path.

'Five minutes earlier, and you'd have saved me sevenpence,' said Mrs Hardaker, watching Flo

102

rumble off down the road. 'And I suppose you'll be expecting tea.'

'Yes, please!' said Maggie brightly, following Mrs Hardaker into the kitchen. There was always a cup of tea for her at Mrs H's, and always a gruff word to go with it: the old lady lived on her own, and although she was Christian kindness itself, she hated to be seen as a soft touch. 'What was she selling, anyway?'

'Luck,' sniffed Mrs Hardaker.

'And how much is that a pound?'

Mrs Hardaker gave Maggie a sour look. 'I dislike gypsies as much as anyone in this village but I won't have anyone starve.'

'Speaking of which – ' said Maggie with a cheeky grin.

'Go on then. You know where they are.'

Maggie reached into the biscuit tin and helped herself to a home-made ginger snap. 'Best ginger snaps in Aidensfield.'

'You should know,' said Mrs Hardaker, trying to hide her pleasure. 'You've had enough of them.' She tossed the sprig of heather on to the table, and hobbled awkwardly over to the stove to put the kettle on.

'So how's the leg been?' asked Maggie, opening her bag.

A terrified squawking and fluttering and ruffling came from Mrs Hardaker's back yard. She stood, kettle in hand, distraught. 'Me hens, they're after me hens!'

'Stay where you are,' said Maggie. 'I'll go.'

Maggie came out of the back door to find Joe,

Frank and Dave chasing the terrified birds round the hen-run.

'Hey,' said Joe, juggling a couple of new-laid eggs, 'how d'you like 'em, boiled or scrambled?'

'Get out of here this minute!' shouted Maggie, taking a step towards Joe. 'Put those back, you stupid idiot!'

Joe's face changed from a grin to a vicious scowl. He swore at her, drew back his arm and threw an egg as hard as he could at Maggie's head. She ducked and it smashed on her shoulder. When she looked up, Joe and the other two were scrambling up on to the coop and over the wall.

Maggie shook her finger at Joe. 'I know who you are, Joe Norton!'

'Guess what?' sneered Joe, standing on top of the wall. 'So do I!'

Maggie retreated angrily into the house. 'I'm not having that! Can I use your phone, Mrs Hardaker?'

Nick took Blaketon's call by the roadside up above Bishop's Dyke. Down below, he could see two of Bob Grant's men loading the carcass of a sheep, victim of a night-time hit-and-run, into a tractor and trailor.

'Where are you, Rowan?' said Blaketon's voice over the radio-telephone.

'Sorry sarge, I got held up. Bishop's Dyke.'

The radio crackled again. 'Well get yourself back to Mrs Hardaker's, Chase Cottage, Aidensfield. Your district nurse has just reported an incident – '

'How serious, sarge?' asked Nick, immediately thinking of Kate having to manage without Maggie.

'Something involving some kids,' crackled Blake-

104

ton's voice. 'Serious enough for her to report, anyway.'

'I'm on my way, sarge.'

Maggie's egg-stained jacket hung over the back of a kitchen chair. 'I wish you'd let me wash that off,' said Mrs Hardaker.

'Sorry,' said Maggie, sipping her tea. 'I can't, it's evidence.' There was a sharp rap on the front door. 'I'll get it,' said Maggie.

'Anyone would think you lived here.' Mrs Hardaker stared at Maggie's jacket, sighed and shook her head.

'What's up, Maggie?' said Nick at the door.

'Come in.' They moved down the hall into the kitchen. 'Kids, I'm afraid,' said Maggie.

'Morning, Mrs Hardaker,' said Nick.

'You took your time,' said Mrs Hardaker, determined to let Nick know exactly how she felt. 'Gangs of lads preying on old folks, rampaging about, doing what they like where they like, and the police doing nothing about it. It's a good job my Sam's dead and out of it.'

Nick could see the old lady was glad of a chance to let off steam; it was better that she was angry rather than frightened. 'What happened exactly?'

Maggie pointed to her jacket. 'Joe Norton and his cronies – '

'Not him again?'

'They were messing about with my fowl,' said Mrs Hardaker.

'I went out there to tell them off,' said Maggie.

105

'Joe swore at me, then he threw that. Hard as he could. He should be playing for Yorkshire.'

'Borstal, more like,' said Nick, 'the rate he's going. Then what?'

'When they'd hopped it, we discovered washing missing from the line,' said Maggie.

Nick frowned. Messing about and making a nuisance of themselves was one thing, but pinching stuff, even washing, was another. 'What's been stolen?'

'Underwear mainly,' said Mrs Hardaker tersely. 'Sheets get done on a Monday in this house.' She paused, making a mental list. 'Six pairs of knickers, white cotton.'

Nick noted it down. 'Anything else?'

'Two vests,' she snapped. 'They left the pink flannelette liberty bodice.'

'Thank you Mrs Hardaker,' said Nick. 'When you went out to them, Maggie, were any of these kids carrying clothing?'

'Not that I saw.'

'Are you sure?'

Maggie thought back. 'They certainly didn't have anything in their hands when they were in the hen-run.'

Mrs Hardaker picked up the sprig of lucky heather, wondered whether to throw it out, then decided that she had had quite enough bad luck for one day. She went to the draining board, ran the tap, put the heather in a glass, placed the glass on the table and looked at it. 'May the Lord forgive me for saying this, but sometimes it's quite hard to make sense of the Divine Plan.'

106

'Don't worry, Mrs Hardaker, we've got their names,' he reassured her. 'I'll catch up with them.'

'I hope so. I don't want them coming round here again.'

Maggie led Nick to the front door. 'It's hit her harder than I thought,' she said quietly.

'It often does, after a bit,' said Nick. 'What bothers me is this washing. It'd be more Joe's style to leave it scattered all over the place. I've had one run-in with them already this morning.'

'Perhaps he's just looking for attention.'

'He's going the right way about it.'

'No,' said Maggie, 'what I meant was, he never seemed to get much at home, not when I used to have to go up there. Mother was too busy with the other two, and Ted was always out on the farm.'

'I always got the impression Ted was really proud of his boys.'

'The first two, maybe,' said Maggie. 'Joe was an unwanted surprise.'

'How d'you mean?'

'Look, I'm coming to see Kate soon. What say we discuss it then?' Maggie looked down the hall to the open kitchen door. 'I can't have my patients thinking I'm a gossip.'

'As if they would,' grinned Nick.

Maggie gave him a firm push through the front door. 'Goodbye, Constable Rowan!'

Kate was breathless by the time she got down the stairs to the front door. 'Yes?'

'Oh dear,' said Flo, taking in Kate's condition, 'I wouldn't have knocked if I'd known. I'm sorry love,

I didn't mean to disturb you.' She turned to head back down the path.

'No,' said Kate quickly, 'that's all right, really.'

'You sure?' said Flo doubtfully.

Kate nodded. 'It makes a change from lying down.'

'Well, if you're sure,' said Flo, scrabbling around in her basket, 'I've got just the thing for you. A sprig of heather to bring you luck.'

'Well, thanks, but not really, no.' Kate began to close the door.

Flo poked her head forward. 'We all need a little luck, dear.'

Kate looked at Flo's crooked, weatherbeaten grin, and relented. 'All right,' she smiled, 'I'll just fetch my purse.'

'You won't regret it, dear.' Flo shifted the basket from her right arm to her left. There was a neat but dirty bandage across the knuckles of her left hand.

'What happened to your hand?' asked Kate.

'Caught it on a bit of barbed wire.'

'It looks like it could do with a new bandage,' said Kate. 'If you'd like to come in, I'll change it for you.'

'No,' said Flo, shaking her head. 'It's all right, thanks all the same.'

'I am a doctor,' said Kate.

Flo took a step back, looking alarmed. 'What sort of doctor?' she asked.

'I'm a GP,' said Kate.

'Oh,' said Flo, looking Kate up and down. 'I didn't think they had lady doctors, not this far out in the country.'

'You'd be surprised,' smiled Kate. 'Are you coming in?'

108

'Well, why not?' said Flo. 'Were you thinking of putting the kettle on, by any chance?'

Ted Norton, a hard, lean-faced man in his late forties, heard Nick's bike from the barn. When it stopped in the yard, he came out and gave Nick a long look and a dour nod. 'Constable.'

'I'm looking for your Joe,' said Nick, propping up the Francis-Barnett.

'Oh aye?' said Ted, his Scots accent unchanged after twenty years' sheep-farming on the moor. 'What's he done?'

'Suspected theft.'

'He didna hurt anyone?'

It struck Nick as a strange reaction. 'Why?' he asked. 'Has he before?'

Ted Norton turned away and began sweeping the yard. 'I canna help ye. He's no here.'

'D'you know where he is?' persisted Nick.

'He's nearly a grown man, constable,' said Ted sharply. 'He doesna need my permission to go out.'

'Maybe not,' said Nick, 'but since he's only fifteen, he's still your responsibility.'

Ted Norton doggedly went on sweeping the yard. 'Joe's not on his own, you know. His pals are just as bad.'

'Don't worry,' said Nick. 'I shall be talking to their parents too.'

Ted leaned on the yard broom. 'Look here, Constable Rowan, no one can say me and his mother haven't done our duty.' A hard, unforgiving expression came across his face. 'He's a mongrel,'

109

said Ted bitterly, 'he's always been a mongrel. He's . . . wilful.'

In that one word, Nick could see the whole, life-long battle between father and son. 'Can you think of any reason for this latest trouble?'

'Aye, I can.' Ted's gaze took in all the farm buildings before returning to Nick. 'I had to tell him there'd be no job for him on the farm. It's already stretched supporting my other lads. Joe . . . took it personal.'

'How does he get his spending money, then?'

'He takes it out of his mother's purse,' said Ted. 'When he can find it.'

Now came the crunch. 'Would you mind if I took a look in his room?' If Ted Norton refused, it would mean a search warrant, magistrates, the Juvenile Court, social workers . . . Luckily, the same thoughts seemed to pass through Ted's mind.

'He shares it with the next lad up.' He smiled, grimly. 'You might need a gas mask.'

There was a smell of sweat, stale tobacco smoke and old socks. The room was in two distinct halves: on one wall a Beatles poster, a couple of album sleeves and a Marilyn Monroe pin-up; on the other, an aircraft recognition chart and several military recruitment posters. Joe's bed was tightly made and his kit laid out, army-fashion, on a folded khaki towel.

'He's got it in his head he's going to get into the Paras,' said Ted. 'What else?'

Joe's possessions amounted to little more than some Army surplus clothes in a wardrobe and a couple of orange boxes full of war story magazines.

Nick looked under the bed: apart from a pair of polished army boots and a single boxing glove, nothing. 'How long before he's sixteen?'

'August,' said Ted shortly. 'Not soon enough for the rest of us. The other boys try and keep him in order, but when they're not around . . .' Ted Norton shook his head and walked over to the window to look out over his land.

'What happens?' asked Nick.

'It's no as if I can take my belt to him any more,' said Ted bitterly. 'Still, the Army will soon sort him out.'

'Does Joe have any weapons?' asked Nick cautiously. 'Knives, or guns?'

'I hope not!' Then, more defensively, 'Not that I know of – he's bad enough with his fists.'

Nick searched through a chest of drawers: socks, shirts, underwear, a couple of khaki sweaters with shoulder and elbow patches. 'This may seem a strange question, Mr Norton, but have you ever seen Joe with any women's clothing?'

For the first time, Ted Norton's dour face cracked into a smile. 'Joe? He may have gone rogue, but he's not peculiar. There's nothing funny about any of my boys.'

'Fair enough,' said Nick, looking at the recruitment posters. 'Were you ever in the Army?'

'Aye,' said Ted. 'The Black Watch.'

# Seven

Flo had drunk Kate's teapot dry. 'Oh, that's better!' She wiped her mouth with the back of her newly bandaged hand, and stood up to leave. 'Thank you ever so much, dear.'

'It's a nasty cut, you know,' said Kate. 'I still think an injection would be a good idea.'

Flo gave a little shudder. 'I'm not keen on needles,' she said. Then she smiled crookedly and put on her wheedling voice. 'D'you think I could beg a favour before I go?'

Kate immediately thought she was going to ask to use the lavatory. 'That depends on what it is.'

Flo pointed at Kate's stomach. 'Could I touch?'

Kate had some vague memory of an old wives' tale about touching bringing luck. 'Yes, of course.'

Flo put her hand gently on Kate's stomach. 'Strong healthy baby.' Her lined old face took on a sad, wistful look; Kate wondered how long she was going to keep her hand there. But after a second or two the old lady seemed to come back to herself; she smiled up at Kate. 'Mustn't forget to give you this.' She took a large spray of heather from her basket and laid it on the kitchen table.

Kate opened her purse and took out a shilling. 'Here.'

'Oh no,' said Flo. 'There's no need. Not after you did my hand.'

'Please,' said Kate. 'I'd like to give you something.'

Flo's eyes lit on the packet of chocolate biscuits. 'One more of these will do.'

Nick came across Joe and his mates in the bus shelter. He pulled into the kerb as Dave was blowing a bubblegum balloon. Joe, seeing Nick get off his bike, popped the bubblegum with his cigarette end and stared insolently up at him.

'I've had enough of your lot for one day,' said Nick shortly. 'You think you're being clever, messing about like this?'

'Nah,' said Joe, 'we ain't clever – we go to Secondary Modern, don't we?'

'Not there now, are you?'

'Lunch hour.'

'Come off it,' said Nick, 'you're playing truant.'

'You going to report us then?' said Joe. 'Take us in for bunking off?'

'I tell you what I could do,' said Nick. 'I could do all three of you for wilful damage and assault.'

'You got to be joking,' sneered Joe. 'One rotten old egg?'

'We were only mucking about,' muttered Dave, shuffling his feet.

'Oh yes?' said Nick, his voice hardening. 'You call criminal damage to other people's property mucking about, do you?'

'Nothing else to do round here,' said Frank. 'We were having fun. You know, F-U-N.'

Joe turned his back on Nick. 'Don't waste your

breath. He's a copper. They got rules to stop us enjoying ourselves.'

'We've also got rules that'll have you put away for stealing clothes,' said Nick.

The three looked at each other in surprise. 'What clothes?' said Frank.

'The ones that went missing from Mrs Hardaker's washing line,' said Nick. 'Which, in case you don't know, is not mucking about, it's theft. And theft means court and court means Remand School.'

Dave swallowed hard. 'That wasn't us,' he said. 'Honest – '

'I don't believe you,' said Nick flatly.

Joe turned on him. 'Look,' he said, 'if I did any thieving it'd be stuff worth having.'

'Right,' said Nick. 'I'm warning you now. If I catch you stealing so much as a blade of grass, you'll be in the next van to Borstal. Understand?'

'Yeah,' said Dave, nodding quickly, 'I do.'

'You?' said Nick to Frank.

'OK,' he said reluctantly.

'That leaves you, Joe Norton.'

'Yeah,' said Joe, eyeing Nick up and down. 'It does, doesn't it?'

'You're not doing yourself any favours, Joe.'

Joe shrugged, insolent to the last. 'Nobody ever done me any.'

Nick thought about it on the ride over to Ashfordly. The other two lads were no problem; a warning was enough. But Joe was definitely spoiling for a fight, and it wasn't hard to see where the aggression came from: neglected at home, a failure at school, and fighting was all he was good at. Nick wondered whether he should have lifted him there and then; on balance he decided he had been right not to. Community policing wasn't about arresting people, it was about persuading them to keep the peace for their own benefit; getting heavy over minor offences only ever succeeded in making things worse. The trouble with Joe Norton was that he really was asking for it . . .

'What did you do?' asked Blaketon.

'I warned them,' said Nick. 'Severely.'

'Did it do any good, though?' asked Ventress.

'Does it ever?' said Bellamy.

'It'll work with two of them,' said Nick. 'I'm not sure about the third, Joe Norton. He thinks he's a hard case.'

'What about the stolen clothes?' asked Blaketon.

'No evidence as yet to prove it was them,' replied Nick. 'And if I arrest Joe for vandalism, he'll only see himself as a hero.'

'So will his mates,' said Ventress.

Blaketon thought it over. 'Clip round the earhole usually works. Used to, anyway.'

'I doubt it in Joe's case, sarge. His dad used to try that, and his brothers. Now I think it's just the excuse he's looking for. The boy needs watching. He's heading for trouble – '

'Come on Rowan,' said Blaketon. 'He's a light-fingered lad who threw an egg, not Jack the Ripper. What about the parents of the other two?'

'Dave's mother works at the chicken factory. I couldn't get to see her. Frank's dad just laughed.'

'Who'd be a father?' said Blaketon drily. 'How is Dr Rowan, by the way?'

115

'She's all right, just getting more and more tired,' said Nick. 'I'm trying to get her to look at prams, but she's got it into her head it's unlucky to buy one too soon.'

Blaketon shook his head sagely. 'No man,' he said, 'will ever plump the depths of the female mind.' Having delivered himself of this pearl, he clasped his hands behind his back and, head still shaking, strode into his office.

'Well,' said Ventress, 'I never thought I'd agree with the old blighter, but he's right this time.'

'How d'you mean, Alf?' said Bellamy.

'You look at my missus. She took a liking for coal and radishes when she was carrying. Amount she ate, I'm surprised she didn't ignite in the delivery room.'

Bellamy frowned, tried to take it in, and gave up. 'I don't think I'm ready for fatherhood yet.'

'Steady on,' said Nick. 'You're not even married.'

'Some of my mates have discovered it doesn't always come in that order,' grinned Bellamy. 'Anyway, what I've heard, babies cost a fortune.'

Nick took a three-year baby book out of its brown paper bag. 'I've just bought this, today. You can record the baby's progress. Look: first step, first word, first tooth, everything for the first three years – '

Bellamy and Ventress exchanged looks and sighed. Nick, oblivious, went on leafing through the baby book.

'Hey,' said Bellamy, 'make sure you get loads of photos of the nipper in the bath.'

Nick looked up from the book. 'Why?'

'Well,' grinned Bellamy, 'later on you can threaten to show them to his girlfriend if he doesn't do the washing-up.'

'It wouldn't work,' said Nick.

'Why?'

'It's going to be a girl.'

'It's no use, Phil,' said Ventress. 'He's a hopeless case.'

The desultory lunch-time conversation in the Aidensfield Arms ground to a complete halt as Flo walked in and parked herself next to Greengrass at the bar.

'I'll have half a pint please,' she said firmly.

George paused, hand on the beer-pull: he'd been caught out by what he considered to be Flo's type before. 'That'll be sevenpence, then.' He waited, hand out for the money.

Flo nodded, knowing full well what he was thinking, and slowly counted out a threepenny bit and four pennies. George took the money, looked at each penny to see if it was Irish, and began to pull the beer.

'Is that your caravan parked on Fletcher's Common?' he asked.

'Yes,' answered Flo, putting her chin up. 'Why?'

Greengrass saw his chance. 'It's an offence against the community, that's why.'

'How d'you mean?' said Flo. 'I'm not harming anyone.'

'You're not paying rates, that's what you're not doing,' blustered Greengrass. 'Unlike the rest of the decent, upstanding citizens in this bar.'

George looked at Greengrass's pint, his fourth since twelve o'clock. 'You're not always upstanding, Claude. How many summonses have you had lately?'

Greengrass took a swig at his pint. 'Bureaucratic irregularities.'

'Swallowed the dictionary again,' said Gina. 'I'm just going out the back, see if me washin's dry.'

Greengrass started on Flo again. 'We're hardworking folk round here, and we object to people living off the land for nowt.'

'From what I've heard,' said Flo, sipping her half-pint, 'you've made a profession out of it.'

Greengrass turned on his grinning cronies. 'And you lot'll be laughing out the other side of your faces before long. Mark my words, you'll be sorry. They bring nowt but trouble, do gypsies.'

'I'm not a gypsy,' said Flo stoutly. 'I just prefer life on the open road. I'm a free spirit, that's what I am.'

'The only free spirit I like comes in a bottle,' retorted Greengrass. 'How long d'you reckon on stopping?'

Flo took another judicious sip, and looked all round the bar. 'Well, it was only going to be a couple of days, but seeing how friendly you all are, maybe I'll stay a lot longer.'

'Hellfire – '

Gina came storming in through the back door. 'Right then!' she shouted angrily. 'Who's the joker? Who's pinched my knickers?'

With one accord, everybody at the bar turned to stare at Greengrass. 'What you all looking at me for?' he said, doing his best to seem affronted. 'Only nickers I'm interested in are green and crinkly and come from the Royal Mint!'

An hour later, Nick was riding across Fletcher's Common towards the dark red and yellow caravan when Greengrass flagged him down.

'You see that?' he said, pointing to Flo stirring a pot on an open fire. 'Look at her, crouched over it like some flaming old witch. I hope you've come to move her on.'

'Why would I want to do that, Claude?'

'She's an eyesore, that's why.' Greengrass belched and waved his arm in the direction of his smallholding. 'She's ruining the landscape, spoiling the view.'

Nick glanced at the piles of old tyres and wrecked car bodies. 'That's rich, coming from you.'

'Apart from that, she's a public danger an' all.'

'How d'you make that out?'

'She's a flaming albatross,' said Greengrass. 'Brings folks bad luck. You want to get rid of the old witch!'

'Come off it, Claude.'

'Oh no, Mr Ronan, I'm serious,' said Greengrass, swaying slightly on his feet. 'You look at it this way. No one has ever accused me of stealing ladies' you-know-whats before she evil-eyed me.' He belched, and stomped off unsteadily towards his smallholding. 'Get rid of her! Nowt but trouble!'

Nick rode over to Flo, saluted and introduced himself. 'Police Constable Rowan.'

'Oh yes?' said Flo, eyeing him warily. 'Is anything wrong?'

'No,' said Nick, stepping off the Francis-Barnett. 'I just wondered how long you intended staying here.'

Flo looked round the open common. 'Just another couple of nights,' she said. 'That isn't a problem, is it?'

'It shouldn't be.' Nick kicked at the singed turf round the fire. 'You'll keep an eye on that? Moorland fires are a real hazard, even in winter.'

'Yes, of course,' said Flo, skimming a few bits of burned grass off the top of the pan of boiled water on the fire.

'How do you manage for water?' asked Nick.

'Don't worry,' said Flo, glancing slyly down towards Greengrass's place. 'I've made my own arrangements.'

Greengrass watched from his kitchen window until Nick had ridden off and Flo had disappeared into her caravan. 'No flaming privacy anywhere,' he grumbled to Alfred, picking up a copy of the *North Yorks Gazette*, and heading off across the yard to the privy.

He hauled open the creaky wooden door – and stopped dead in astonishment. Everything had been swept clean: there wasn't a spider's web or a woodlouse to be seen, and a large pot of fresh daffodils stood on the immaculate flagstone floor. He scratched his head and frowned. What the flaming heck was going on?

'Rub my back, Nick.' It was after supper, about half-past eight in the evening, and Kate and Nick were sitting together on the sofa. The stove was drawing well, there was a comforting red and yellow flicker from the logs, the Righteous Brothers sang softly in

120

the background, and Nick was out of uniform, relaxing in his favourite Arran cardigan.

'How's that, love?' he said, massaging Kate's shoulders.

'Mmm,' said Kate dreamily.

They sat peacefully for a while, content with each other's company. Nick went over the events of the day: Joe Norton, Flo, Greengrass . . .

'You know,' he said, 'old Claude honestly thinks this Flo's hexed him.'

'She seemed perfectly harmless to me,' said Kate.

Nick sat up. 'When did you meet her?'

'Oh,' said Kate, 'she came here selling lucky heather this morning. There, on the mantelpiece.'

Nick went on gently rubbing Kate's neck.'First we can't buy the pram too soon, then we're buying lucky heather – what happened to the level-headed doctor I married?'

Kate smiled at him. 'I know, it's stupid, isn't it?'

'Superstitious, that's all.'

'I tell you what,' said Kate, turning to face him. 'Why don't you go ahead and buy a pram?'

'What? Without you?'

Kate leaned her head against him, and sighed. 'I'm not sure I'm up to a shopping trip. Whatever you choose will suit me fine.'

'Well, if I do,' said Nick, getting up to reach the brown paper bag from the table, 'I'll hold you to that. I bought this today. See what you think.'

Kate took the grey and gold baby book from its bag. 'Oh, Nick – '

'Don't tell me that's unlucky too.'

Kate snuggled herself back into his arms. 'No, of course it isn't. It's lovely.'

He watched her leafing through the pages. 'It'll be something to look back on,' he murmured into her soft blonde hair, 'when we're old and grey, and our children are having their children.'

Kate closed the book and set it aside, lost in thought.

'What d'you think?' he asked.

'I think it's lovely.'

He put his arms round her and held her close. 'You, me and our baby. I can't wait.' He felt Kate's arms very tight around him.

'It won't be long now, Nick. It can't be . . .'

# Eight

Nick had gone by the time the mail arrived next morning, and when Kate opened the letter she had been waiting for, her world collapsed in ruins.

The brown NHS envelope lay ripped open on the surgery table. Kate stood by the phone, willing someone to answer quickly, willing it to be good news. The ringing stopped: Kate could hear her heart thudding. 'Hallo,' she said, striving to keep her voice level and professional. 'This is Dr Rowan here, Aidensfield. You sent a letter asking me to ring for the results of a blood test on a Mrs Betts . . . Yes, that's right, Betts . . . Don't worry, I'll hold.'

Waiting, Kate felt herself growing hot and dizzy. She wondered whether she was going to pass out or, worse, go into labour at this of all moments. 'Oh come on, come on, for God's sake.' She pushed a hand through her hair. It felt as if she'd just come out of the shower.

'Dr Rowan?' said the light, pleasant voice at the other end of the line.

'Yes, yes, I'm here.'

As Kate listened, part of her, the professional medical practitioner, was on automatic pilot, checking and rechecking the results. 'What? . . . Yes, yes, I got that . . . Thank you . . . Bye-bye.' The rest of her, the part that felt, loved, moved with new life, was sinking like a stone into cold, black despair.

As her world collapsed around her, she heard the line go dead at the other end. There was no one she could tell. Not Nick. Not Maggie. No one.

When she finally remembered to replace the receiver, the silence around her intensified the emptiness she felt within.

There was no pain, she noted, just a deadness, an absence, as if she had suddenly been robbed . . .

Nick and Maggie were in the kitchen when she finally, somehow, got herself home. She tried to listen to what Maggie and Nick were saying, in the hope that their familiar voices would somehow pull her back to normality, up out of the blackness, out of the well, into the warm, safe light of ordinary everyday life – but her mind wouldn't, couldn't, focus: nothing they said seemed to make sense.

Maggie glanced at the breakfast things littering on the table. 'Where is she then?'

'She must have popped into the surgery to pick up the mail.'

'More bumf to wade through.'

'She won't be long,' said Nick. 'Tell me about the Nortons.'

'Well,' said Maggie, moving the striped mugs and cereal bowls to the sink, 'the last couple of times I've called, Ted Norton had bruising to the face and eye. Reckoned he'd walked into the barn door.'

'Can you remember how long ago that was?'

'About a month, six weeks at most.'

'Could it have been an accident?'

Maggie shook her head. 'You walk into a door,

you'll either cut the skin or raise bumps on the cheek or forehead. You won't get bruising to the eye. This was a real shiner, Nick, and I've seen enough of them to know.'

Nick nodded thoughtfully. 'If Joe is beating up his father, he's well out of control.'

Step by step, Kate forced herself to move down the hall, towards the kitchen. She could hear their voices clearly now.

'I'll have a word with Ted Norton,' Nick was saying.

'He's a proud man,' said Maggie's voice. 'He'll deny it. You know what Ted's like. He'd never be able to hold his head up in the pub again.'

Kate pushed a hand through her damp hair, took a deep breath and walked into the kitchen. She closed the door, keeping her back to them.

'Oh hi, Kate,' said Maggie. 'How are you today?'

Kate forced herself to turn round and smile. 'Bored, tired, the usual.'

'You haven't been working?'

'I wouldn't dare.'

'Are you sure you're OK, love?' asked Nick anxiously.

'Nick, how many more times? I'm fine.'

'You don't look it – '

'You should try carrying this great lump round all day.'

'Sorry, love – '

Maggie decided it was time to step in. 'Have you had the results of your blood test yet?'

'No.'

125

'Are you sure?'

'Of course I'm sure – what d'you take me for?'

'They should have been back by now, Kate,' said Maggie.

'I can't see why you're so concerned,' snapped Kate. 'We both know all it's going to indicate is anaemia.' She swung round sharply and caught her thigh on the corner of the kitchen table. 'Damn – damn everything!' she said, slamming out.

Nick looked at Maggie. 'What was that all about?'

'Well,' said Maggie, 'I'd say it probably means it's on the way.'

'What?' said Nick, looking alarmed. 'Now?'

'Very close,' said Maggie. 'It's the difference between the baby's clock and her clock that's making her irritable. It'll be some time today, mark my words.'

'Today?' echoed Nick. 'I'd better get the pram then.'

When Kate heard Maggie laughing, the tears began to flow unbidden down her face.


Greengrass's truck was parked on the side of the road, its bonnet up and most of Greengrass's big-bellied bulk underneath it. Alfred sat in the passenger seat, delicately sniffing the morning air. Flo came up on the driver's side: dogs and Flo didn't get on.

Greengrass was grunting and cursing to himself as he fiddled with the electrical contacts on the petrol pump. 'Flaming nuts, either too flaming small or too flaming tight – '

'It's probably the carburettor,' said Flo casually.

Greengrass shot bolt upright at the sound of her

126

voice and banged his head on the greasy underside of the bonnet.

'What the – ?'

Flo leaned forward to look into the engine. 'I was only saying, it's probably the carburettor, or the air filter. I can hear the petrol pump ticking from here – '

'I'll thank you to keep your head out of my bonnet!'

'Only trying to help.'

Greengrass slammed the bonnet shut, and reached down to crank the starting handle. 'Why don't you go and sell some pegs?'

'I don't sell pegs,' said Flo equably. 'I told you, I'm not a gypsy.'

Greengrass grunted and swung, and swung and grunted, all to no avail. He grabbed the starting handle in both hands and cranked with all his might. The engine kicked back on him and the handle flew round, twisting his wrist and clouting him on the shin. He let out a howl of rage, stood up, his face purple, and launched a flying kick at the radiator. All that produced was another howl of pain. Flo watched Greengrass hopping around on one leg, rubbing his wrist and cursing the air blue.

'Oh dear,' said Flo. 'You're not going to get very far in life if you're always so bad-tempered.'

Greengrass let out an agonised roar. 'I only want to go to flaming Ashfordly!'

'Well,' said Flo, 'why not catch the bus like the rest of us? There's one going in ten minutes.'

Greengrass, lost for words, watched her march stoutly off down the hill into Aidensfield.

As soon as the bus pulled in, Joe and his two mates

barged to the front of the queue past Flo and Mrs Hardaker, up the steps on to the bus. Joe's transistor started blaring out 'Hippy Hippy Shake'. The slightly-built middle-aged conductor stood in their way. 'You're not getting on here playing that racket.'

'Why not?' Joe towered over him. 'My kit, I'll do what I like with it.'

'Not on my bus you won't.'

Nick rode up on his bike. 'Any trouble?'

Joe immediately switched off his transistor and moved quickly down the bus, grinning at Frank and Dave. Flo, Mrs Hardaker and the other passengers climbed on board while Nick chatted to the conductor and kept a careful eye on Joe and his mates. Gina came running over from the pub.

'Late as usual,' said the conductor.

'Always in a rush, me,' said Gina. 'Thanks for holding him up, Mr Rowan.' She clambered up the steps. ''Ey, you any closer to catching the Knicker Nicker?'

'I'm working on it.'

'Yeah, well you better get him. I can't get lacework like that in Ashfordly, y'know.'

The conductor pulled the bell-cord and the bus drew away. It hadn't gone five yards before Nick heard 'Hippy Hippy Shake' belting out of Joe's transistor.

Greengrass had siphoned off a cupful of precious petrol from the tank of his truck and was washing the carburettor jets in it when the bus sailed past. He looked up just in time to see Flo waving the back of her hand at him, smiling and nodding like the Queen Mother. He was so taken aback he spilled

128

half a cupful of petrol down the front of his trousers. 'Now look what she's made me do!' he yelled at Alfred. 'By heck, I am flaming hexed!'

Ventress picked up the phone. 'Ashfordly police station.' Bellamy noticed him flinch and hold the receiver several inches from his ear. From the resigned, long-suffering expression on Ventress's face and the shrill tirade emerging from the earpiece, Bellamy surmised it was Mrs Ventress on the line. 'Yes, of course it's me,' said Ventress. 'What? . . . Now then, calm down, love, I can't make out what you're saying . . . What? . . . Did you see anyone? . . . No, I see . . . All right, love, now just tell me what's missing.' Ventress picked up his ballpoint and started to make a list.

Blaketon came out of his office with Nick. 'It might be worth checking the dress agencies – '

'All right!' shouted Ventress into the phone. 'I'm coming, I'm coming! I can't be in two places at once, can I?' He slammed the phone down and blew out a long, heartfelt sigh.

'Trouble, Ventress?' asked Blaketon.

'Mrs Ventress. Washing's missing down our street, sarge.'

'I see. Do we know what, exactly?'

'Well,' said Ventress, consulting his list, 'what's gone from our place is two shirts, couple of petticoats and . . . six pairs of bloomers.'

'Right,' said Blaketon, 'you'd better get yourself over there then, as a matter of some urgency.'

'Yes sarge.'

'Find out if anyone saw anything.'

'I will, sarge.' Ventress hurried out, pulling on his helmet.

'Our thief is widening his area of activity,' said Blaketon. 'First Aidensfield, now Ashfordly.'

'I saw Joe Norton and his mates getting on the Ashfordly bus this morning,' said Nick.

'Right,' said Blaketon decisively. 'What we need to find out is what they're doing with the stuff once they've nicked it.'

'I'll try the second-hand stall on the market,' said Nick. 'They could be selling it there.'

'Good thinking,' said Blaketon. 'I'll come with you, Rowan. I shall quite enjoy a run-in with these flowers of our youth. You're in charge, Bellamy.'

'Yes, sarge.'

Joe, Frank and Dave sauntered past a flower stall massed high with daffodils and anemones, and homed in on the fruit and veg stall next to it. With a routine practised since childhood, Frank asked the stall-holder how much the swedes were while Joe nudged Dave into the other end of the stall with his shoulder. A few seconds later, once they had turned the corner into the next aisle, all three were biting into big, dark-red Canadian apples.

Nick and Blaketon were patrolling the opposite side of the market. 'So Nurse Bolton thinks it'll be today, does she?' said Blaketon.

'Haven't even got the pram yet,' said Nick. 'Not that I know anything about prams anyway.'

As they strolled on through the stalls, making their presence felt and keeping an eye out for Joe and his mates, Blaketon considered the problem. 'When you

130

come down to it, it's just another form of transport, Rowan. Approach it the same way you would if you were buying a car and you won't go wrong.' They came to a junk stall, beside which stood a battered old pram, its hood in ribbons and its wheels buckled. 'Which means avoiding wrecks like this,' said Blaketon.

A couple of yards further on was the second-hand clothes stall, its trestle table piled high with a jumble of skirts, blouses and shirts. Underneath were cardboard boxes full of underwear.

'Are you the owner of this stall, madam?' asked Blaketon.

'You've just missed him,' said the woman behind the table. 'He's gone to a house clearance. Could be all day.'

Nick was rifling through one of the boxes of underwear. He pulled out a pair of black frilly knickers and looked for the label. A short frayed stub was all that remained. 'The label's been cut out of this pair, sarge.'

Blaketon took the knickers and held them up for the woman to see. 'Have you got any idea where you got these?'

'Sorry,' said the woman. 'The boss does most of the buying.' She leaned forward confidentially. 'Is it black lingerie you're particularly interested in then, sergeant?'

Blaketon let the knickers fall on to the stall. 'Purely in a professional capacity.'

'Because if you are,' said the woman, 'there's a box of it round the back here, just arrived.'

As Blaketon and Nick came out from behind the

stall with the box of black underwear, they saw Greengrass holding out a Hawaiian-style shirt to the woman. He dropped it as soon as he saw them.

'Got something to sell, Greengrass?' asked Blaketon.

The eyes began to blink. 'Me? No, nothing – '

'Don't tell me you're putting your hand in your pocket and actually buying.'

Greengrass managed to blink and look hangdog at the same time. 'I'm thinking about it.'

'Maybe we can help you make your mind up?' said Blaketon, picking up a lurid green and orange palm-trees-in-the-sunset number. 'How about this?'

'No, no thanks,' said Greengrass. 'Very kind of you an' all, but it's personal.'

Blaketon watched him shambling away from the stall. 'Greengrass and tropical shirts – one of the great unsolved mysteries of our time.'

'Perhaps he's thinking of going abroad, sarge,' offered Nick. 'Somewhere hot.'

'The hotter the better,' said Blaketon. 'Let's get that box of ladies' articles in the car.'

On the way back along Ashfordly's main shopping street, they came to a display of prams in a babywear shop. Blaketon looked cautiously up and down the street. 'Fancy a look inside?'

'We're on duty, sarge,' said Nick, taken aback.

Blaketon propelled Nick firmly through the double doors. 'If your conscience bothers you that much, Rowan, I can always put you down for some unpaid overtime.'

Kate sat on the living-room floor surrounded by

132

medical textbooks she hadn't consulted since she was a student. She felt a slight twinge – and then the shock of a real contraction. As it hit her, she gasped in involuntary panic, and then, as the wave of pain went through her, she began her deep-breathing exercises, heaving lungfuls of air in and out through her mouth until the contraction moderated sufficiently for her to relax and glance at her wristwatch.

Twelve-thirty.

Just before one o'clock, she had the second big contraction. When it had passed she hauled herself to the phone and dialled Maggie's number.

'Maggie, it's Kate. I've started.'

'Are you sure?'

Kate smiled, despite herself. 'I'm a doctor, aren't I?'

'This is no time to pull rank,' said Maggie. 'How fast are the contractions coming?'

'Every half-hour. There's no hurry, my waters haven't broken yet. I just thought I'd let you know.'

'Right. I've got a couple of quick visits to make, then I'll see you at the hospital. Is Nick with you?'

'I'm just about to ring him.'

Maggie put her lunchtime egg and cress sandwich to one side. 'OK, but no showing off and giving birth *en route*. I booked tickets for this one months ago.'

Kate dialled the station and got Bellamy. 'If you could just tell Nick I've started – '

'Started what?'

'Having the baby, Phil.'

'What?' yelped Bellamy, leaping to his feet and looking round as Ventress clomped heavy-footed into the duty room. 'Yes ... No ... The hospital ... Right, I'll tell him – '

'And tell him there's no panic. Everything is perfectly normal.'

'Right,' said Bellamy. 'There's no panic. Understood.' He put the phone down and stared wild-eyed at Ventress. 'Panic? Why should I panic?'

Ventress sank into his chair with a sigh of relief. 'What about?'

'Kate,' said Bellamy, rushing round his desk and picking up his helmet. 'She's only having the baby!'

Ventress leaned back and lit a dog-end. 'Oh, is that all?'

'Well, don't just sit there! This is an emergency! We've got to find Nick!'

The bus was returning from Ashfordly. Flo was hemmed in by Joe Norton on one side and Frank and Dave kneeling on the seat in front, listening to 'You Really Got Me' at full volume on Joe's transistor. She tried to shut the din out of her mind, peering through the bus window for a glimpse of her caravan on Fletcher's Common. As soon as she caught sight of it, and her old horse Peg safely tethered, she stood up. Joe took no notice, the radio jammed to his ear.

'Excuse me,' said Flo. 'I'd like to pass. I've got to get off here.' Joe made no attempt to move. Flo tried to squeeze past him. Her progress was further impeded by Frank and Dave hanging over the seat back. 'Did you hear me?

'Yeah, I heard,' said Joe, staying put. 'You're scum, you are.'

'I'm getting off this bus now,' said Flo firmly. As

134

she pushed past him, her shopping jogged his elbow and the transistor radio crashed to the floor. The battery cover flew off and the battery flew out. In the sudden silence, Joe looked at the broken radio – and went berserk.

'You stupid cow!' He lashed out at Flo, knocking her to the floor. Hands bunched into fists, he was about to go for her again when the bus pulled up suddenly and Frank and Dave dragged him away from her.

'Leave her!' shouted Frank in Joe's face. 'You're mental!'

'Come on!' Dave picked up the radio. 'Move!'

As the conductor came up, Frank and Dave heaved Joe down the aisle and off the bus. Flo tried to stand, but collapsed into a seat.

'Are you all right, love?' asked the conductor.

'Yes, fine.' She took the conductor's arm and tried to stand. 'Ta – '

'Stay where you are a minute,' said the conductor, looking out of the window at the fleeing lads. 'You've got to report them. We'll take you down to the Police House – '

Kate was halfway down the narrow staircase, hospital bag in hand, when another contraction overwhelmed her. She clung on to the rail, bent double, panting desperately through her open mouth, telling herself whatever she did, not to fall now –

There was a knock at the front door. As the pain moderated, Kate was able to hobble, ashen-faced, to the door. She leaned against it to get her breath. When she opened the door she found Flo standing there. Neither of them saw Joe, watching from behind the garden wall.

'Oh my God,' said Flo. 'Are you all right?'

'I've gone into labour.'

Flo stepped inside and closed the door. 'Ambulance?'

'I've just rung.

'Bag packed?'

'Yes.'

'Right then,' said Flo, helping Kate down the hall, 'now you make yourself comfy, and I'll wait with you.'

'Thanks.'

Flo settled her into a kitchen chair. 'There we are,' she smiled at Kate, and patted her hand. 'I had a baby once. All on my own I was . . .'

When the ambulance came, Flo insisted on carrying Kate's bag out for her. Flanked by two ambulancemen, and watched by Joe and several other villagers, Kate made her way slowly down the path. At the door of the ambulance, Flo handed Kate her bag. 'When you can't bear it any more, just think of that beautiful baby.' She pressed Kate's hand warmly and stood aside. Joe ducked out of sight.

'Ready to go, Dr Rowan?' asked the ambulance driver.

Kate smiled. 'Thank you.'

Bellamy and Ventress screeched to a halt. Blaketon and Nick were coming out of the babywear shop looking pleased with themselves. 'Beige, you see,' Blaketon was saying, 'doesn't show the muck so much – '

136

'Kate's having the baby!' shouted Ventress.

'Been all over looking for you!' panted Bellamy.

'Where is she now?'

'On her way to hospital – '

'You better get yourself down there, Rowan!'

'Right!' Nick piled into the Anglia.

'And no speeding, constable!' shouted Blaketon. 'Parents come better in pairs!'

Nick took off with a shriek of tyres and a smell of burning rubber. Five minutes later, he was running through hospital corridors.

He had never run so fast, or felt so nervously exultant. He plunged through doors, down one corridor, up another, past orderlies, patients in dressing gowns, porters washing floors, until, rounding a corner, he ran slap-bang into a staff nurse.

'No running in the corridors please!'

'I'm looking for Dr Rowan! I'm her husband – '

'I'm in here, Nick!' said Kate's voice.

Nick whirled round and saw Kate lying on a trolley in a small treatment room. Ignoring the staff nurse, he rushed in to her.

'Are you OK?'

'I'm fine,' smiled Kate, reaching for his hand. 'The baby just got bored waiting.'

The staff nurse came in with two nurses and bustled Nick aside. 'Come on, Dr Rowan, we'd better get you down to the delivery room.'

Nick was allowed to hold Kate's hand as the stretcher trolley was trundled rapidly down the corridor. Another contraction came. Nick saw Kate tense and cry out involuntarily. He felt stricken and useless; then full of admiration as Kate forced herself into the deep-breathing routine. How could anyone bear such pain? He found himself breathing in sympathy. Kate smiled up at him wanly, her hair plastered to her flushed and glistening skin. 'I'm all right.'

'I feel so helpless.' Nick heard the staff nurse clear her throat disapprovingly at this show of emotion. Kate, taking no notice, squeezed his hand.

'You're a lovely man, Nick Rowan. Have I ever told you that?'

The staff nurse pointed to a cubicle across from Delivery Room 1. 'Wait in there, please.'

'I'll try not to be too long,' said Kate.

Nick kissed her on the mouth. 'I'm not going anywhere.'

The nurses wheeled Kate into Delivery Room 1. The staff nurse gave him the briefest of smiles, then the doors closed.

Greengrass decided to wear his new shirt to the pub that very evening. 'Nice shirt, Claude,' said George, shading his eyes from the eruption of red and yellow covering Greengrass's paunch. 'Very – colourful.'

'Aye,' said Greengrass, showing it off round the bar. 'That's because it's new.'

Fred Brickwood, a big, heavy-set lorry driver wearing a fisherman's blue woolly hat, turned to take in the sight. His eyes bulged in his thick, fleshy face. 'New to you, maybe.'

'What d'you mean?'

'That shirt went missin' from our line two days ago.'

'Don't talk daft. I only bought it yesterday.'

'Our Ernie brought us that back from Hong Kong.'

'Your brain's short-circuiting,' said Greengrass, turning away. 'This shirt came from Ashfordly market.'

Fred swung Greengrass back round to face him. 'Take it off.'

'Why should I?'

'Because I'm telling you.'

Greengrass's eye fell on Flo warming her mittened hands by the fire. 'I can't, there's females present.'

Fred looked round. Flo gave him her crooked smile. 'I'm sure there's been some misunderstanding –'

'Butt out, you,' said Fred. 'You don't belong here.'

'Don't you talk to her like that!' shouted Greengrass.

'And as for you, you thieving skunk,' said Fred, unperturbed, 'take that shirt off or I'm taking it off for you.'

Bellamy stuck his head round the door of Blaketon's office. 'Pub brawl, sarge.'

Blaketon sighed. 'There should be a law banning market traders from public houses –'

'It's not here, sarge,' said Bellamy. 'The call came from the Aidensfield Arms.'

George had ordered that nothing should be touched until the police arrived. Tables and chairs were still overturned, glasses lying in pools of beer where they had smashed. An uneasy silence fell as Blaketon and Bellamy entered and marched up to George. 'What happened here, then?' asked Blaketon, sardonically

139

casting his eye over the damage. 'A bunch of bikers passing through?'

'No,' said George. 'A couple of cloth 'eads, and they're still here.' He indicated Fred and Greengrass, sitting on opposite sides of the room. Fred looked more or less undamaged; Greengrass's face was bruised, his hair all over the place and his brand-new red and yellow shirt ripped to pieces. Flo dabbed at Greengrass's forehead.

Blaketon allowed himself a smile of satisfaction. 'Long time since I did you for a bar-room brawl, Greengrass,' he said. 'Quite like old times.'

Greengrass grunted.

'Poor Mr Greengrass,' said Flo, slyly needling him. 'You're not having the best of luck, are you?'

Nick paced up and down outside Delivery Room 1. He had seen it dozens of times, on films and television, but only now did he realise how all first-time fathers felt: a mixture of fear, elation, tension, boredom, and the restless, futile knowledge that there was nothing, absolutely nothing, he could do to help.

The staff nurse came out and hurried down the corridor carrying a blood sample. Nick followed her. 'How's Kate? What's happening?'

'Still busy,' said the staff nurse.

Maggie came running up. 'I'm not too late, am I?' she said to the staff nurse.

'I think she's been waiting for you,' replied the staff nurse, hurrying on.

Maggie patted Nick's arm. 'Don't worry. Kate'll be fine.' She went into the delivery room.

140

'You will tell me what's going on?' said Nick to the door closing behind her.

Another contraction. Kate heard voices and the tinkle and clatter of instruments coming through a fog of pain, and then Maggie was leaning over her, full of solid, smiling reassurance, wiping her brow with something cool.

'What time is it now, Maggie?'

'Just after seven, love.'

'Still Friday?'

'Yes, love.'

Kate struggled against the pain to remember the childhood rhyme. 'Friday's child is loving and giving.'

'And Saturday's child works hard for a living,' Maggie reminded her.

Kate forced a grin. 'I'd better hurry up, then.'

Ten minutes later, as Nick sat in the corridor wondering why everything had gone so deathly quiet in the delivery room, there was the sound of a baby crying.

Maggie came out, still gowned, eyes sparkling. 'It's a girl, Nick. Seven pounds two ounces.'

'Is Kate all right?'

'They're both fine.'

An overwhelming sense of love and gratitude swept through him. 'Can I see them?'

Maggie opened the door. 'Course you can.'

Kate was sitting up, holding the baby. Their baby. It stopped Nick in his tracks. He stood there, absorbing the picture. Kate, and the baby suckling her finger. Kate looked up. Her face was tired, sweaty

141

and triumphant. She smiled teasingly at Nick. 'Aren't you coming in?'

In a daze, he moved to the bedside. Slowly he reached out his little finger to the baby's tiny red fist. His finger brushed the amazingly soft new skin, and then the baby's fist opened and clasped his finger. 'Hello, Sarah Rowan,' said Nick, trying out the name for the first time. His heart had never been so full. 'You're magnificent,' he said to Kate, 'd'you know that?'

He bent forward and gave Kate a kiss; then he sat beside her, and gazed in wonder at baby Sarah. 'She's the most beautiful thing I've ever seen,' he murmured, taking hold of Kate's hand. 'Next to her mum.'

There was a knock on the door, and Maggie came in holding up a small pocket camera. 'First for the album?' Nick squeezed himself close to Kate, Kate lifted up baby Sarah, and Maggie pointed the camera. There was no need to say 'smile'.

# Nine

Kate slept for more than twelve hours after Nick left; the deep sleep of total physical exhaustion. When she awoke to the hospital dawn chorus of clattering metal trays, trolleys and teacups, she saw her daughter lying peacefully asleep in her cot. For a few seconds she felt an overwhelming sense of peace and fulfilment. She had given birth, and her baby was whole and healthy.

Then the realisation dawned, like a dark cloud moving across the face of the sun, slowly blotting out and soaking up its light. She began to weep, quietly and uncontrollably, prompting the woman in the next bed, who was in to have her fourth child, to tell her not to worry, it nearly always happened after the baby was born. Kate knew it was too soon for post-natal depression to set in, but was unable to stop the flood of silent, bitter tears.

After breakfast she and baby Sarah were transferred to a small, sunlit private ward. When she complained about preferential treatment, the staff nurse told her that only the best was good enough for her, and the room was empty anyway. Now would she kindly hurry up and put some make-up on before the consultant haematologist, Mr Faber, arrived.

Mr Faber, an imposing man in his late forties wearing a three-piece dark blue pinstripe, bustled cheerfully in, followed by a white-coated junior houseman.

'How are you feeling, Kate?'

'Not too bad, thanks, Mr Faber. I didn't know hospital consultants worked on a Saturday.'

Mr Faber smiled. 'We try not to, but you're a special case, Kate. Did you sleep well?'

'Like a log.'

'And baby Sarah?'

'No trouble so far.'

'Excellent.' The consultant's smile was replaced by professional seriousness. 'Now, I suggest we have a think about where we go from here.'

Discreetly, the junior houseman closed the door, and handed Mr Faber the folder containing Kate's notes.

Nine-thirty, and no sign of Greengrass about in his yard.

'Nursing a sore head, I reckon,' said Bellamy.

'That or wounded pride,' said Nick. 'Ready? On three – '

They thundered in unison on Greengrass's kitchen door. He appeared, groaning and bleary-eyed. 'If you've come about ladies' undergarments,' he said in a thick, morning-after voice, 'I always ask before removing them.'

'You were behaving very suspiciously in the market yesterday, Claude,' said Nick.

Greengrass hitched up his baggy trousers. 'I'm telling you I bought that shirt fair and square.'

'Then you'll have nothing to hide,' said Nick. 'Can we come in?'

144

'No, you can't,' said Greengrass, filling the doorway with his bulk.

'Why not?'

'Because it'll spoil things.'

'Who for?' put in Bellamy.

'Never you mind. Nowt to do with you.'

'We can always come back with a warrant, Claude,' said Nick.

Greengrass reluctantly moved aside. 'Flaming hell,' he grumbled, 'and they tell you an Englishman's home is his castle.'

Alfred got up from his sack near the stove, wagged his tail at Nick, turned round a few times and collapsed back on his sack again.

'Have a look in the hall,' said Nick.

'Right,' said Bellamy.

'You can't go in there,' said Greengrass, following him out of the kitchen.

Bellamy pulled a battered pram out of the mess of newspapers, orange boxes, coal, logs and wellington boots Greengrass kept in the hall. The last time Nick had seen that torn hood and buckled wheels was at Ashfordly market.

'Is that it?'

'All there is here,' said Bellamy.

'I don't get it,' Nick said to Greengrass. 'Why all the secrecy? It's only a pram – '

Greengrass's unshaven face twitched into a weak smile. 'It's supposed to be for you, right? For the new babby.' He scratched his stubble. 'It's an antique.'

'I can see that, Claude.'

'I were going to do it up, like.'

'Well,' said Nick charitably, 'I'm touched.'

'I know you think I'm an old villain – '

'Not all the time.'

'But I care about you and the missus,' said Greengrass, with every appearance of sincerity.

'I didn't mean to be rude about it just now – '

'So you'll take it?' said Greengrass quickly.

'Well,' said Nick, 'the thing is – '

Grass slapped his hands together, horse-dealer style. 'A bargain at ten bob.'

'Ten bob?'

Greengrass stood back, looked at the pram appraisingly. 'Course, it'll cost you a bit extra if I do it up.'

'You expect me to buy that thing?'

'You won't get many perambulators of that quality,' said Greengrass.

'No,' said Nick, wryly, 'you're right there.'

Nick watched Bellamy drive off to interview the second-hand clothes stall-holder in Ashfordly. Feeling full of the joys of spring, he rode over Fletcher's Common on his way home to give the hospital a call. Flo saw him as she was shaking a sheet out of the caravan door. She laid it aside and waved Nick down.

It was exactly what Joe, hiding behind a drystone wall some thirty yards away from the caravan, had feared would happen. After following her down to the Police House and watching the ambulance arrive for Kate, he was pretty sure Flo hadn't reported him. Nick wasn't there for a start, and Flo had other things to think about. This morning she was bound to tell him: why else would she flag him down?

Joe had had a bad night. Something, he knew, had

come over him in the bus, a fit of uncontrollable rage or something, and if his mates hadn't stopped him, he would have lammed into her. And if he had been picked up and charged, that would have been the end of his chances of getting into the Army.

Now Joe was sure the old cow was going to drop him in it. On all fours he leopard-crawled along the base of the wall to get within hearing distance. He came to a gateway with a BEWARE OF THE BULL sign on it, and then stopped, cursing his luck. There was no way he could cross the open gateway without Nick spotting him, and that meant he couldn't hear what she was going to say. He watched Nick walk up to the caravan. There had to be another way of getting rid of the old cow. Scare her off somehow, stop her giving evidence, even if she did report him . . .

'I heard in the shop it was a daughter,' said Flo. 'Congratulations.'

'Thanks very much,' said Nick.

Flo reached into the basket resting on the top step of the caravan, and offered Nick a sprig of heather. 'I wanted to give you this,' she said with a toothy smile, 'for luck.'

Nick hesitated, wondering what police regulations had to say about the matter, then decided to wear it anyway. 'Thanks.'

Joe wasn't the only one watching Flo's caravan. As soon as Nick had ridden off, Greengrass's truck came spluttering up from his smallholding, its exhaust popping and banging.

'Morning,' he said, politely wiping his nose on the back of his sleeve.

'You're right,' said Flo warily. 'It is.'

Greengrass shifted from one foot to the other, hummed and hawed to himself, and generally lunged about like a bullock in a stall, undecided whether to go or stay. Flo maintained a watchful silence.

At last he blurted out. 'I want you to do us a favour.'

'Get on with it, Claude,' said Flo drily.

'Ey?'

'I said get on with it.'

'That hex you hexed me, can you unhex it? Only I've had a bellyful of dog's breakfasts, broken-down vans, false accusations against my person, house-proud poltergeists in the khazi – '

Flo saw her chance and jumped at it. 'It'll cost you.'

'How much?'

'Free use of your lav and I'll throw in the floral arrangements for nothing. What d'you say?'

The light dawned on him. 'Why, you sneaky old – '

'I couldn't use it in the state it was in,' said Flo. 'It was disgusting.' She put out her mittened hand. 'Deal?'

Greengrass thought about it. There was no way out. 'Have to be.' Reluctantly, he took her hand, shook it once and stomped off without another word. Flo watched him drive away. Humming a snatch of 'We'll Gather Lilacs', she went back into the caravan to finish off her chores.

Peg, who had been peacefully cropping the grass, lifted her head and pricked her ears. She whinnied, jerking at her tether and shifting her old head this

148

way and that, alarmed by the human presences she could detect behind the drystone wall.

While Greengrass and Flo had been negotiating, Joe had gone back to the village to fetch Frank and Dave.

'You two are in this as well,' he said. 'And if all three of us say we were miles away when it happened, they'll have to believe us.'

'When what happened?' said Frank. 'What are you going to do?'

Joe grinned, pulled out a Zippo and flicked it alight on the leg of his camouflage trousers. 'Scare her off. Right out of it.'

'How?'

Joe looked at the caravan. 'How d'you think?'

'You can't do that,' said Dave, already scared sick. 'She's inside it – '

'Tough.'

'Look Joe,' said Dave, trying to make him see reason, 'she's just some old biddy. She's harmless. You're only making it worse – '

Joe gave him a backhander to shut him up. Dave fell against the drystone wall. 'You don't even know if she's reported it – '

'He's right,' said Frank. 'All you said was – '

Joe grabbed Frank by the throat and banged his head against the wall. His eyes had clouded over the way they had on the bus. 'I thought you reckoned you were hard?'

Frank rubbed the back of his head, and looked at his fingers for blood. 'Maybe she didn't say owt.'

'She's been to the Police House, and she was talking to him up here a half-hour since. Course she's told him.'

'You're bloody mad, you are,' said Dave, backing off.

'Shurrup!' hissed Joe, ducking down.

Flo came out of the caravan, spoke to Peg, settling her, then headed off down towards Aidensfield with her basket full of washing.

Joe turned to the others, his voice full of vicious sarcasm. 'That make it any easier for you?'

'No,' said Dave bluntly. 'I'm off.' And before Joe could lay hands on him he was away at a low, crouching run along the side of the wall.

Joe watched him go, his face set hard. 'He'll regret that. Come on.'

Frank swallowed, and nodded. Joe took out his Zippo and climbed through the gate. Frank, his face white with fear, followed. Joe moved round the frightened, whinnying mare. Frank stopped, looked enviously at Dave's fleeing back, then moved forward a couple of more paces. Joe was at the caravan now, Zippo alight, gesturing to Frank to get a move on.

Frank turned, ran for the gate, flung himself headlong over it and landed in thick tractor-churned mud. His hand was bleeding and his trousers had ripped on the barbed wire but he didn't care: anything to get away from Joe. Dave was right, he was a bloody maniac.

'Right, thank you, we'll get somebody down there.' Bellamy replaced the receiver, glanced at his watch and noted down the time: 10.30. 'Report of an old lady in the river this side of Aidensfield, sarge. Near Fletcher's Common.'

Blaketon, who had been listening to the progress of the call, was already at the station transmitter. 'Ventress, get out there. I'll radio Rowan to join you.'

Ventress followed the path down to the riverbank. Petticoats, slips and baggy drawers were draped over the bare branches. If it *is* a suicide, thought Ventress, barging his way through the bushes, it's a bloody funny way to go about it –

Then he heard singing. And splashing. A high, cracked voice trilling out 'The Sun Has Got His Hat On'. Wondering how he had ever got into this job, and why it always seemed to be him who got the crackpots, he forced his way to the river's edge.

There was Flo, right out in midstream, the fast-running water up to her thighs, cheerfully splashing about in her combinations. Ventress coughed politely and averted his face. 'Are you in need of any assistance, madam?'

'No, thank you!' shouted Flo cheerily, 'not unless you fancy scrubbing my back!'

Ventress carefully considered his duty, and decided it did not involve getting soaking wet and struggling with eccentric old ladies in the middle of a freezing river. 'Perhaps it would be a good idea if you came out and put some clothes on.'

There was a crashing in the bushes behind him, and to Ventress's relief, Nick appeared, grinning all over his face. 'Hello, Flo!' he called. 'Are you all right?'

'I'm fine,' she replied, splashing the freezing water

up her arms and around the back of her neck, 'but your colleague's gone a funny colour!'

Ventress, as usual, defended himself by stating the obvious. 'She's only got her combinations on.'

'Better than nothing,' grinned Nick. 'Flo!'

'Yes?'

'Why don't we all go back to the caravan and have a cup of tea? Have you got a towel?'

'I don't usually bother!'

'We'll turn our backs!'

As Flo emerged, dripping but otherwise undaunted, Nick and Ventress made their way back through the bushes to the lane where the car and bike were parked.

'I don't see why it has to be the car,' grumbled Ventress. 'She'll drip all over the upholstery.'

Nick pointed to the Francis-Barnett. 'She can hardly ride pillion, can she?'

Flo appeared, not so much dressed as draped, carrying her soaked combinations. 'I don't know,' said Ventress. 'It'd be one way of drying her off.'

But the caravan, when they got there, was a smouldering, burnt-out shell. Nothing at all remained of the cabin, and the wheels, frame and shafts were charred beyond repair. Peg had broken her tether and was standing terrified, head up, ready for flight.

A look of horror on her face, Flo jumped screaming from Ventress's car and ran towards the smoking ruin of her home. Nick leaped from his bike and sped after her. He caught up with her and held her. 'It's too late, Flo.'

She let herself be held, shivering in Nick's arms.

Ventress cautiously backed round Peg and urged her towards her owner. Flo broke away from Nick and made her way to the badly frightened old mare, talking quietly all the while to calm her down, soothe her, win her confidence again.

'Shush. It's all right. I'm here now, Peg. There we are. Yes. All right now.' She caught hold of Peg's head-rope, dug a wrinkled yellow apple out of her motorcycle coat pocket, and led her gently upwind, away from the smoke.

When Nick joined them, Flo was gazing dry-eyed at the charred remains. 'That was my home.' Her voice was calm, but the look on her face was bewildered, lost, completely devastated.

'Come on, Flo. We'll take you to the Police House. Then we'll see about finding you somewhere to stay.'

The old lady looked at him blankly, and allowed herself to be led away.

Leaving Ventress to drive Flo to the Police House, Nick rode down towards the village. Frank and Dave, scared to go home in case Joe came looking for them, were slouched against a wall on the edge of Fletcher's Common. When they saw Nick coming, they flagged him down.

Nick climbed off the Francis-Barnett, his face grim. 'I was coming to look for you. I'll leave you to guess why.'

'It wasn't us,' said Frank.

'It wasn't us who did what?' said Nick.

'It was Joe,' said Frank, 'he was the one who set fire to the old bird's van.' He looked to Dave to back him up.

'We got out of there,' said Dave. 'He's gone completely barmy.'

'How?' asked Nick.

'Same way he went on the bus,' said Dave.

'He just goes mental,' said Frank.

'First he started knocking me about for arguing with him,' said Dave.

'Then he had a go at me,' said Frank.

'I hopped it,' said Dave. 'I'd had enough.'

'Then he comes out with this lighter, and starts going on about how hard he is,' said Frank, 'and how he's going to scare her off.'

'Why?'

'So she can't drop him in it over what happened on the bus.'

'What did happen exactly?' asked Nick.

'He threatened her, said she bust his radio,' said Frank.

'Then he went right off his head,' said Dave. 'He had his fists up and he was going to lambast her, but we dragged him off, didn't we Frank?'

'Yeah.'

Nick nodded. He'd got his witnesses: all they were interested in was saving their own necks. More to the point, what was Joe up to? 'Where d'you think he might be now?'

The two lads looked at each other. 'He'll be down by the quarry,' said Frank. 'It's where he always goes.'

Nick rode into the grassed-over quarry and saw Joe some distance off. He was hurling chunks of rock at a row of tin cans perched on top of a low wall. 'Die, pig!' he was shouting. 'Die, you pig!'

As soon as he saw Nick he was off, running low and zigzagging across the shallow grassy bowl. Nick went after him, flat out. Hampered by his heavy greatcoat, Nick had little chance of catching Joe until the boy leaped for the top of a wall, lost his footing on the loose shale and went rolling down the slope on the other side.

Nick was on to him before he could get up. As soon as Joe's first punch landed on the side of his head, Nick knew he had a fight on his hands. Over and over they rolled, punching and kicking at each other until Nick found himself sitting astride Joe's midriff.

'That's enough, Joe!'

With an almighty heave, Joe bucked Nick off and dived on top of him. He sat up, a rock in his hand the size of half a brick. He raised his arm and the mad, clouded look came into his eyes.

'It'll be murder, Joe,' said Nick. In response, Joe raised his arm higher. 'Put it down, Joe,' said Nick quietly. 'Put it down, and let's see if we can sort this out.' Joe stared at him uncomprehendingly; then, as suddenly as it had flared, the fit of rage seemed to burn itself out.

He laid the lump of rock down and collapsed off Nick, shaking like a leaf. Nick grabbed him in an armlock, taking no chances. Joe winced. 'I wouldn't have done it.'

'Touch and go,' said Nick, dragging him to his feet. 'What the hell d'you think you're playing at?' He shook him hard, his own anger and relief coming out. 'Come on! What's all this about?'

'Showing them,' muttered Joe.

'Showing them what?' Nick swung Joe round. He lifted his head to meet Nick's gaze. The arrogance was still there. 'I'm somebody,' he said. 'They got to respect me.'

'Respect what?' said Nick. 'A bully who burns down people's homes?'

'The old tart's dirt. She was asking for it.'

'You're the one who's dirt, Joe.'

Joe tried to struggle free. 'My dad used to say that! Not any more though – I taught him!'

Nick switched the armlock, taking Joe's arm up behind his back. 'By beating him up? Very smart.' He pushed Joe back along the floor of the quarry towards the Francis-Barnett, where he could cuff him and radio for a car. Both of them were covered in mud from head to foot.

'I wouldn't have hit you,' said Joe, scared now Nick was getting the cuffs out. 'Honest.'

Nick gave him a sideways look. 'You sure of that?'

Joe hunched his shoulders, scuffling his combat boots clean on the thin grass. 'Yeah.'

'More than I am.' Nick clamped him to the front forks. 'You didn't know what you were doing. You'd gone, Joe, hadn't you?'

Joe remained silent as Nick radioed for help.

After Mr Faber had taken another blood sample down to the haematology lab to oversee the test results for himself, Kate felt oddly reassured. Now it was out in the open, at least she was getting all the attention she could wish for. 'Kate,' he said, 'I give you my word that anything that can be done, will be done.' When he left, she relaxed, and spent her time

156

either dozing or looking at baby Sarah sleeping peacefully beside her.

There was nothing more Kate could do. Even the slim chance that Mr Faber had held out to her was better than no chance at all. Another weight off her mind was that there was no longer any need for pretence. She still had Nick to face, but by then there might be something positive to tell him; she hoped and prayed there would be.

A knock on the door, and Maggie came in. 'Hi,' said Kate, genuinely pleased to see her, 'this is a nice surprise. I thought you were bound to be working all day.'

Maggie closed the door; instead of moving to Kate's bedside, she stood where she was, just inside the door, her arms folded, her face cold and set. 'How long have you known?'

Kate was stunned by the bluntness of the question. After all she had been through, the strain of concealment, the feelings of utter hopelessness she had endured, Kate thought that Maggie, of all people, would be the first to understand. 'I got the results two days ago,' she said.

'You're a doctor, Kate,' said Maggie, angrily. 'You must have realised before then.'

'I can see you're upset, but – '

'Upset! I'm furious! I had to find out from a colleague!' Seeing the distress on Kate's face, Maggie relented slightly. 'I thought you were my friend, Kate.'

Kate sighed, wondering if she could make Maggie understand. At least she could try and explain, she

157

decided; she owed her that much. 'I wanted to tell you,' she said, 'but it seemed so disloyal.'

'Disloyal?'

'To Nick.'

Maggie stared at her in disbelief. 'You haven't told him?'

Tears filled Kate's eyes and her face began to crumple like a smacked child's. 'I couldn't, Maggie, I couldn't.' She looked up at Maggie, desperate for understanding. 'He was so excited.'

Maggie's anger melted away. Cursing her quick temper, she moved to Kate and hugged and rocked her in her arms. 'I'm sorry, love, I didn't mean to shout, it's just – oh, I don't know – the shock.' She tilted Kate's chin up and kissed her. 'You're the last person I should be angry with.'

'Have you got a tissue?'

'Here.'

'Thanks.'

Maggie waited for Kate to pull herself together. 'How did you manage to hide the results of the blood test?'

'I ran it under someone else's name.'

'Why didn't you do it earlier? You could have been induced. Started treatment sooner.'

'I wanted everything to go normally,' said Kate, looking over at Sarah in her cot. 'She's a baby. This isn't her fault.'

'It isn't yours either,' said Maggie firmly.

'I had the blood transfusion last night. Mr Faber's doing another test now.'

'Well, that's something,' said Maggie. 'What about Nick?'

'He's coming this afternoon. I'll tell him then.'

Maggie looked at her. 'You've got some guts, girl.'

Kate shook her head. 'No I haven't. I feel scared, Maggie, scared and lonely. I look at Sarah and I can't bear it.' Her voice began to break. She swallowed, recovered, and for the first time let her own anger show. 'It's so unfair, Maggie. We don't deserve this.'

Shortly after Maggie left, Sarah began to cry. Kate picked her up and was unbuttoning her nightdress to feed her when there was a knock at the door, and Mr Faber came in.

'How was it?' asked Kate.

Mr Faber gave her the faintest of encouraging smiles, and said, 'We're going to start you on metho-trexate straight away.'

'OK.' It meant there was some hope.

He put his hand over hers. 'This does mean you won't be able to feed little Sarah, I'm afraid.'

Kate looked down at the baby in her arms.

Blaketon sat in his office, going through Nick's report. In front of him stood Joe, Nick on one side, his father Ted on the other. As far as Blaketon could see, there were no mitigating circumstances whatso-ever. He looked up at Joe. 'These are very serious charges. Do you understand that?'

Joe stared insolently back, saying nothing. His father lost his temper and clouted him across the back of the head. 'You're not at home now! Answer the question.'

'Get off me!' He attempted to hit back.

Nick stepped in, separated them, and pinned Joe's arms. 'Now you're both making it worse – '

'He's beyond help, this one.' Ted Norton's voice was full of scorn. What he said next revealed the depth of his loathing for his son. 'He was born a maggot.'

Nick watched for Joe's reaction. There wasn't one. 'Arson, assaulting a police officer,' said Blaketon. 'I've no choice but to charge you.' Joe stared at the wall above Blaketon's head with complete and utter indifference.

In the silence that followed, Bellamy tapped, and stuck his head round the door. 'Can I have a word, Nick?' Nick waited for Blaketon's nod, and left with relief.

'How's it going?' asked Bellamy.

'I'm getting a really good lesson in parental care,' said Nick cynically. 'My mum called me a few names, but she never said I was born a maggot.'

'Stroll on – '

'How about you? Are you getting anywhere?'

'Yeah,' said Bellamy. 'It wasn't Joe and his mates who sold those clothes to the stall-holder. I've just been to see him.'

'Did he say who had?'

'He said he gets so much stuff brought in, he can't remember one lot from the next.'

'That's helpful.'

'And Greengrass did buy that shirt. The woman on the stall confirmed it.'

'So we start again.' Nick looked down at the bedraggled sprig of white heather, and straightened it. 'Not having much luck, are we?'

'Hang on a minute,' said Bellamy. 'He had a bit of that in his lapel – '

160

'Who did?'

'This bloke I went to see, the one with the second-hand clothes stall.'

He caught up with Flo on the narrow moorland road leading north out of Aidensfield. She was leading Peg, both of them trudging wearily uphill. As Nick drew alongside, he saw her eyes dart quickly across to the open moor.

'Where are you going, Flo? Where's there to run to?'

'Whoa, Peg.' Her voice sounded tired, full of resignation. She led the old mare to the verge and let her crop the short, springy grass. Nick dismounted and went over to her.

'I had you down as an honest person, Flo.'

'I've got to eat.' Still not looking at him.

'Stealing those clothes could get you locked up,' he warned.

She jerked her head round, panic in her eyes. 'Oh no! No, I couldn't stand it. Please, Mr Rowan,' she tugged at his sleeve. 'I'm sorry, but not again. No, never again!'

'So you've been sent down before?'

'I didn't do anything wrong,' she pleaded. 'There was nothing wrong with me. They let me out.'

'Out of where?'

She shook her head, unable to bring herself to say the name.

'Flo?'

'Spring Hill.' Her voice was scarcely audible.

'The mental hospital?'

161

Flo nodded, then shot a hunted and fearful look at him.

'I think you'd better tell me about it,' said Nick.

They found a sheltered spot out of the keen moorland wind. Flo spent a long time looking back into the past before she spoke.

'I had a baby when I was fourteen,' she said flatly. 'They said I couldn't keep it.'

'What happened?'

She shook her head, overcome by her memories. 'Never even got to hold him.'

'How did you come to be in Spring Hill?'

'After they took the baby away . . .' She looked away. 'Well things were difficult, for a bit.'

'How long were you in there?'

'Nearly forty years,' she said bitterly. 'It was an "administrative oversight", apparently. They were very apologetic.' It was only too clear what she thought of their apologies.

'Didn't you speak to anybody, tell them?'

'Oh no. It doesn't pay to complain in those places. They only increase the medication.'

'And you started stealing when you were released?'

'No, I didn't!' said Flo indignantly. 'Only in the last few months. There isn't much seasonal work about in the winter. I like to be out in the fresh air, Mr Rowan.'

'I can understand that, after what you've been through.'

'I'm glad somebody can.'

'All the same,' said Nick, 'you're going to have to come with me, Flo.'

162

Flo glared at him defiantly. 'If you lock me up, I'll do myself in.'

Nick knew she meant it. 'I'll have a word with my sergeant,' he reassured her. 'Maybe we can work something out.'

She reached out a hand to his face, patting his cheek and giving him a crooked smile. 'You're a kind boy, you know that? You're going to make a smashing father.'

With Flo in the kitchen and Peg tethered outside, Nick explained the situation over the phone to Blaketon.

'Right, Rowan,' he said when Nick had finished, 'as I understand the matter, this old lady's done forty years without the option for the simple crime of motherhood. Enough is enough.'

'What I thought, sarge.'

'No point in sending her down again for a boxful of bloomers. As you say, it'll probably finish her off.'

'That's what she said, sarge, and I'm sure she meant it.'

'Right,' said Blaketon decisively. 'If ever a case warranted a bit of ear-bending, arm-twisting and string-pulling, this is it. Leave it with me, Rowan, and I'll see what I can do.'

'Right sarge, thanks.' Nick replaced the receiver and smiled to himself.

Within the hour, Blaketon had arranged with the Magistrates' Court to have Flo bound over on appearance, and informed the Council and Social Services that she had been made temporarily home-less by reason of arson and was in need of suitable accommodation for herself and horse. Furthermore, if by any chance there was a suitable property in the vicinity of Mr Claude Greengrass's smallholding, then that would do very nicely.

'Thank you.' Blaketon put the phone down, and felt like a man who had struck a blow for freedom.

Nick left Flo and Peg to their own devices while he went off to visit Kate in hospital. 'Don't stray too far, Flo. I'll let you know what's been arranged when I get back.'

'Thank you, Mr Rowan, you've been most kind,' said Flo. 'Give my best to your wife, won't you?'

When Greengrass came out of the Aidensfield Arms holding a pint in one hand and a meat pie in the other, Flo was standing with Peg on the far side of the car park, looking pensive. 'So would you,' he told himself, 'if your house had just been burned to the flaming ground.' He went over to her.

'Morning, Flo.'

'Afternoon, Claude.'

'Always morning in the pub.'

'I'm not in the pub, am I?'

'Any road,' he said, offering the pint and pie, 'I bought you these.'

Flo hesitated.

'Bought and paid for,' he said. 'Come on, you've got to have your dinner, got to have summat inside you, whatever happens.'

'Ta.' She set the pint and pie down on top of the wall.

Greengrass took out his battered old hip-flask. 'If you happen to be passing, like, and you need a brew-up, give us a knock. There'll be no charge.'

164

'Thanks,' said Flo, 'but I don't know what I'm going to do, or where I'm going to be.'

'No,' said Greengrass thoughtfully, 'I don't suppose you do.' He unscrewed the top of the flask. 'You any good at washing and ironing?'

'No.'

'That's good,' grunted Greengrass, 'otherwise I might be tempted to propose.'

'Only because you know I wouldn't have yer.'

He raised his flask to her. 'Cheers, Flo.'

'Cheers, Claude.' She picked up her pint and gave him a sad, crooked smile. 'I suppose it could be worse.'

Kate's room was already full of cards and flowers when Nick came in with his own large bouquet. 'For you,' he said, bending over his wife and kissing her.

'They're gorgeous, thanks.'

He moved over to look at Sarah in her cot. 'And how are my two beautiful girls? Everyone's dying to visit. Perhaps we should draw up a rota – '

'Nick. We need to talk.'

There was no mistaking the seriousness in her voice. 'What is it? It's not Sarah? Not something wrong with Sarah?'

'No,' said Kate, taking a deep breath. 'It's me. I have acute leukaemia.'

Nick shook his head, half smiling, refusing to take it in. 'Why don't I just go out and we'll start again?'

'It's true, Nick.' She watched him cast around for something, anything, to grab and hold on to.

'No, Kate. It can't be. I mean, you've just had our baby – ' He searched her face, looking for help,

165

reassurance. When all he saw was her own calm acceptance, it began to sink in. The silence lengthened between them. 'When did you find out?'

'Two days ago.'

'It's a mistake – '

'I only wish it was.' She watched painfully as Nick struggled to understand, to cope, to get things into some sort of order.

'Why didn't you say something?'

This, Kate knew, would be the hardest part. 'I didn't want to spoil things,' she said finally. 'We were both so happy, planning for Sarah. I just wanted to concentrate on having a healthy child.'

Nick looked unconvinced. 'But we share everything, Kate. We agreed that when we got married. Good or bad, we'd share it.'

She shook her head. 'Remember when I first knew I was pregnant? I was so selfish – '

'No you weren't – '

'I was,' said Kate firmly. 'I was thinking about my career, whether it was the right time. It should have been special and I ruined it. I wasn't going to ruin the birth of our only daughter as well.'

He took her hand. 'There'll be others, love.'

'No, Nick.'

There it was. In all its awful finality.

'But what about the doctors?' said Nick desperately. 'Why didn't they do something?'

'They didn't know.'

Nick saw, or thought he did, with sudden clarity. 'You did though, didn't you? The swollen ankles, the breathlessness, the bruising. They're all part of this,

166

aren't they? Why did you tell me there was nothing to worry about?'

'Sarah's life is just beginning. She had to come first.'

Now Nick truly understood what she had sacrificed. He gazed into her eyes, overwhelmed by the selflessness of what she had done. As their eyes met and held, he found himself struggling against the pain that filled his own heart, and fought for the strength to overcome it. Then, with a glow of certainty, he knew that he had. He took hold of her hand. 'I love you, Kate Rowan.'

She felt the love between them begin to flow again, to re-establish itself, bringing her renewed strength. 'I'm going to fight this, Nick.'

He squeezed her hand. 'You're the most precious thing in my life. *We're* going to fight this.'

# Ten

It was ten days since Kate had left Aidensfield. Now she was on her way home.

She sat in the back of the Triumph Herald, baby Sarah in her arms, drinking in every view, every hill, vale, cloud and clump of grass, trying to seize and absorb into herself every detail of the vast immensity of the moor.

She was aware now, more acutely than ever before, that life, her life, everybody's lives, hung by a thread, and it was this that gave her such a thirst for the sombre early spring beauty all around. It was this freedom, this freshness, this sense of life returning, that she so desperately wanted to share with Sarah, to show her and share her new-found joy. She nuzzled and cuddled her, gazing outwards and inwards at the same time, and cradled the baby against every bump in the road.

As Nick drove off the moor and down towards Clouds End bridge, more memories came flooding back: memories of hot summers, picnics, swimming in the cold clear pools, drying off in the sun, making love, walking home through the heather-scented dark with the stars thick as daisies overhead.

It seemed so long ago, another world.

The course of methotrexate had brought about enough of an improvement for Mr Faber to agree to

Kate's request to be discharged; the onset of the disease had been halted, and so long as Kate continued to build up her strength there was a good chance of complete remission. The danger was, as Kate well knew, that the leukaemia had lowered her resistance to all kinds of other diseases: even a cold could prove critical.

They came over Clouds End bridge; Kate saw clumps of daffodils and crocuses on the greensward by the old log where they had had their picnics. The primroses were out on the banks, even though the willows were still bare and there were drifts of snow-drops in the shade. It was amazing how spring had leaped forward in the days she had been away. A sudden, panicky surge of fear gripped her: how much longer, how much more would she get to see of it? She fought the feeling down. Enjoy it, my girl, enjoy every moment while you can –

Nick, concentrating on his driving, did not notice Kate's eyes misting over as they drove down the familiar streets of Aidensfield. She had not realised how much she had missed the place, ordinary though it was. She saw Mrs Hardaker, and Netty Pickard, and the buxom, cheerful figure of Rita Stirling Mansion-polishing her front step a dark and gleaming red; then they were past the telephone box, round the village green, and home.

Now Nick and Maggie were fussing round her. They meant to be kind but Kate somehow found it offputting. She was determined to show them she wasn't going to be an invalid all her life. As Nick helped her out of the car, Maggie took Sarah. 'I can

169

manage, Nick, I'm fine.' As soon as she was standing, she held out her arms to get her beloved Sarah back.

'Welcome home!' said Maggie. 'How does it feel?'

Time to be a bit brisk, she thought, show them whose house it was, who was in control. 'Let's just get this baby in out of the cold, shall we?' Kate marched up to the front door and in, leaving Nick and Maggie to deal with her case and the bags of baby things.

'Watch out,' grinned Nick, 'Bossy Boots is back.'

'Good!' said Maggie staunchly.

The stove was going well, there was a tray of tea things set in front of it, with buttered muffins and crumpets, and the entire living room was a sea of flowers, cards, layettes and presents. Kate gazed round full of emotion, all her brusqueness melting away. 'Oh Maggie, you shouldn't!'

'It wasn't me, it was Rita Stirling,' said Maggie. 'She insisted on getting the place ready for you.'

'Look at all these!'

'Presents from grateful patients,' said Nick.

'Bootees by the dozen!' Maggie held up several pairs by their pink satin laces.

'Look at all this!' Kate showed Sarah round the room, her face beaming with pleasure, eyes bright with tears. 'Oh, Nick!'

'I'll just put the kettle on,' said Maggie tactfully.

Nick put his arms round Kate and Sarah and hugged them both. 'It's lovely to have you back.'

She put her cheek against his. 'Mmmm.'

'Oh Kate – '

Kate drew her head back a fraction. 'You haven't told anyone?'

170

'Promise,' said Nick. 'How are you feeling?'

She laid a finger against his lips. 'Now then. No doom and gloom. I'm fine.'

While Maggie was noisily filling the kettle in the kitchen, she let Nick draw her into a long, warm kiss.

The duck was fighting back. Bellamy scored it two rounds even and the third going the duck's way. It was a large yellow plastic object which Ventress, smoke in his eyes and ash drooping from the end of his cigarette, was attempting to wrap in a smallish piece of brown paper. If he got it round the head, the tail stuck out, and if he got it round the tail, there was the problem of the bill to contend with. He was still attempting to strangle the thing into submission with unbreakable self-tangling Sellotape as Blaketon quietly crept up on him. He had never seen Ventress concentrate so hard to achieve so little.

Bellamy watched with childish delight as Blaketon leaned on Ventress's desk to observe the unequal struggle.

Ventress managed to stick the paper to the desk and his hand to the duck. He sighed in exasperation and looked up to see Blaketon lugubriously contemplating him. 'Ventress.'

'Yes, sarge?'

'I do not expect my men to waste valuable police time wrapping plastic ducks.'

'No, sarge.' Ventress removed the cigarette from his mouth. It stuck to the Sellotape on his fingers.

'Life,' said Blaketon, ignoring Ventress's predicament, 'does not stop just because someone has a baby. In China, there's one born every minute.'

171

Ventress privately thought it was more frequent than that, but now was not the time to contradict the sergeant. 'Yes, sarge.'

'Has our absentee constable rung in yet?'

Ventress and Bellamy simultaneously contradicted each other.

'No, sarge. He's fetching Kate back from the hospital.'

'Yes, sarge. He's busy over at Aidensfield with firearms certificates.'

'I see.' Blaketon gazed at them in weary disbelief. 'One more day I'll give him. One more day.'

The police phone rang at midnight. Cursing softly, Nick stumbled downstairs to answer it.

'Constable Rowan?' said a crusty, middle-aged voice.

'Yes?'

'Henry Copeland here, Moor View.'

Nick struggled to put a face to the name. Moor View had just changed hands; the chap who bought it was a retired bank manager. Nick had seen him a few times, walking a couple of Yorkshire terriers. Like a lot of retired bank managers, Copeland affected a brigadierish style of dress and manner, all tweed caps and nettle-slashing. Give him six months, Nick reflected, and he'd be on the parish council complaining about litter and dog mess. 'What can I do for you, Mr Copeland?'

'You can come over here straight away, constable.'

'Could you tell me a little more first, please sir?'

'Very well. I'd like to report a break-in.'

'Is this in your house, Mr Copeland?'

'In my driveway, constable!'

'Actually that's trespass, Mr – '

Copeland's voice rose several decibels. 'I don't care what it is! There was definitely somebody banging and clanking – '

'Did you see them, Mr Copeland?'

'Almost certainly after our new wrought-iron gates – '

Nick stifled a yawn. 'Are your gates still there, sir?'

'What? Yes of course they are!'

'I'll have a look round in the morning. I think you'll find it was probably a cat.'

Kate started to get out of bed to go and look at Sarah. As soon as she got to her feet she felt dizzy and hot. The room began to swing round her. She sat heavily back down on the bed, the walls still scrolling up past her like a faulty TV set. She heard Nick coming upstairs, and lay back on the pillows, willing the nausea to go away. Nick looked in on the baby, then climbed into bed.

'Is she all right?' asked Kate.

'Fast asleep,' said Nick. 'Wish I was.'

'What was it?'

'Mr Copeland. New chap at Moor View. Thought he heard someone in his driveway.'

'Are you going out?'

'Does it look like it? I told him it was probably a cat.'

'Nick!'

'Oh come on, Kate. I'm not leaving you and Sarah on your first night home.'

He switched the light out. Kate lay in the darkness, listening to his breathing, surreptitiously checking her pulse and respiration rate. They slowed, and she began to breathe more easily. It wasn't like Nick to turn down a call, she thought; he must be more worried about her than he was going to admit.

The baby began to cry.

By the time Kate reached the nursery, Nick was already lifting Sarah out of her cot. He looked at Kate, leaning against the door frame. 'All right,' he said gently, 'I'll do it love. You go on back to bed.'

The next morning, Nick took a stroll past the Copelands' house. A neighbour told him they had gone off to the golf course. 'Up there two or three times a week, they are. All right for some, eh?'

Nick took a look at the borders round the driveway. No footmarks. He examined the gates; the hinge-posts were secured with nuts and washers and still smeared with grease. There was, however, a chip in the new black paint near the fancy sugartwist handle, so maybe Copeland had heard something after all. On the other hand, it was nothing to get excited about, and nobody else had reported anything amiss, so it could be that Copeland just fancied throwing his weight about a bit. Or perhaps his missus was the nervous type: newcomers often found the silence of the countryside at night unnerving.

Nick had had a broken night, up with Sarah at three, then again at six. She didn't seem to want anything in particular, except possibly reassurance against the dark. He wondered whether they ought to get a night-light, one of those small orange five-watt bulbs, or have the cot in their room. The problem was that Kate was against either measure, and

174

there was no point in upsetting her unnecessarily, particularly since she didn't seem to be nearly as strong or as well as she claimed to be. Both times when he had got out of bed, he had found her so hot that her hair was sticking to the nape of her neck. She was restive too, constantly altering position, and making odd little noises in her sleep. Maybe it was just the change from the hospital routine, and not being used to sleeping in her own bed . . .

He turned the corner on to the main street, stifling a yawn, and realised that his concentration was all over the place: he had walked at least a couple of hundred yards without noticing a thing.

Come on, Rowan, he told himself, you're not the only bloke with a newborn baby in the house, so get on with it.

David Rendle, a plump, moon-faced lad, was industriously polishing the bonnet of an old MK 10 Jaguar. It was dented here and there, with only a month's tax on it and not much tread left on the tyres, but it was still an impressive motor to find in this part of Aidensfield. Nick strolled over.

David's head was inches away from the bodywork, wagging away with his arm movements. Although he wasn't very bright or particularly well coordinated, he was a willing, good-natured lad, more like a big, plump baby than a twenty-two-year-old.

'Nice car,' said Nick.

'It's not mine, Mr Rowan,' said David, beaming away happily. 'It's Gary's. Grand, in't it?'

'Who's Gary, David?'

David's smile grew even bigger. 'My old mate from school o' course! He's come back to see me!'

A figure rose up from the other side of the car, adjustable spanner in hand. A sharp, flash-looking character with thick eyebrows and a self-assured manner. 'Come on birdbrain, get a move on.'

'This is Gary,' said David.

'Morning,' said Nick.

Gary gave Nick a cocky little grin. 'Morning, constable.'

'He's done right well, Mr Rowan,' said David, bathing in Gary's reflected glory. 'Got his own business in Leeds.'

Gary came round to inspect David's handiwork. There was a pale grey smear of dried polish on the chrome. Gary wiped it off with his finger and showed it to David. 'What did I say? No ride unless you do a proper job.'

'Sorry Gary, I didn't notice it.'

Gary glanced at Nick and tapped the side of his head. 'Hopeless.'

Nick watched David, head down, rubbing away anxiously at the chrome. 'And what are you doing here, Gary?'

'Oh, you know, just back to give the old place the once-over.'

'Well,' said Nick amiably, 'it's nice to know somebody from Aidenfield's doing well in the outside world. What sort of business are you in then, Gary?'

'Bit of this, bit of that.'

Nick strolled on towards the terraced cottages at the top of the village. It was the sort of answer a lot of cocky young lads would give, he thought, some of them straight, others less so. He made a mental note to find out Gary's surname.

'Mr Rowan!' It was Rita Stirling, calling to him from her front step.

Nick turned back to speak to her. 'Thanks for tidying the place up for me, Rita.'

'My pleasure.'

'You should have seen Kate's face when she saw all the presents.'

'Well,' smiled Rita, 'she's always been one of Dad's favourites.'

Joseph Walker was a spry old chap in his mid-seventies, hard of hearing now but still active and sociable. He joined his daughter on the front step, and waved a bottle at Nick. 'I've got a little something for her!'

Nick raised his voice so Joseph could hear. 'Looks like a drop of your home brew, Joseph!'

'Best blackcurrant cordial, it is. With my congratulations.'

'Give it to me, Dad,' said Rita. 'Mr Rowan can't go on his rounds with a bottle stuck out of his pocket. What would folk think?'

'I've tried your cordial before, Joseph. Powerful stuff.'

'Aye,' said Joseph, 'just the thing to perk Dr Rowan up when she needs it.'

'I'll take it round for you, Mr Rowan,' said Rita. 'I'm going up anyway to see if Dr Rowan needs any shopping.'

'Thanks Rita. Very kind of you, Joseph. I'm sure Kate'll be very pleased.'

'Aye, well, she's always been a good doctor to me, she has.'

'Come on, Dad, let Mr Rowan get on,' said Rita.

'You'd chat all day, you would.' She began to close the front door.

'No, wait a minute, wait a minute, Rita, I want to tell him about our prowler.'

'Not now, Dad. Come on – '

Joseph pushed her hand away. 'I heard him, I'm telling you!'

'What's this then, Joseph?'

'Strange noises outside me bedroom window, Mr Rowan – in the dead of night!'

'He's dreaming again,' said Rita. 'I didn't hear a thing.'

'Well, let me know if it happens again, won't you, Joseph.'

'Aye, I will that!'

Bellamy pulled up outside the Police House, tucked the two parcels under his arm, and rang the bell. Kate, still in her dressing gown, opened the door, looking deathly pale. Bellamy cursed himself for being a tactless idiot: she'd probably been up all night with the kiddie. 'I'm sorry, Kate,' he said, 'I can see it's not a good time, I'll come back – '

'No, no,' said Kate. 'Come in.'

Gina ran up the garden path, heels clacking, waving a large fluffy pink elephant. 'Ey! Wait for me!'

On the way to the living room, Kate surreptitiously rubbed her cheeks to try and put some colour in them. Bellamy looked round at the mass of presents and baby clothes and wondered if he and Ventress hadn't been a bit on the mean side. Oh well, it was too late now . . .

Gina had burst in and was hugging Kate, bubbling

over with vitality. To Bellamy the contrast could not have been more marked: Kate, pale and tired, and Gina, fresh-faced and full of life. Even their clothes emphasised the difference: Kate in her dressing gown, and Gina in a loud black and white lambskin jacket with blue suede patches.

'Well done, Kate!' Gina stood back to look at her. 'You are ever so pale, though. Here, was it as bad as they say it is?'

Trust Gina, thought Bellamy, praying he would be spared the gynaecological details. Luckily, at that moment, the baby started crying. 'Oh!' said Gina, coming over all motherly, 'Listen to her, the poor little mite! She doesn't like being left out, does she? Let me go and pick her up, Kate. Can I?'

'Thanks.'

'Don't drop her!' called Bellamy.

'And you!' retorted Gina, pounding up the stairs. Kate sighed with relief.

'I know what you mean,' grinned Bellamy. 'Like living in a house with the doors wide open.' He handed over Ventress's much-Sellotaped parcel, and watched as Kate unwrapped it.

'I don't believe it!' laughed Kate, squeaking the duck. 'Thank Alf very much for me, won't you?'

'You should have seen him trying to wrap it.' Bellamy handed over his own present. 'And this is from me. I hope it's all right.'

Kate unwrapped a musical box surrounded by blue rabbit cut-outs that revolved as the music played.

'Oh Phil!'

Bellamy glowed with pleasure. 'I mean, she probably won't enjoy it yet, but she will when she's a bit older.' They watched the rabbits twirling slowly round to the tinkling tune. 'Good, isn't it?'

'Yes it's – ' A picture rose into her mind of Sarah aged two or three, playing with the musical box. A lump rose in her throat and suddenly Kate was close to tears. Blinking them back, she turned away from Bellamy and fumbled for her handkerchief in the sleeve of her nightdress. 'Sorry . . . It's absolutely lovely . . .'

'Here, are you all right?' said Bellamy, concerned.

'Fine.' Kate blew her nose hard, wiped away the tears and tried to put a bright face on it. 'It's just, you know, baby blues or something. The slightest thing sets me off, I don't know why.'

For a moment, neither knew what to say. Then they heard Gina thudding down the stairs, cooing to baby Sarah. 'Phil,' said Kate urgently, suddenly deadly serious. 'Can I ask you something?'

'Course.'

'Look after Nick for me – '

Gina waltzed backwards through the door with the baby in her arms, gazing at it adoringly. 'Oh Kate, she's beautiful. And she's just like you!'

Bellamy left and made his way down the garden path, puzzled and preoccupied by what Kate had said. How could he look after Nick? Nick could look after himself, couldn't he?

Maggie's Land Rover drew up. Bellamy waited for her as she came up the path, medical bag in hand.

'Morning Phil!'

'Maggie – '

'What is it?'

'Is Kate all right?'

Maggie paused before switching on a big smile. 'Course she is!'

Bellamy sat in his car. No matter how he tried, things just didn't add up.

Gary drove David out to Greengrass's place in the newly polished Jag. 'Hellfire,' said Greengrass when he saw David getting out. 'That's the first time I've ever seen a pheasant plucker with a chauffeur!'

'That's my mate Gary, Mr Greengrass.'

'Aye, lad, I know,' muttered Greengrass, watching Gary reverse at speed out of the yard. 'He were good for nowt when he were here, and I'd be surprised if he were owt better now.'

'Oh he is,' said David. 'He's got his own business, in Leeds.'

'Has he? Well now I'm going to show you your business.' Greengrass tossed a sackful of pheasants to David. 'Time you've done them, you'll be a fully qualified pheasant plucker.'

An hour passed. David gamely tried to get the hang of it but the coordination just wasn't there. 'No, no, no!' fussed Greengrass. 'Not like that, you'll tear the flesh. Careful! No, you don't throw the tail feathers away! I get fourpence a time for them – '

Two-tone horn blaring, Gary's Jag swept into the yard, scattering the chickens all over the place.

'Ey you!' shouted Greengrass. 'What d'you think you're doing!'

Gary ignored him. 'Hop in, birdbrain.'

David dropped the half-plucked pheasant on the dirt floor and lumbered over to the Jag. Greengrass followed. 'Oi!' he shouted at Gary. 'You hear what I said?'

'I need to speak to him,' said Gary insolently. 'All right?'

'No it's not all right! He's in the middle of a job – '

'In,' said Gary. David obediently climbed into the Jag. Gary gave Greengrass his cocky little smile and accelerated out of the yard. Greengrass picked the bird up and brushed the dirt off it, watched hungrily by Alfred. 'And you can gerroff an' all!'

Nick and Kate were in bed by nine; by eleven, Nick was up again, giving baby Sarah what he hoped would be her last feed until morning. He put her over his shoulder to wind her, then padded up and down in his bare feet, softly singing her to sleep. After laying her down and tucking her in, he gazed down on her, love pouring through him. Feeling relieved and looking forward to a good night's sleep, he backed away from her cot – and trod on the plastic duck. It let out a long wheezing squeak; Nick held his breath and said a silent prayer. Sarah's tiny fingers twitched but she didn't wake up.

Kate lay flat out on the bed, feeling drained of every ounce of strength. She forced herself to raise a smile as Nick came in. 'You're a genius,' she whispered.

'Yes, well . . .' Nick glanced at his watch. 'With any luck she might go through till five.' He got into bed, careful not to disturb Kate's worryingly slight form. It wasn't just that he had spent the last nine months sharing a bed with a woman who was getting bigger and bigger; Kate's lack of energy, her total exhaustion after the slightest effort, made her seem smaller, more fragile. 'How are you feeling?'

'Fine.'

'No,' said Nick, leaning up on his elbow to see her face. 'Really.'

Kate put on her bright voice. 'Just a good night's sleep and I'll be a million dollars.'

Nick sighed. There was no sense in cross-questioning her, it only made her more stubborn. He turned over to put the light out.

'Nick.'

'Mmm?'

'D'you know what I'd really like?'

'What?'

'To go out for a day, just you and me and the baby. Get right away from everyone.'

Nick hesitated before replying, hating to disappoint her, but worried about all sorts of risks. 'Isn't it a bit soon?'

She put a hand on his shoulder. He could feel the heat of it through his pyjamas. 'Please, Nick. I'm getting stronger every day.'

Nick stared out into the darkness, his heart breaking with love for her.

'Just the three of us,' she whispered against his neck, 'like a proper family.'

He turned over and hugged her gently. 'We *are* a proper family.'

She smiled, snuggled up close, and fell asleep in his arms.

# Eleven

Winter returned overnight. Banks of grey cloud thickened over the hilltops and rolled down off the moor. By midday, a cold rain wept incessantly from the lowering sky.

Nick had taken his lunch break early to have a word with Mr Faber after he had examined Kate and taken another blood sample. He walked the haematologist through the rain to his car. 'What d'you think, Mr Faber?'

'We'll know more when we get the results of the latest blood tests.'

It was neither encouraging nor discouraging. Nick pushed a little harder, needing to get the consultant to commit himself. 'We thought of going out for a day. She's been cooped up so long, first in the hospital and now here. Would that be all right?'

'Not thinking of today, I hope.'

'No fear, I'm not looking forward to being out in it myself.'

'The main risk is infection: crowded places, shops, pubs, that sort of thing.'

'We were thinking of a picnic, just the three of us, out in the country.'

Mr Faber pondered. 'In the car, and if she's well wrapped up, I can't see any problem.'

As Nick opened the gate, the phone started

ringing. Nick ignored it. There was one question he still had to ask, and even if it took all his courage to ask it, he was determined to get a straight answer. After the fifth or sixth ring, the phone stopped. They stood beside Mr Faber's car, rain drumming on its black roof.

'Mr Faber.'

'Yes?'

'How long have we got?'

It was a question the haematologist had been asked many times before; he was still stumped for the best way to answer it. Despite all the advances in leukaemia research, and research into cancer generally, no one knew for certain why one patient went into remission and another did not. It wasn't simply a matter of treatment, or diet; nor was it the particular individual's psychological make-up, important though the will to live had proved to be.

To put it baldly, in the opinion of Mr Faber and most other specialists, remission seemed to be largely a matter of luck. As he was acutely aware, this was not what patients or their loved ones wanted to hear. They wanted to have faith, and they wanted certainty, and no responsible, right-minded medical practitioner could provide either. Kate knew that. Mr Faber was less sure of Nick. Undoubtedly he knew the facts concerning remission; what was debatable was whether he accepted them.

The best thing, as always, was to be as straight as possible, and err on the side of optimism. 'Well, given the present evidence, I'm pretty hopeful,' said Mr Faber.

'Of a cure?' asked Nick quickly.

185

Mr Faber ducked into his car. 'She's a fighter, Nick. I've got a feeling she may surprise us all.'

'Surprise us all!' What was that supposed to mean? How would she surprise them all? By staying alive, getting better, or what? Only slightly encouraged and still uncertain, Nick trudged back into the house for his greatcoat.

'That was Rita,' said Kate, indicating the police phone.

Nick nodded, looked round to see that everything was all right, then decided to build up the fire.

'Nick, you better go,' said Kate, trying to hurry him. 'Rita sounded in quite a panic.'

He clanged the fire door shut and set down the scuttle. 'Sure you'll manage?'

'I'll be fine. Now go on.'

He kissed her. 'I'll be back as soon as I can.'

Kate watched him go. Feeling tearful, and telling herself that she was being over-emotional, she sat on the sofa to blow her nose. A gush of bright red blood stained the tissue.

It was a good twenty minutes before the nosebleed stopped. Kate lay on the sofa, her head back, surrounded by a mass of blood-soaked tissues. She put yet another tissue to her nose. No more blood. She stood up, felt wobbly, and reached out a hand to steady herself on the arm of the sofa. Then, with despair drenching through her, she gathered up the bloody tissues and knelt by the stove to burn them.

The heat from the open stove almost made her faint. She closed the fire door and with an enormous effort, her whole body a dead weight, forced herself upright.

186

Once the dizzy spell had passed, she took a deep breath and looked round for something to do. Anything to take her mind off it. She began to fold the baby clothes on the airer. It didn't work. The dark gulf was still there, waiting for her. What she needed was love. She laid down the last tiny soft woollen cardigan, picked up Sarah from her cot and held her close. When Sarah's tiny head turned towards her breast, and her mouth made little suckling movements, the tears that Kate had held back for so long began to flow.

She shuddered at the hopelessness of it all, the hopelessness even of her love for the poor innocent child in her arms, and tearing sobs racked through her heart.

She had no idea Maggie had entered until she found herself and the baby buried in Maggie's starched embrace. 'There, love, there,' murmured Maggie, feeling Kate's distress as if it were her own. 'Come on, love. Come on, tell me.'

Kate sniffed back her tears, the pain still aching in her. 'I love her so much. More than I thought possible.'

'Of course you do.'

'They don't tell you about that, do they? Mother love.' She looked up at Maggie, her voice breaking. 'I'd do anything for her, anything in the whole world. And yet the one thing she wants, the one thing she really needs, I can't give her.'

'Oh, come on,' said Maggie. 'That's not true.'

'Maggie, it is.' Kate closed her eyes, seeing once more Sarah's mouth seeking her breast. 'I can't be a mother to her.'

'You are a mother to her,' said Maggie stoutly. 'A wonderful mother. I'd soon tell you if you weren't, my girl.'

Kate tried to smile, but there was no disguising the desperation in her voice. 'Yes, but what about in six months' time? A year, however long I've got? What sort of start in life is that? Who's going to be there when she takes her first steps? Says her first word?' Kate glanced down at the three-year baby book. There was a splash of blood on the cover.

'Look,' said Maggie briskly, 'you're down in the dumps. It's natural after having a baby.'

Kate turned away angrily. 'Oh please Maggie, don't! This isn't just post-natal depression, we both know that. Let's just be straight with each other, shall we? I'm going to die.'

'Nonsense!' said Maggie. 'That's absolute rubbish, Kate, and you know it. You've responded brilliantly to treatment. You know you have.'

'My glands hurt.' Kate's voice cracked slightly as she spoke, reminding Maggie of a frightened child desperate for reassurance.

'Let's have a look.' Maggie gently felt Kate's neck and throat; the lymph glands were hot and swollen.

'Well?'

'You're right, as usual,' said Maggie. 'They are enlarged, but you know as well as I do these things often get worse before they get better.'

Kate's half-smile expressed her disbelief. When it faded, she looked Maggie straight in the eye. 'Don't tell Nick. Don't tell him about any of this.'

Rita was waiting on her step. As soon as the Francis-

Barnett came into sight, she ran out into the rain to meet Nick. 'It's Dad,' she said, breathless with anxiety. 'He went off in his car after breakfast, Mr Rowan, and he's not come back.'

'Any idea where he went?'

'To see his pals, he said,' She pushed a hand through her damp hair. 'I mean, he's always back for his dinner on the dot of twelve.'

'D'you know which pals?'

'Ernie Shawcross of Upper Toft Farm and Ginger Roberts at Clouds End. I wouldn't worry only he had that stroke six months back.'

'Stay by the phone, Rita. I'll get a call through as soon as I find him.'

'Oh, thank you Mr Rowan, thank you ever so much.'

Nick pressed on through the rain up on to the moor. The wind blew in vicious gusts, shoving the Francis-Barnett all over the road and lashing Nick with cold, stinging rain.

Glad to get the wind behind him, he turned off the top road and bumped along the track to Upper Toft Farm. There was something up ahead, stuck on the highest part of the track and out of sight of the valley-sheltered farm. Nick wiped the streaming rain from his goggles. It looked like an old Austin 10 with the bonnet up. Nick accelerated up the rock track towards it.

Joseph was bent double over the starting handle, breathing heavily, trying to work up the strength for another swing. Nick, seeing the old chap was blue with cold and just about at the end of his tether, leaped off his bike. 'Come on, Joseph!' he shouted over the wind and rain. 'Leave it!' The old man looked up at him, his wits dulled by cold.

Nick threw his greatcoat over him and bundled him into the car. 'Let's get inside out of the wind!' Joseph slumped in the back seat, his teeth chattering and his voice incoherent.

'I was – I was on my way to see Ernie – you know, Ernie Shawcross – '

'All right, Joseph, save your strength!'

'She just conked out. I tried . . . I tried starting her, on the handle – '

'You just sit there, try to warm up, Joseph. I'll have a look.' Nick hung on to the driver's door against the gusts of wind and eased himself into the seat. He turned the ignition key. The oil pressure, temperature and battery indicators flickered. The petrol gauge stayed dead, on zero. Nick tried the key again to make sure, and then, the car rocking in the wind, turned to Joseph.

'Joseph!'

'Aye?' A little colour had returned to his face.

'It's very simple, really!' Nick shouted so the old man could hear. 'You've run out of petrol!'

Nick borrowed a gallon can from Ernie Shawcross, left his bike in the barn and drove Joseph straight back to the Police House.

He sat huddled in blankets while Kate took his temperature. Nick and Rita looked on. 'Hmm,' said Kate, frowning at the reading. 'You've had a touch of hypothermia, Joseph.'

'Aye, but I'm all right now,' muttered Joseph doggedly.

'No you're not,' said Kate firmly. 'When you get

190

him home, Rita, just put him to bed and let him warm up gradually. A drop of soup won't do any harm, but no alcohol.'

'Oh Dad,' said Rita wearily, 'you must be more careful.'

Joseph looked up out of his blankets, stubborn as ever. 'I was. I filled her up Monday. I've hardly been anywhere since then, and I checked before I set off. Three-quarters of a tank, I had.'

Rita, standing behind Joseph made a face at Nick: 'You see what I've got to put up with.'

'Of course you did,' said Kate. 'You've just had a nasty shock, that's all.'

Joseph took Kate's hand. 'Ey, Dr Rowan, it's grand to have you back.'

Kate smiled at him warmly. 'Thank you, Joseph.'

'Best little doctor in the world, you are,' said Joseph.

After they had gone, Kate insisted on getting supper ready. Nick could see that dealing with Joseph had boosted her confidence, made her feel useful again, given her something to look forward to; Nick hoped she wasn't going to try and do too much too soon.

When he went up to bed, he found Kate sitting up, writing.

'What's that, love?'

'Oh,' said Kate vaguely, putting the pad away. 'Just thank you letters.'

'You must be feeling better, then.'

'I am. I tell you what I'm really looking forward to.'

'What's that?'

'Our little walk. Getting out in the fresh air, showing Sarah around.'

'Have to see what the weather does first.'

'It's going to brighten up.' She kissed him as he got into bed. 'Everything is, you'll see.'

By eleven o'clock next morning, the wind had blown the clouds away and it was a bright cold spring day. Nick, in uniform because he was supposed to be working, pushed the pram along the path and waited for Kate. He wasn't too happy about their little jaunt, but Kate had been excited from the moment she had woken up and seen the sunshine streaming in, and there was no way he could refuse her.

She came out of the house carrying the picnic set they had been given as a wedding present and wearing her full-length sheepskin-lined suede coat.

Nick waited at the gate for her to catch up. 'Are you quite sure about this, Kate?'

'Yes, of course I am. Why?'

'I still think a day in the car would've been better. You know what Mr Faber said – '

'I don't want to be cooped up in a car!' She put her face up to the fresh cold air and breathed in the smell of the morning. 'I want to go for a walk, the three of us, up into the hills like we used to.' She looked at him archly. 'Time was, Nick Rowan, you couldn't wait to get me up there.'

She was trying to put a good face on it, but under the make-up she was alarmingly pale. 'Right as usual,' he smiled back at her. 'Let's go.'

He wheeled the pram through the gate and looked exaggeratedly up and down the village street.

192

'What are you doing?'

'I'm in uniform, aren't I? If anyone sees us, I'm on a case.'

'You fool!' She linked her arm through his, and they set off. Nick reflected that it was the first time he had ever driven a pram. He was considering whether to dip the front wheels over the kerb first or keep them in the air until the back wheels were safely down, when they came to their first corner and bumped straight into Greengrass.

'Well, I'll be blowed,' he said, looking at Nick in astonishment. 'Here, I hope you've got L-plates for that.'

'Ssh,' said Kate seriously. 'Don't tell anyone. He's on a case.'

'You what?' Greengrass scratched his scruffy pate and watched them walk past, thoroughly mystified. When they burst out laughing, he bellowed out after them, 'It's all right for some!'

They reached Clouds End bridge just on noon, and scrambled down the bank to their favourite patch of green between the old log and the stream. Nick spread the rug and Kate set out the blue picnic set.

Once she had her bottle. Sarah settled back peacefully in Kate's arms. Out of the breeze, it was warm and sheltered, and Nick, seeing the pleasure glowing on Kate's face, began to relax for what seemed the first time in weeks. He put one arm round Kate, and held Sarah's bottle with the other.

'Oh Nick,' breathed Kate, snuggling up to him, 'it's wonderful.'

'Not bad, is it?'

'Primroses, look, Nick. Over there. And those

must be globe hyacinths – they're early. Spring's coming – I can't wait!'

Nick leaned back against the log, the feverish intensity of her enthusiasm saddening him. Sensing this, she turned to him. 'We've been very happy, haven't we?' There was a pleading note in her voice, a need for reassurance.

'We are very happy, love.' He kissed her hot cheek.

'Mmm,' she sighed contentedly. 'And things'll be even better now.'

'How d'you mean?' said Nick.

'Now I'm not going to be spending half my life in Whitby.'

'Oh, right,' said Nick, relieved. 'That's what you're thinking about, is it?'

'I've also been thinking about the Aidensfield practice.' She shifted position so she could see his reaction. 'How about if I went part time and just held one surgery a day?'

'Sounds great,' said Nick, hiding his surprise.

'I could take Sarah to the surgery with me, and get Rita in to mind her. Then I wouldn't have to leave her at all.' She waited eagerly for Nick's approval.

'Kate,' he said, hating himself but knowing that it would be wrong to let her start rushing into things. 'Don't make too many plans yet.'

It was as if he'd slapped her across the face. She took the bottle from him abruptly, and turned all her attention to her baby. 'Come on, Sarah. Your first picnic, isn't it? The first of many. We'll have lots in the summer, won't we? Just you and me, and we won't care what silly old Daddy says, will we?' She gave a sudden shiver inside the thick sheepskin coat. 'And I shall make as many plans as I want.'

'I didn't mean that, Kate – '

She was not listening. Her eyes closed and another spasm of shivering ran through her. He got to his knees and began to clear up blindly, clumsily, all his love and sorrow flowing through him, cursing himself for giving in to her. He closed the picnic case and tried to make his voice sound casual. 'Are we off, then?'

After what seemed like an age, her eyes opened. 'I'm sorry,' she said dully. 'Could you fetch the car?'

'What's the matter?'

'I'm a bit tired, that's all. Bit cold – '

'Right. Fine.' Smiling as though nothing was amiss, Nick took his jacket off and wrapped it round her. 'You just sit there and I'll be back in a jiff!' He ran up the steep bank on wings of panic.

Kate watched him go, and leaned back against the log, exhausted. Below her, the stream ran fast and dark.

The Triumph Herald was low on petrol but it got them home. Neither of them spoke much about what had happened, and with Kate asleep most of the afternoon and evening, Nick had no option but to stay at home and look after Sarah.

Kate woke at half-past two, her throat raw and her skin burning. She slid quietly out of bed, trying not to wake Nick. Breathing heavily, and suppressing the fit of coughing she felt coming over her, she tiptoed out of the bedroom. Nick, immediately awake, watched her move through the door. Instead of going to the nursery, as he thought, her bare feet went padding down the stairs . . .

He found her in the kitchen, trying to hide the thermometer she had taken from her medical bag.

'What's up?'

She shook her head, swallowing a cough. 'Nothing.'

He felt her forehead. 'You're hot, Kate. Really hot.'

'I've got a tickly throat, that's all. I'll just have a drink of water – '

The phone rang. 'Leave it, Kate! Let it ring!'

She had already picked it up. 'Yes? Yes he is.' She covered the mouthpiece and handed it to Nick. 'Mr Copeland.'

'Tell him to go to hell!'

'No, Nick, you'll have to go. You must, you've got a job to do.'

Nick dragged on his uniform over his pyjamas. Ten minutes later he was shining his torch round the front of Moor View. The front door was unlatched and Henry Copeland came out in dressing gown and slippers, carrying a walking stick. 'Same as the other night,' he said, pointing with the stick. 'Noises over there by the garage, and footsteps on the gravel.'

Nick kept his mouth shut, and went over to try the garage doors. Locked. He shone his torch carefully over the gravel. Nothing. He moved to the gate: it was shut but the latch was up.

'Well?' asked Copeland from the porch.

Nick trudged back. 'There's nothing to see at the moment. I'll come back in the morning when it's light and have a good look round – '

'Not good enough,' said Copeland sharply. 'I need you out here now, in case he comes back again – '

Nick glanced at his watch, and before he could help it the accumulated tension of the day boiled over. 'Mr Copeland. It's twenty to three. No crime has been committed. Nothing's been stolen and nothing's been damaged. I'm sorry, but there are people in this world with real problems, and I need to get back home now to deal with one of them.' His angry outburst over, he scrunched his heel in the gravel, and left Copeland with his mouth hanging open.

Nick twisted the thermometer to catch the light. Kate, hot and shivering under her blanket, looked up helplessly. 'A hundred and three,' said Nick quietly. Kate bit her lip to stop her teeth chattering. There was no use pretending any more: this was serious.

The kitchen clock's second-hand jerked inexorably round. Nick knew he had to make a decision now, while there was still time. 'I'll phone Faber.'

'It's the middle of the night.' She glanced up at the clock. 'Ten to three.'

Nick was already dialling. 'I don't care.' The number began to ring.

Kate reached out a hand. 'Nick,' she said, admitting it for the first time, 'I'm frightened.'

# Twelve

Kate insisted on talking to Mr Faber herself. Nick stood by her side worried sick while she and the haematologist calmly discussed her symptoms over the phone. To Nick, it seemed as if they were talking about some other patient altogether. Their diagnosis, reached with the same impersonal moderation, was that Kate had contracted a throat infection, either at home or in hospital, and that due to her reduced immunity it had spread to her chest. They agreed on a course of antibiotics, to be started immediately, and after apologising for waking him up, Kate put the phone down.

'I thought you said you were frightened?' said Nick.

'I was,' said Kate, 'I still am.'

Nick shook his head in admiration. 'You didn't sound it, love.'

She smiled patiently. 'Shouting and screaming doesn't help, Nick. Get my medical bag, would you, please? I need the keys to the drugs cupboard.'

Maggie was round by a quarter to nine next morning. Kate sat propped up in bed, giving Sarah her bottle. Although the antibiotics had not had much effect so far, Kate seemed to Nick to have discovered a new, steely calm. Whether it was resignation or determination he found hard to tell. Irked most of

198

all by his own uselessness, he knew his anxiety was beginning to irritate Kate, but there was absolutely nothing he could do about it. Emotionally shattered as he was, he felt he had to be there.

He watched Kate's rapid, shallow breathing as Maggie took her pulse. Compared to him, the two women were taking it all as a matter of course, part of the day's work.

'Uh-uh,' said Maggie, checking her watch.

'What is it?' asked Kate.

'Too fast.'

'Respiration rate is thirty-four, by the way.'

'Thank you, doctor.' Maggie leaned Kate forward to puff up her pillows.

'It started with a sore throat,' said Nick, trying to help, 'which of course she didn't tell me about.'

'Typical,' said Maggie. She gave Kate a glance: Men.

'Made me take her for a walk up to Clouds End instead.'

'Nick,' cut in Kate edgily, 'could you do something for me? Go and ask Rita Stirling if she could come in and tidy the place up a bit.'

'I can tidy up. All I've got to do is ring Blaketon –'

'Nick. I'd rather you went to work and Rita came in.'

'I think Kate would feel easier that way,' said Maggie.

Faced with the pair of them, Nick knew he had no option. 'OK.' He went out to get his jacket, and came in again straight away. 'What time's Mr Faber coming?'

'Nine-thirty,' said Maggie.

'Right.' Out he went again. Kate sighed with relief.

'Poor Nick,' said Maggie.

'Oh I know, Maggie. But there's nothing he can do, and it just makes it worse for both of us.'

'Rita's a good idea,' said Maggie, considering. 'She could help with the baby, too.'

Kate pushed herself up off her pillows indignantly. 'I'm not having anyone else touch my baby, Maggie –' She tried to smile at the strength of her own reaction. 'Oh, you know what I mean.'

'All right, I'm sorry I mentioned it –'

'It's only an infection, I'm not incapacitated.'

'No, ma'am.'

'Could you pass me that pad and pencil from the dressing table, please.'

Maggie did as she was told. 'Anything else, ma'am?'

'Yes. Leave me in peace. I've got work to do.'

'I do love a nice polite patient, don't you?'

'Oh you know what I mean,' sighed Kate.

'No, I don't, actually.'

'I don't have any time to waste, Maggie.'

Maggie took Sarah from her. 'Sorry, love.'

Henry Copeland had arrived at Ashfordly station in his black banker's overcoat and homburg to lodge a complaint. Having done so once in the privacy of Blaketon's office, he was determined to say it all again on the way out. Bellamy and Ventress bent industriously over their desks and listened. Blaketon, they noted, was looking particularly pale and long-suffering.

'I've called him twice and he's done nothing.'

'Right, Mr Copeland – '

'His manner has been offhand in the extreme.' Copeland looked distastefully round the cramped, untidy duty room. 'I'm tempted to say downright rude.'

'As I said, Mr Copeland, I'll look into it – '

Copeland ignored him. 'And to discover this morning that someone has stolen a tankful of petrol from under my very nose, and that there is a veritable spate of such thefts throughout the village – '

Blaketon decided that was it. 'Mr Copeland, I have taken note of everything you have told me and I will be investigating the matter fully. Goodbye!' He opened the door and steered Copeland through it. 'Right!' Blaketon swung round and glared at Bellamy and Ventress. 'That's it! Try him on the phone, Ventress. I've turned a blind eye long enough. Bellamy, his radio.'

'Yes, sarge!'

'Yes, sarge!'

Blaketon watched them jump to it with a measure of satisfaction. 'And if we can't raise him as per usual, I'm going over there!'

Nick had no intention of setting a foot outside the Police House until he had had a word with Mr Faber. He sat in the kitchen with the phone off the hook and his mind blank. The haematologist had already been up there half an hour. How much longer was he going to be? Nick took a sip from the mug of tea in front of him. It was stone cold.

Mr Faber sombrely folded his stethoscope, giving Kate time to absorb what he had just told her.

'Pneumonia?'

'I'm afraid so.' He took hold of her hand. 'Only in one lung, at the moment. Have you started the antibiotics?'

'Straight away last night.'

'Sod's law, isn't it?' he said, for once giving vent to his feelings. 'You were coming into remission so well. The blood tests were looking better. This is just what we didn't need.' He patted her hand and stood up. 'I think the best thing I can do now is call in Charlie Morrison.'

'Do you have to?' said Kate. 'It'll only worry Nick.'

Mr Faber frowned. 'With all due respect, Kate, that's hardly the point. I'm only a humble haematologist. We need an expert opinion.'

Blaketon parked his car and strode up the path to the Police House. A familiar tinny chatter distracted him. He found the Francis-Barnett dumped behind a bush, its radio twittering away to itself. He picked up the receiver and pressed TRANSMIT. 'All right, Bellamy, I'll handle this.'

Nick had been cleaning out Sarah's bottles. He stood just inside the front door with Mr Faber, bottle-brush in hand, unable to take in what the haematologist had just told him. 'Could you say that again?'

'Hypostatic pneumonia,' said Mr Faber. 'Congestion of the lung.' He watched Nick, knowing that the more he tried to explain, the less Nick would understand. 'I want our chest man, Morrison, to come over.'

'Right.'

'I'd better warn you, he'll probably want her in.'

'Back to hospital?' Nick's heart sank at the thought of being separated from Kate. In addition, as far as he was concerned, it was probably where Kate had picked up the infection in the first place. Before he could tackle Mr Faber on the subject, there was a sharp rat-tat-tat on the door. He opened it and came face to face with Blaketon.

Blaketon looked Nick up and down. Tieless. Jacketless. Holding a bottle-brush.

Mr Faber eased his way between them. 'I'll ring you later.' He gripped Nick's arm reassuringly: 'let you know what's happening.' When he had gone, Blaketon stepped inside. Nick shoved past him. 'Wait a minute,' he said over his shoulder, and hurried down the path after Mr Faber.

'Wait a minute.' That was a bit bloody offhand, thought Blaketon. He made his way into the kitchen. What he saw stopped him dead.

A fastidiously neat man whose own house was tidy to the point of bleakness, Blaketon had rarely been confronted with such a truly terrible mess. Blankets were hanging out of the pram, baby clothes were festooned all over the airer, unwashed breakfast things were piled at the foot of the stairs, the sink was filled with crockery, the fire was unlit, ashes had spilled out of the grate on to the hearth, and baby clutter of all kinds and descriptions, including Ventress's plastic duck and Gina's pink elephant, lay scattered all over the floor and made it impossible to put one foot in front of the other.

Blaketon picked his way through the mess, his face souring with disapproval and affront. When he saw that the phone had been left off the hook, disapproval turned into pent-up rage. What the hell was going on?

Nick, dazed by the implications of what Mr Faber had told him, wandered in. Blaketon swung round and stuck his glowering face inches from Nick's. 'So this is what you're up to, is it? Playing mummies and daddies. While drawing full pay from the North Riding Constabulary!' Nick turned away: there was nothing he could tell Blaketon, so the best thing was to let him rant on. 'I, Rowan, receive complaints about rudeness, about incompetence, about the village constable being permanently out of contact!' He glanced sharply at the phone, making sure Nick followed suit, and continued in a low, threatening tone, 'I don't care if your wife's a doctor or Chancellor of the Exchequer: once she has a baby, that's her job. And yours is to bring in the bacon. And there'll be precious little bacon to bring in if you don't pull your finger out! So put that telephone back on its hook immediately! Do I make myself clear?'

'Yes, sarge.' Wearily, Nick did so.

'Where is Dr Rowan anyway?' said Blaketon.

'Resting.'

Blaketon made his way into the hall, and turned to survey the chaos. 'Well, when she's finished "resting", this place could do with a woman's touch!'

Nick listened to the front door bang. He supposed, since Blaketon had come over in person, he had been given a Grade A rollocking. Thinking about it, he realised he couldn't care less.

'I heard all that.' Kate made her way slowly into the kitchen, and held on to a chairback to get her breath.

Nick helped her into the chair. 'You shouldn't be up.'

She gazed levelly at Nick. 'You've got to tell him. I was the one who wanted to keep it secret. I was wrong.'

'No, love – '

'Nick,' she insisted, 'it's better now if everyone knows. For your sake.'

That was the hardest thing, he thought. You were out there, out of your depth, drowning, and back on the shore, life went on as usual. Kate had got hold of that; she always had been much quicker on the uptake. 'What'll I tell them?' he asked.

Kate looked up at him calmly. 'Everything.'

Blaketon's Anglia coughed, spluttered and died just as he reached Ashfordly Woods. Cursing volubly, already in a foul temper, he tried the starter. One, twice, three times. Nothing. He got out to look under the bonnet. As he fiddled with the catch, Copeland's words came back to him. 'A veritable spate of thefts . . .'

He got back in the car to check the petrol gauge. Empty. A police vehicle. Done in broad bloody daylight.

He switched on the radio. 'Delta Alpha Two Zero to Control.'

Ventress's voice answered. 'Go ahead, sarge.'

'Ventress, get a can of petrol and get out here!'

David Rendle took the half-full jerrycan out from under his duffel coat and set it on the ground by Greengrass's truck. He looked round carefully. A small flock of sheep was trailing slowly down the road. Good. That meant there'd be no traffic along for a couple of minutes. His moon face beaming at his astuteness, he drew out a length of blue agricultural plastic hose and inserted it in the truck's red-painted tank. He began to suck, keeping a careful eye on the petrol sluicing up the hose so he wouldn't get more than a mouthful before he siphoned it into the jerrycan. Now then –

'Ey you, you bugger!' roared Greengrass, storming round the end of the truck. David gulped and swallowed in fright. Raw spirit burned into his mouth and down his gullet. He dropped the hose and cavorted about with the can, clutching his stomach. 'Help!' he spluttered. 'Help! I've swallered it!'

As Greengrass collared him and swung him round he was coughing and hacking and retching until tears streamed down his face.

'After all I've done for you!' Greengrass shoved him against the side of the truck.

'I'm sorry – I'm sorry!'

'Gimme that!' Greengrass wrenched the jerrycan off him. There was a good couple of gallons in it.

David began to blubber. 'No! I need me can! I need it – '

'Not likely,' growled Greengrass, shaking him by the scruff. 'Not after you've nicked my petrol!'

'I didn't take any from you, it all came from Mr Blaketon!'

Greengrass's shrewd little eyes glinted with sly amusement. 'Never mind where it came from.' He put his face close to the cowering David. 'Stealing's a mortal sin! Now get out of it – before I chop your arms and legs off!' He flung David away from him and watched him disappear at a whimpering, uncoordinated run. He uncapped the jerrycan, and, grunting with satisfaction, upended Blaketon's petrol into his tank.

Bellamy was alone in the station when he took Nick's call. He listened to the brief, controlled account, the tears springing to his eyes. 'I don't know what to say, Nick – '

'Just tell the others for me, will you, Phil?'

'Nick?' There was a click, and then the disconnected tone.

'Broad bloody daylight!' Blaketon's voice rang out as he and Ventress entered the station. Bellamy found he was still stupidly holding the disconnected phone. He put it slowly down, and stared into space, stunned.

'And now what have I got?' grated Blaketon, striding into the duty room. 'A mucky carburettor and a car that sounds like fireworks night gone wrong . . . I'm in Aidensfield for precisely twenty minutes and what happens?'

'A crime wave, sarge,' said Ventress dolefully.

Bellamy was still staring into space. 'What's the matter with you?' snapped Blaketon.

'I've just been speaking to Nick.' Bellamy swallowed, trying to steady his voice. 'Kate's got leukaemia.'

Blaketon, remembering what he had just said to Nick, fell silent.

'Kate?' said Ventress. 'Kate Rowan?'

Bellamy, unable to speak, nodded.

'Leukaemia?'

Again Bellamy nodded.

'But she can't have,' said Ventress doggedly. 'She's only just had the baby.'

Bellamy braced himself to tell them the worst. 'They don't think she's going to pull through.'

Without saying a word, Blaketon walked into his office and leaned against the door. He heard Bellamy's voice. 'I mean, she's so young, only a year or two more than me.'

For the first time in years, Blaketon sat down and wept.

Kate lay back on her pillows, her face pallid, her eyes dull and ringed with dark shadows, her body limp. Maggie, a towel over her shoulder, was tepid-sponging her limbs to bring her temperature down. 'The pad, Maggie.'

'What's that, love?'

'The writing pad, on the side there. Under the books. There's some instructions.

'Oh yes?'

'I want you to take them.'

'Now look here,' said Maggie, trying to make a joke of it, 'if it's your Last Will and Testament, I'm having nothing to do with it.'

'It's not. It's about the arrangements, you know, afterwards.'

'That's even worse!' Maggie sponged away vigorously. 'We're not at that point yet, Kate. Stick that other leg out.'

'Please. Just take them.'

Maggie looked at Kate and saw she was serious.

She wiped her hands on the towel, and took the loose sheets from the writing pad. 'Oh come on, Kate,' she said, glancing through them. 'Where to get the ham, who to ask . . . I've heard of forward planning, but this is ridiculous!'

'It's only to make life easier for Nick.'

'Only to get your own way, more like,' said Maggie, determined to jolly her out of it. 'Bossy to the bitter end!'

Kate started to giggle, and then went into a painful coughing fit. Maggie put a glass of water to her lips. 'Sorry, love.'

'Maggie.' Nick poked his head round the bedroom door.

'Yes?' said Maggie, shoving the loose sheets in her skirt pocket.

'Mr Faber and Mr Morrison are here.'

Downstairs, Rita Stirling was putting the final touches to the living room and kitchen. Both rooms were now immaculate. Footsteps creaked overhead. A muffled sound of low voices. The mantelpiece clock, ticking louder than usual, increased the tension. Sarah began to cry. Rita hurried to her, plucked her out of her cot, held her close and rocked her. 'Ssh, ssh, now Sarah, it's all right,' said Rita softly, knowing it was anything but.

Mr Morrison, the consultant from Ashfordly Hospital, finished listening to Kate's chest. He exchanged a glance with Mr Faber, then turned to Nick, his voice grave. 'Things aren't looking good, I'm afraid. The congestion is getting worse fairly rapidly.'

'We'd like you back in hospital, Kate,' said Mr Faber gently. Kate sank back in her pillows and closed her eyes. The two consultants looked for Nick's reaction.

'I'm not taking any decisions without Kate.'

Blaketon, seeing the consultants' cars outside, knocked softly on the front door. Rita opened it, baby Sarah in her arms. 'You'll have to wait in the kitchen,' she said quietly. 'There's doctors upstairs.'

Nick moved to the bedside. 'Kate?'

Kate looked at the two consultants. 'No. It's very kind of you, but no.'

'It might give you a better chance,' said Mr Faber.

Kate smiled and shook her head. 'Time is very precious to me now, Michael, and I want to be here. With my husband and baby.'

Nick was in despair. 'But Kate, if there are other treatments – '

'They wouldn't work. They'd only delay things. I don't want to linger.' She smiled as though she were talking about nothing more serious than catching a train, and then added lightly, with a mischievous glance at Maggie. 'Besides, it's playing havoc with my looks.'

Nick saw the two consultants to the door. He knew they were doing their best to be supportive, but now Kate had made her decision he didn't want them in the house any more.

Mr Faber put a hand on his shoulder. 'You'll let us know if she changes her mind.'

'Yes.' said Nick shortly. 'Thank you for coming.' He closed the door and leaned his head against it, wishing he could accept what was to come as serenely as Kate, knowing that he never could.

Rita came into the hall with Sarah in her arms, and waited, unwilling to intrude. Nick, sensing her, turned round. 'What is it, Rita?'

'Sergeant Blaketon's here to see you ... He insisted on waiting. He's in the kitchen.'

Nick walked past her without a word. Blaketon got to his feet awkwardly. 'I came to apologise.'

No expression whatsoever crossed Nick's face; it was, thought Blaketon, like looking into the eyes of an accident victim: no recognition, no emotion, only a dull, wounded, uncomprehending stare.

'Had I known how ill Kate was, I would never have said the things that I did. I am extremely sorry.'

Still no reaction.

'I want you to know that if there's anything I can do, or Bellamy, or Ventress, you only have to ask.'

This time, there was a faint nod. Encouraged, Blaketon relaxed into a more familiar mode. 'For a start you can take that uniform off. You're on compassionate leave. Three days official, and after that we'll bend the rules.'

'Excuse me,' said Nick flatly. He turned on his heel and moved quickly up the stairs.

Ventress sat in the driving seat of the Anglia watching Blaketon's grim-faced approach. He came straight round to Ventress's door and wrenched it open.

'How is she?' asked Ventress.

'Until further notice,' said Blaketon curtly, ignoring him, 'Aidensfield's your patch. So hop out and get cracking.'

★

After he got off duty, Bellamy went home, changed, and drove over to Aidensfield. He felt, without knowing exactly why, that he ought to be near Nick, and needed to be among friends.

They were a sombre group that night in the Aidensfield Arms: it was as if a black cloud had settled over the whole village. Since Nick had said that Kate wanted everyone to know, Bellamy told George and Gina and a few other regulars about the phone call. When he finished, he was close to tears. 'I mean, I only saw her the other day, to give her the presents.'

Ventress, in uniform, deputising for Nick, put a sympathetic hand on his shoulder. 'Aye, well – '

'She looked ill then, but I thought it were, you know, just having the baby, like.'

The door opened. Everyone looked round quickly, fearful of bad news. Greengrass barged in, cheerfully rubbing his big red hands together against the cold. He took in Ventress's uniform, and winked at his cronies. 'Evening all!' Not one of them smiled. 'Oh well, Scotch please, George.' George turned to the optic without a word. Greengrass looked around the bar; set, serious faces everywhere. 'By 'eck, what's this then, an undertaker's funeral?'

'Claude,' snapped Gina. 'Just shut up, will you?'

'Eh?' said Greengrass, taken aback. 'What have I done now?'

'It's the upset about Kate Rowan,' said Ventress.

'What? She's only had a babbie, hasn't she? What's that to get upset about? More t'other way round, I should've thought – '

George placed Greengrass's Scotch in front of him. 'Kate's very ill, Claude.'

'She's got leukaemia,' said Gina.

Greengrass looked from face to face, still grinning uncertainly, not sure whether they were having him on or not. 'Pull the other one!' he said, knocking back his Scotch. 'I saw her only the other day, happy as a sandboy, going up to Clouds End. Laughing away, she was . . .' He trailed off, finally aware that everyone was willing him to shut up. 'It's not true, is it, George?'

George nodded, and Greengrass too fell silent.

The passage of time had done nothing to dull Nick's anger or resentment. To give Kate the best chance of an undisturbed night, he had decided to sleep on the spare bed in the nursery. At eleven o'clock he came in to see her. He straightened her bed and began to tidy her bedside table with small, angry movements. 'Right,' he said. 'There we are. Have you got everything you need?'

Kate, propped up in pillows, watched him fiddling with her water glass and medicine bottles. 'Yes, thanks.' He went on shifting them around, an inch here, an inch there. She put her hand on his to stop him. 'Nick, please.'

'What?'

'Come on. Don't be bitter.'

'Don't be bitter? Kate, my whole life's been turned upside down. I'm not a saint!'

'Feeling angry won't help. You need to be calm, for your sake and the baby's.'

He took his hand away and started fiddling with things again. 'Yes, well, if it hadn't been for her – '

'Nick!' said Kate sharply, 'I had to make sure the

baby had the best chance. Having her made no difference. I would've got this illness anyway. You must never think that, ever!'

Nick stuck his hands in his dressing-gown pockets, and sighed heavily. 'I'm sorry, love. I don't know what I'm saying.'

'Go and get some sleep. You look exhausted.' Kate could see the strain he was under. In many ways, it was worse for him than it was for her. She had, after all, made the decision: it was Nick who had to put up with it. 'Sure you'll be all right in there?'

'Yes.' He bent down and kissed her. 'Just tap on the wall if you need anything.'

She smiled up at him. 'Is that a proposition?'

Nick crept into the darkened nursery, looked in on Sarah's cot, saw that she was sleeping peacefully, felt a surge of love conflicting with the anger and bitterness in his heart, and climbed wearily into the narrow bed. He lay there, dead beat but unable to sleep, staring into the darkness.

# Thirteen

It had taken the best part of a day for Maggie to persuade Kate to let Gina take Sarah out in the pram. 'She needs the fresh air, Kate.'

'Yes, but Gina – '

'Gina is a very sensible young woman,' insisted Maggie. 'She may not look it, but she is. Apart from that, she's been wheeling her brothers and sisters and cousins out round the streets of Liverpool since she was barely high enough to see over the end of the pram. She's never lost one yet, Kate.'

'I'm not the only determined woman in this house, am I?'

'No,' smiled Maggie, 'you most certainly are not.'

Gina took Sarah out late that afternoon. Passing Rita's terrace house, she saw her cleaning the inside of her front window. 'Hiya!'

Rita came out for a look at the baby. 'Oh, isn't she a little poppet?'

'Yeah, she's lovely,' beamed Gina. 'And just like her mum.'

'Poor wee thing, lying there all innocent.'

'Oh Rita,' said Gina, her eyes suddenly brimming. 'It's so awful.'

'I know, love, I know.'

After Rita had comforted her, Gina fished out a bunch of coloured tissues and blew her nose. 'Well,' she said, rallying, 'I better get on or I shall be in real trouble.'

'Bye, love.'

Nick sat on the bed, watching Maggie give Kate oxygen. Her pallor, alternating with flushes and sweats, was now virtually translucent. Taking off the oxygen mask, temporarily revived, she turned her head to the window, listening. 'Is that them?' she said anxiously.

There was a faint clack of high heels on the stone slabs of the garden path. Maggie looked out. 'Yes, here they are!'

Kate tried to lever herself up in bed. 'I want to see the baby.'

Nick lifted her as Maggie plumped up the pillows. She felt oddly light in his arms, her skin hot and sticking to her nightdress.

'There we are,' said Maggie.

'Not Gina,' said Kate. 'I'm not up to Gina.'

'Right.' As Maggie bustled out of the room Nick began to sponge Kate's lips and forehead, tenderly moving the damp locks of hair off her face.

'Nick,' said Kate, 'I want to say something.'

'What's that, love?'

'If you remarry – '

'Nick – '

'No, I'm serious.' She took his hand. 'I want you to find someone else. But I want you to remember . . .' She stopped to get her breath.

'Ssh,' he said, 'don't talk so much.'

'No, it's important.' Weak as her body was becoming, there was no doubting her strength of will.

216

'Sarah's your firstborn.' She gripped his hand tightly. 'She must never take second place.'

'She won't, I promise.'

'And you must give her enough love for both of us. Double rations.'

They gazed into each other's eyes. 'Lots and lots of love,' she murmured, laying her head back on the pillows.

Maggie came in with Sarah. 'Here we are, safe and sound!' She eyed Kate and Nick with mock suspicion. 'And what have you two been up to? You're both looking very smug all of a sudden.'

'She's been at it again, Maggie,' smiled Nick. 'Telling me what to do.'

'I should hope so, too.'

Nick leaned towards Kate and ticked off her instructions on his fingers. 'Lots of cuddles and bedtime stories. No smacking, no leaving her to cry. No forcing her to eat things she doesn't like, or do things she doesn't want. Never say no without an explanation . . . Any more?'

'Fresh air and exercise,' prompted Kate.

'Oh yes, that's right, and take her to all our favourite places,' Nick faltered, remembering.

Maggie came to his rescue. 'And when she's older, help her with her homework . . . See, even I know it by now!' said Maggie, pleased to have made Kate smile. 'And with your brains and his looks, how can she possible fail?'

'Excuse me!'

'I beg your pardon!'

Kate held out her arms for the baby. Nick looked

217

to Maggie, wondering whether Kate was strong enough.

'Oh, come on,' said Kate impatiently, 'I won't drop her!'

Nick passed Sarah carefully into Kate's arms and Maggie repositioned the pillows. Kate held her baby, satisfied at last. She smiled lovingly at Nick.

'Right,' said Maggie breezily, knowing they wanted to be alone, 'I'll go and make up some bottles for the night.'

As she was mixing the Cow and Gate in the kitchen, Maggie, overcome by everything at once, suddenly began sobbing uncontrollably.

The light began to fade. Nick sat in the semi-darkness with Kate and the baby. There was a sheen on Kate's skin. She was breathing ever more rapidly to overcome the congestion in her lungs. 'I meant to do so many things,' she said with a sad, reflective smile. 'Have lots of children.'

Nick felt the knife go in, cold as ice.

'Tell her about us, will you?'

'I will.'

'Tell her . . .' She paused, heaving for breath.

'Yes, love?'

'Tell her her mum and dad . . . quite liked each other.'

Her head fell back exhausted into the pillows; their look held, and a tide of love flooded between them. 'Come on,' said Nick, 'you're tired out.' He stood to take Sarah. 'I'll put her in her cot.'

Kate clung on to her baby. 'No. Wait.' She bent

forward with agonising slowness to kiss her. 'Night night darling.'

He lifted Sarah from her arms. 'Back in a minute.'

Kate watched them go. The ones she loved most, moving away from her, into the darkness. She closed her eyes.

When Nick came back from the nursery he found Kate, her face a mask of sweat, in a restless sleep. He sat by her to keep watch, and took hold of her hand. She stirred, moving into delirium. Her eyes opened, vague and unfocused. Her mouth made low, indistinct sounds, trying to speak.

'What was that, love?' he asked quietly.

'Alex . . . Call Alex.'

'Sorry, love?'

'Alex . . . Call Alex Ferrenby . . . I feel terrible . . .'

Her eyes closed again and her face relaxed once more into sleep.

'Kate?' he waited. Her breathing became more regular.

He found Maggie in the living room. 'She's asleep, and so is Sarah. We're all OK now, I think.'

Maggie gave him a long, critical look. 'Are you sure, Nick?'

'As sure as I'll ever be.' He sighed wearily. 'Thanks for staying, Maggie. I'll ring you if I have any problems.'

'OK.' Maggie put her coat on. In the mirror she saw him sink his head in his hands. 'What's the matter?'

'She asked for Alex.'

'Dr Ferrenby?'

Nick tried to smile it off. 'I mean, he died three years ago.'

Maggie nodded, tight-lipped. It was something she had come across before: the dying calling upon the dead, as though there were no difference, no distinction to be made.

She stopped at the door and turned back. 'You need some sleep too, Nick. Get to bed.'

When she had gone, Nick put more coal on the fire and fell back into the sofa, watching the flames and listening to the clock tick away.

After he had run away from Greengrass, David Rendle hid in the woods till it was well and truly dark. He made his way home through the back streets of the village, avoiding the streetlamps and sticking to the shadows until he could see the comforting glow of the curtained light in his mother's front room. Only a few more steps and she'd be giving him his tea and asking him where he'd been all day . . .

Gary stepped out from the entry wall and grabbed David by his duffel coat. 'What you think you're playing at?' He swung him round into the entry. 'You were supposed to meet me an hour ago!' He looked for the jerrycan. 'Where is it?'

'I didn't get any – '

'What?'

'I lost it,' David whimpered. 'I can't get any more, Gary. It's stealing – '

'What you talking about?'

'Mr Greengrass. He caught me. He said it was wrong, he said he'd – '

Gary shook him. 'Never mind what he says. You

220

listen to me. You get me more petrol or I'll tell your mum what you've been doing!'

'Don't tell Mum! She'd kill me! I'll get you some, I promise – '

Gary slammed him against the entry wall. 'You'd better!'

Nick woke with a start. Upstairs, Sarah was crying. He heaved himself up off the sofa, yawned, stretched, looked at the clock: 3 a.m. Oh God . . . He stumbled up the stairs in his stockinged feet. Luckily, Kate hadn't moved.

It took him half an hour to feed and change Sarah and get her off to sleep again. He undressed and went in for another look at Kate.

She had slipped sideways off her pillows. Her hair was matted with sweat and her breathing faint. When he lifted her up, she was floppy and unconscious. He moistened her flannel and wiped her face and neck. She made no move. He looked down on her, and knew there was not long to go.

'Well,' he said in a calm, matter-of-fact voice, 'I'm sick of the spare bed, so if Madam doesn't object, I think I'll sleep in my own bed for a change.' He climbed in beside her. 'Come on. Move over a bit, you're all on my side . . . Well, if you won't budge you'll just have to have a cuddle.' He put his lips gently to her neck. 'I see. I don't get a kiss. Oh well. Night, Kate.' He put out the light, and held her in his arms.

He was still holding her, loving her and mourning her, as dawn lightened the sky.

Something inside him refused to believe it, would not take it in. She couldn't be dead, not Kate, not his Kate, she looked so peaceful, so free from pain.

It was only when Sarah began to cry that the full realisation came. Alone and heartbroken, he stumbled downstairs, his eyes swollen red and painful from the tears that constantly, achingly, welled up from the reservoir of grief inside him. Automatically, he put the kettle on for Sarah's bottle and drew the downstairs curtains shut. He felt impelled to go to the front door and open it, but whether it was to let the warm flood of grief out or the cold chill of reality in, he had no way of knowing. He stood, barefoot and solitary, on the threshold he had carried her over five years before, his eyes red-rimmed, wet, the skin around them bruised violet and mauve from grief and lack of sleep, and stared uncomprehendingly at the world outside.

A few desultory, haphazard snowflakes fell and melted as they touched the ground.

In the midst of his desolation he could not understand why or how the outside world, the world of Aidensfield, the world that he and Kate had loved, could remain so deaf, ignorant and indifferent to his world, the vaults and chasms of dark and empty pain he felt forever opening up inside him. He wanted to howl, storm, scream and rail at it, rouse it from its bleak inertia to share his own appalling loss, even though he knew it would do no good: it would not bring her back. Nothing could.

The flakes continued to fall and melt. From the kitchen, the kettle whistled, calling him back to a life which had changed for ever.

# Fourteen

Kate's funeral took place four days later on a sunny, blustery March day in Aidensfield.

The greystone church was full, every pew packed and more mourners from the village and the moorland farms crowding in to stand at the back. Everybody whose life Kate had touched seemed to wish to pay their last respects. Nick, in uniform, was the last to arrive.

As the undertaker closed the heavy wooden doors behind him, the church fell silent. A few heads turned, and a swell of heartfelt sympathy went out towards him. He made his way down the centre aisle, his head up but his face pale and tense, to the front pew where he sat alone. People noticed that he did not kneel to pray as he took his place, but many, if not all, put this down to the shock of bereavement.

Everyone knew that Kate had chosen the psalm and hymns: the familiar, heart-rendingly beautiful Crimond setting of 'The Lord Is My Shepherd', 'To Be A Pilgrim' and finally, 'Abide With Me'. Wholeheartedly, they joined with the choir and organ, and by the time the last soaring harmonies of the Twenty-Third Psalm died away, every single member of the congregation felt that their hearts were full, united in a grieving love for Kate, and tears filled the eyes and flowed unchecked down the cheeks of men and women alike.

It was not just Nick, the whole community had suffered a great loss, and the outpouring of their sorrow filled the small grey church. During the Lesson from St John XIV, 'In My Father's House Are Many Mansions', a child in arms began to cry. People's thoughts turned as one to baby Sarah, at home with Rita Stirling; until the mother succeeded in stilling her child's piercing wails, the poignancy was all but unbearable.

After the Blessing, the majority of the congregation broke up and filed away from the church, silent and heavy-hearted. Meanwhile, the vicar, a bluff, balding grey-haired man in his late fifties, led the bleak funeral procession of close friends and relations through the churchyard for the Burial Service at the graveside.

As Nick walked along behind the vicar through the blustery sunshine and cloud-shadows racing across the tombs and gravestones, he found himself listening to the tread and crunch of boots and shoes on the gravel and flagstone paths behind him. The vicar's soles and heels, underneath the frayed edge of his windblown cassock, were thick with yellowish clay: Nick supposed he must have already inspected the grave. Part of the job, no doubt.

He looked up at the blue sky, bruised with fast-moving grey cloud. A couple of rooks flew off down the wind, cawing raucously over the silent procession below. The trees were still almost bare, their branches swaying in the gusts of wind. Behind him, a woman was trying to stifle her sobs. He listened; it was almost certainly Kate's Aunt Eileen. He caught a hint of old-fashioned eau-de-cologne, a sharp scent on the damp wind, and concluded she had taken her handkerchief out.

Since Kate's death his senses seemed to have sharpened, become preternaturally acute: he could remember every single detail of the undertaker, the registrar, their faces, clothes, the look and smell of their offices, with intense clarity.

On the emotional front, however, the events of the last four days registered nothing, meant nothing. It was as if part of him had withdrawn in an act of self-protection, and left the rest of him to carry on with a life that had duties and responsibilities, but no centre, no meaning. Today was just another day as far as he was concerned, something to be got through, got over with, finished. Let other people cry and mourn, find whatever emotional comfort or release they could; Nick considered he was already cried out, bone dry, and so far he had found no release whatsoever.

Reaching the graveside, he steeled himself for the final ordeal by recalling what Wally Atkinson, his old sergeant in the Met, had told him on the way to his first serious traffic accident. 'When you go in there, Rowan, you're going in to do a job. As far as the rest of it is concerned, just try and think nothing matters very much, and very little matters at all.' That was it, in a nutshell. Go through the motions, and try to stop anything else getting through.

What Nick failed to realise was that resentment was building up inside him like steam inside a boiler.

The vicar intoned his way through the Burial Service. 'Man that is born of a woman hath but a short time to live, and is full of misery. He cometh up, and is cut down, like a flower . . .'

Nick, stony-faced, let the sonorous phrases roll over him and remained cold and cynical, emotionally inert. How very, very true, vicar. And what a load of rubbish. It seemed to him that this whole grisly thing was set up to make the dead feel guilty for dying, and the living guilty for living. It wasn't a ceremony of love, of being glad for someone's life. It was punitive, the last punch in the gut, designed to make everybody feel worse so they could go to the booze-up afterwards with a clear conscience. It was nothing to do with him and Kate. Nothing at all.

It was as if he had a fist of ice inside him. Life was arbitrary, callous, malignant, and since that was the way it was, he would never allow anything past his guard again. Love made you soft. You became a hopeless emotional sucker, helpless prey for what life had in store, a victim and nothing else.

As the long nights since Kate's death had dragged by, Nick considered he had cauterised his grief and come to see things clearly, exactly as they were. Pitiless. That being the case, it was better to live in a state of contemptuous indifference. If you didn't care, it didn't matter.

He glanced round at the other mourners. Faber and Morrison were there. Great. He'd have a word with them later.

Blaketon. Ventress. Bellamy. All three in their best parade uniforms. Bellamy had tears in his eyes; he'd learn.

People Kate had worked with. Maggie. Gina. Kate's Aunt Eileen: she'd brought her up, so at least she had a right to be there.

Then there was his mother, standing next to Eileen in fluorescent pink lipstick and a big fur hat. That was something else he wasn't particularly looking forward to. She was bound to have something to say; she always had. Outspoken was the word for Ruby Rowan, outspoken, basically good-hearted, but a bit too brassy and flash for North Yorkshire. Already she stuck out like a sore thumb. Oh well, he thought, the whole thing was a bloody farce, so why shouldn't she play a part?

The vicar threw in a handful of earth; it rattled on the shiny coffin lid. He looked up and nodded meaningfully at Nick. Nick returned the look, coolly polite, and did nothing. To throw earth on Kate, he felt, would be like spitting in her face. It was wrong, all wrong. The whole thing was wrong – how could it be his Kate lying in that cold grave?

After an awkward pause, the vicar signalled to the mourners that it was all over. They began to disperse, some of the women sniffing into their handkerchiefs and holding on to their hats, the men with bare heads bowed and hands clasped behind their backs.

Nick remained alone at the graveside, staring down at the earth-spattered coffin. Having withdrawn to a tactful distance while the others departed, the vicar returned to lay a hand on Nick's arm. 'Sometimes life seems so very unfair, Nick, doesn't it?'

'Oh, I don't know, vicar,' said Nick harshly. 'God moves in mysterious ways, and I dare say this is a case in point.' His bright, insulting smile drove the vicar away, as it was meant to.

Down at the far end of the churchyard, sheltering under a dusty-smelling old yew, Greengrass and David Rendle leaned on their spades and watched the small procession file out through the lych-gate into the waiting funeral cars. Even Alfred, lying with his head on his paws, was looking more mournful than usual. David, who had never dug or filled a grave before, was snuffling into a large dirty handkerchief. Greengrass, wearing a black armband gone greenish with age, cuffed him round the back of the head. 'Shurrup, will you. Show a bit of respect.'

'I don't know whether I can do this, Mr Greengrass – '

'If I can, you can,' said Greengrass. Then, more sympathetically, 'Come on, lad, nobody said it were easy, but it's got to be done.'

Blaketon and Ventress were overseeing the mourners into the funeral cars. Kate's Aunt Eileen turned back for a last look at the grave. Seeing Nick's lone figure standing there, she began to weep. Ruby Rowan put her arm round her and lent her a handkerchief. 'Come on Eileen girl, what's done is done.' Eileen, still weeping, allowed herself to be helped into the car.

Blaketon stepped out into the road to make sure it was clear, and waved the first car forward. 'Drive on.' The undertaker hesitated, looking back at Nick. 'One of us will bring him along later,' said Blaketon. The gleaming black Austin Princesses slid away in convoy.

'I'll wait for him, sarge,' offered Ventress.

'Right.' Blaketon strode over to Bellamy, who was standing by the Anglia, sniffing and wiping his eyes. 'Get a grip, Bellamy. Remember you're in uniform.'

Nick took a single iris from his wreath and let it fall on to the coffin. It seemed more appropriate than earth – Kate had always loved irises. He stood for a moment, head bent, feeling nothing but anger and loss, then slowly walked away.

Ventress opened the gate for him. 'Would you like to go home for a bit first, before the wake?'

Nick glanced sideways at Ventress. 'Sorry?'

'Go home and see the baby. It might make you feel a bit better.'

'I doubt it,' said Nick coldly. 'Anyway, Rita's with her.'

He set off up the road, away from the village. Hearing Ventress coming after him, he turned round. 'You go on, Alf. Don't miss the bunfight on my account.'

Ventress watched him go, striding off into the wind. He could quite see why Nick wanted to be on his own. On the other hand, he couldn't let him ignore everybody and not turn up at the wake: duty was duty, even at a funeral. He waited until Nick went out of sight round the top bend, then set off after him.

Greengrass, with Alfred, went to scout round the churchyard to make sure everybody had left before he started work. When he came back for the spades, David had gone. 'David?' He looked round the other side of the yew. 'David! Where the flaming hell are you!' He stomped off to the church, looked inside, round the back. No sign of the little blighter. Hellfire. The lad might be a bit thick in the clear, but he wasn't that dumb, was he?

He picked up his spade and contemplated the pile of heavy, stony, yellowish clay. Now he'd have to shift the whole lot singlehanded. He dug his spade into the base of the pile, grumbling to Alfred. 'You bend over backwards to help someone, open up life's opportunities for them . . . and they flaming well scarper! First sign of hard work, they scarper – '

Spade loaded, he looked down into the grave and saw the iris that Nick had placed on the coffin. It stopped him in his tracks. It was all too much, all too bloody much. It was Kate Rowan lying down there. A young woman and a mother. He closed his eyes, and asked her forgiveness. With tears in his eyes he dug away like mad until the top of the coffin was covered and there was no longer that sickening bone-like rattle.

After that, it was easier. He blew his nose hard on his grubby handkerchief.

Nick had taken the narrow high-walled lane behind the back of the churchyard. It twisted and turned here and there, so Ventress was able to keep an occasional eye on him. As far as Ventress could recall, it came out somewhere between the pub and the Police House. He decided he would wait till Nick had walked it off a bit and then catch up with him, see how he was, and get him round to the Aidensfield Arms.

Halfway down the lane, Nick saw a figure in a

fawn duffel coat shambling awkwardly towards him carrying a petrol can. Nick's first thought was that some poor bloke had run out of petrol. Then he saw the length of blue plastic hose. 'Hey, you!'

David Rendle turned and legged it. That was enough for Nick. Resentment flaring into overpowering rage, he tore after him. David, scared to death and encumbered with the can and hose, found himself rugby-tackled to the ground, can and hose flying.

'Right, David Rendle!'

'No, you're hurting!'

Nick hauled him to his feet and slammed him furiously against the wall. 'So it's you, is it?'

'No!'

Nick twisted his arm up behind him. 'You're the little thief!'

'No, please!'

'You're the one's been nicking petrol!'

'Don't – ow!'

Nick dragged him round and made him look at the can and hose. 'What's all this then?'

'Ow! Me arm! Let go!'

'It's you, isn't it?'

Ventress turned the corner to see Nick yelling and shouting at the top of his voice, thumping David repeatedly against the wall. 'You! Prowling about at night! Getting me out when my wife was dying!'

'No! It wasn't me!' David sank to the ground, covering his head with his arms.

'You dirty little liar!' Nick was about to put the boot in when Ventress threw himself between them and pinned Nick against the wall, one arm each side of him. 'That's enough, Nick!'

David rolled up into a ball, shuddering and blubbing. 'No, don't! Don't send me to prison! Please don't send me to prison!'

Ventress, his hands full with a struggling Nick, shouted at David. 'Get up lad! On your feet!'

'Leave go of me, Alf!'

'No bloody fear!' Ventress hung on to Nick and roared at David, 'Hop it! Go on! Off!'

David scrambled up and lumbered off, half-limping, heaving himself into a run. Nick broke free of Ventress's grip, breathing hard, beside himself with anger. 'What the hell d'you think you're playing at, Alf? I was about to make an arrest – '

'Is that what you call it?' Calmly, Ventress picked up the can and hose. 'You know who he is?'

'Course I bloody do – '

'Well, it'll keep then, won't it?' Ventress brushed the dirt and wet leaves off Nick's uniform, and then his own. 'Come on, Nick lad,' he said quietly. 'Let's get to the wake, shall we?'

The sign on the door of the Aidensfield Arms read CLOSED FOR PRIVATE FUNCTION. Inside, people stood around in their own small groups, surreptitiously eyeing each other and the spread of food laid out on two cloth-covered trestle tables along one side of the room.

Pride of place went to a magnificent York ham, ordered and cooked to Kate's specifications. Around it were piles of sandwiches, plates of bread and butter, dishes of beetroot, bowls of onion rings, beer mugs of celery, a trifle, rock cakes, sponge and fruit cakes. Lined up along the bar were serried ranks of cups and saucers, and several trays of filled port and sherry glasses.

Ruby Rowan, in gold earrings, matching necklace and a black, frilly-collared silk dress which she thought showed a suitably modest amount of cleavage, decided it was time to start breaking the ice. She took Kate's Aunt Eileen by the elbow and piloted her towards Blaketon and Bellamy. 'We can't wait for Nick for ever, Eileen, nobody'll ever get anything to eat. I've been up since five o'clock this morning, and all I've had is a cup of British Rail tea. You're the senior relative, so go on, ask him.'

'I can't just walk up – '

'Can't you? I can.'

'Who's that, Bellamy?'

'No idea, sarge.'

Blaketon watched Ruby approach. Forty-seven if she was a day, he thought, and coming to a funeral half-naked.

'That was a very nice gesture, boys, wearing your uniforms,' said Ruby, patting her permed blonde hair. A waft of Blue Grass enveloped Blaketon and Bellamy. 'This is Nick's Aunty Eileen.' Abruptly, seeing a tray of port passing by, Ruby veered off after another glass.

'I was wondering if you knew where Nick was,' said Eileen.

The same thought had occurred to Blaketon: Ventress should have been able to get him here by now. 'He'll be along in a moment, ma'am, he's getting a lift with one of my other officers.'

'Oh, I see,' said Eileen, relieved. 'In that case, I

wonder if you'd care to start carving for us, Sergeant Blaketon.'

'My pleasure,' said Blaketon, gratified. He prided himself on his carving skills and it was a long time since he'd had the chance of exercising them on a whole ham.

Ruby found herself standing next to Maggie and the vicar. 'The Lord giveth and the Lord taketh away, Mrs Rowan.'

Ruby gave him a sharp, glittery-eyed look. 'Well, He's taken away a bit too much this time if you ask me,' she said tartly, turning away to speak to Maggie. 'I shall have to get meself some ham, love. I've already had one port and if I don't get something to eat soon I shall fall over.'

Maggie watched her go. 'Well, I knew she'd be upset, but . . .'

'Like mother, like son,' commented the vicar dourly, remembering Nick's comments at the graveside.

Blaketon ran the carving knife expertly up and down the steel, sharpening it to his satisfaction. 'It's a good spread, George. That I will say.'

'All done by the WI,' said George. 'On Kate's instructions.'

'Kate?' said Blaketon, surprised.

'Oh aye. She left lists for everything, with Maggie. Who to invite, what the menu was to be. She even ordered this ham.'

'Well, I never.'

'She thought it'd make it easier for Nick.'

Blaketon nodded reflectively. 'It's time he was here, George,' he said quietly.

'I know,' muttered George.

Ruby pushed her way forward and held a plate out under Blaketon's nose. 'I'd better try and force a bit down.' Blaketon gave her a disapproving stare: according to his way of thinking, the rule was that the family of the bereaved should be served first. His disapproval bounced straight off Ruby. She leaned forward confidentially. 'You must be Alf Ventress.'

'The name is Blaketon, madam,' he said icily.

Ruby put a hand to her bosom. '*Sergeant* Blaketon? Never! I mean, you're quite nice-looking! Nothing at all like Nick said in his letters.' She held out her be-ringed hand. 'I'm his mother, by the way. Ruby Rowan.'

Blaketon's mouth fell open in astonishment.

'Oh look!' said Ruby. 'Here he is now!'

Nick, his face set, entered with Ventress. People stood back to let him pass, unsure what to say. Maggie, seeing his tense expression, moved quickly to him. 'Everybody's here,' she said, giving him a hug. 'Just as she wanted.'

'Good,' said Nick woodenly.

'Fancy a cuppa, Nick?' said Bellamy.

'No thanks.' Nick's gaze roved over the groups of people, and lighted on his mother trying to balance her glass of port on her plate of ham. His face remained expressionless.

Ventress made his way to Blaketon's side. 'Sorry about that, sarge. Took longer than I thought.'

Blaketon didn't take his eye off Nick. 'He's going to need a close watch, Ventress.'

'You're telling me. I've already had one bit of a do

with him.' Ventress lowered his voice. 'He doesn't seem that keen on the baby either, sarge.'

Blaketon shot Ventress a sharp, appraising glance. 'Right,' he said, 'just give me a minute with this ham.'

Greengrass cleaned up round the edges of the grave and set a jam jar full of snowdrops at its foot. Alfred, having waited patiently, began to whine anxiously, circling Greengrass, his ears cocked, waiting. 'What is it, boy? Where?'

Alfred bounded off in the direction of the old yew. Greengrass shouldered his spade and followed. Behind the tree, slumped in a heap against it was David, snivelling and blubbing heartbrokenly, his head between his knees. Seeing Greengrass, he threw himself at his feet, and clutched him round the legs. 'Save me, Mr Greengrass, save me! Don't let them send me to prison!'

'Go on, Ventress,' said Blaketon, carving.

Ventress kept his eye on Nick and his voice down. 'He went bananas, sarge. Absolutely bananas. I mean, the lad's not all there, can't read or write apparently, but Nick really went for him.'

Blaketon laid a slice of ham on old Joseph Walker's plate, and considered what Ventress had told him. 'All the same,' he said judiciously, 'the lad was carrying a petrol can and siphon.'

'It was still no way to treat him,' insisted Ventress. 'Shouting and banging him against the wall. I've never seen Nick lose his temper like that before.'

'No.' Blaketon looked up. Across the room, Gina and a couple of village girls were taking round trays of port, sherry and fruit cake. He saw Ruby take a port for herself and a sherry for Nick. 'We can't say anything here,' said Blaketon. 'Not yet, anyway. Let his mother have a word with him, see what happens. Meanwhile, you keep an eye on him.'

'Right, sarge.'

'Here you are,' said Ruby. 'Get that down you, lovie. Come on, you haven't had a thing yet.' Nick downed the sherry in one, and reluctantly let his mother steer him to a table. 'Now then, sit down a minute. I want a serious little chat.' She plonked herself down opposite him. 'About the baby.'

Nick turned his head away. 'Mum,' he said dully. 'Not yet.'

She pulled at his arm, treating him like a recalcitrant child, determined to get his full attention. 'Listen to me now. It's got to be decided. You won't be able to cope, not on your own, and Kate had no family to speak of apart from her Aunty Eileen and she's all alone, no relations to help out, so it's down to us, our family, isn't it?'

Well as he knew his mother and her ways – always first to get her oar in, always in a rush to get things sorted – he couldn't believe it. Kate was hardly in her grave, and here was his mother, his own mother, preparing to tear what was left of his life apart, and telling him it was all cut and dried.

'I've talked with your Aunty Lil, and she said she'll give me a hand, she's only just round the corner, so all that's settled. I could take her back to London with me.'

Nick stared at her. 'Take who, Mum?'

'The baby. Sarah.' Ruby sank her port. 'So what d'you say?'

Nick knew he had to get away from her. He scraped his chair back. 'I'll think about it, Mum.'

After that, Ventress noted as he followed him around, Nick kept away from family and people he knew well, preferring to speak, when he spoke at all, to acquaintances from the village or Kate's colleagues from work. It was a depressing business all round, decided Ventress, and got stuck into the sherry.

Ruby was on her fourth port when she cornered Eileen. She looked round the room to make sure she was not being overheard. 'Look, Eileen,' she said, waving her glass about, 'there's something I want to tell you. It's only right you should hear it from me, and I want to know what you think.'

'Go on, then.'

'I've offered to have the baby.' She looked at Eileen combatively. 'Well, it's the only solution, isn't it?'

Eileen sipped her tea and smiled politely. 'It's a solution, yes. But perhaps not the only one.'

# Fifteen

After he had dragged David's story out of him, it took Greengrass less than half an hour to track down Gary and his Jag. He'd parked the car off the road, outside a disused lock-up. Greengrass waited, spade in hand, until Gary turned his back against the wind to light up a Guards. In three strides Greengrass was on him, pinning him against the car, spade at his throat. 'Out!'

'What?' The shiny steel edge pressed into Gary's windpipe.

'You heard! I want you out of here! Now! Before this spade and your motor have a serious accident!'

'What you talking about?'

'I'll show you what I'm talking about!' Greengrass reached a meaty red fist down and grabbed hold of the wing mirror.

'No!' Gary struggled in panic. 'Leave it alone!'

Greengrass twisted and snapped it clean off. 'Now then,' he grunted, 'I'm giving you five minutes to get your stuff together and clear off!'

'Now look here – '

Greengrass leaned his weight on Gary's chest, and kept the spade at his throat. 'Five minutes, or you'll lose your other mirror. And there'll be flaming great dents in *your* bodywork, let alone your motor's.'

Gary looked wildly over Greengrass's shoulder. A jerk of the spade deterred him from shouting for help.

'No one's going to help you, Gary Knight. Because you're a bully and a thief.' Greengrass lowered his spade a couple of inches. 'I'm timing you from now. Five minutes.'

Gary gulped, rubbed his throat. 'I've not got any petrol – '

'Go and buy some then.'

'I'm skint – '

'Skint?' jeered Greengrass. 'The famous business-man from Leeds, skint! Well, you do surprise me!' The spade came swiftly back at Gary's throat. 'There is no business, is there, Gary?' said Greengrass, taunting him. 'You're just a bigmouth, aren't you? A bigmouth with nowt except a damn silly car you can't afford to run! Aren't you? Answer me!'

'Yeah,' said Gary brokenly.

Greengrass took the spade away, satisfied. His tone became threateningly friendly. 'Out of petrol, are we? Well, nobody's looking, lad. There's a funeral on and cars all over the shop. I'm sure a bright spark like you will think of summat.'

Nick downed his sherry. It was only his second, but on top of the emotion of the funeral, the adrenalin of the chase and the fact that he had had nothing to eat, it was enough to make him feel oddly light-headed. He saw Maggie talking to Faber and Morrison near the door. It looked as if they were about to leave. What the hell, he thought, it was time to say what he felt, time to put *them* on the spot. He walked over feeling dangerously invulnerable, looking forward to getting some real answers at last, and tapped Faber familiarly on the shoulder. 'Well, well, well. The medical profession.'

Maggie sensed his mood immediately. 'Don't Nick – '

He ignored her. 'May I put a question to you, as doctors?'

Faber concealed his unease well. 'Of course.'

'May I ask how it happened?' He dropped the politeness, his tone hardening with every word. 'How my wife managed to get through a whole pregnancy with leukaemia and nobody noticed?'

'Look – '

'I am looking, Mr Faber, and it looks like medical negligence to me.'

'Oh come on, Nick,' said Maggie. Now she was siding with them. The medical profession sticking together, as usual.

'No,' said Faber, 'I understand how he feels – '

'I doubt it, Mr Faber!' Nick's resentment burst into bitter anger. He knew he was going over the top, knew people were turning to look, but he didn't care. It was time Faber and Morrison knew what they'd done to him. Time everybody did. 'I watched her die!' His voice was harsh with accusation. 'I lay with her as she died. And all through the night do you know what I thought? That this needn't have happened. She must've been ill for ages – '

Maggie tried to placate him. 'Look – '

He brushed her aside. 'If you'd spotted it, any of you, you could've treated it earlier – '

Maggie took hold of his arm, trying to draw him away. 'Let me try and explain –'

'I don't need explanations!' He threw her hand off, glaring at her. 'You're as much to blame as they are!'

Maggie looked at him, eyes blazing. How could he say a thing like that? How *dare* he? Taking a breath to hang on to her self-control, she opened the door. 'Come outside a minute,' she said in a firm, quiet voice. When Nick hesitated, she more or less shoved him through it.

As soon as they were out in the car park, she rounded on him angrily. 'You're quite wrong! We all did our best.'

'Oh yes,' said Nick scornfully. 'When it was too late.'

'Because we didn't *know*!'

'Well, you damn well should have!'

'How could we?' Maggie wondered how much he knew, how much Kate had told him. Well, there was no point in concealing anything now. The state Nick was in, only the truth would help, hard as it was. 'She hid the symptoms from us.'

Nick looked at her, bemused. 'Hid what symptoms?'

'Look, Nick,' she said patiently. 'I don't know how much you know, but early on in the pregnancy the hospital did a blood test. She was anaemic and she told them she'd treat it herself. I made her have another test at thirty-six weeks because she looked so awful.' She paused, waiting for his reaction. When there was none, she decided to come right out with it. 'She sent that one off under another name and kept the results to herself until she was about to have the baby. She didn't tell me, she didn't tell you, she didn't tell anyone. Not until she was actually in labour. Even after that it wasn't too late. If she'd been stronger – '

Nick looked at her, too choked to speak.

'She did it for Sarah, Nick. You've got to see that. To give her the best chance.'

Nick's anger welled up again. 'You should have seen what she was up to. You and the doctors. You're supposed to be the experts.'

Maggie sighed. There was no shaking him, no point in talking to him. If he didn't understand now he never would. He didn't want to understand, that was the problem. He wanted somebody to blame.

She turned on her heel and walked back to the pub. At the door, relenting, she turned and said, 'And you should wise up and realise what a fantastic thing she did.'

After she had gone, Nick paced the car park, hands deep in his pockets, hoping the cold wind would clear his head. He tried to make sense of what Maggie had told him. According to her, Kate had deliberately sacrificed herself for her baby. Well, he could see that, he knew that. Kate had told him. He could even see why she had kept her symptoms secret and avoided treatment for the baby's sake. What he could not see, and probably never would, was how she had hidden it from everybody for so long. Was mother-love such a desperate, powerful, all-consuming force?

Maybe Maggie was right, and it was a fantastic thing that Kate had done. Chastened but unconsoled, Nick went back into the wake.

★

243

After sending Gary on his way with a graphic description of what would happen if he dared show his face in Aidensfield again, Greengrass tidied himself up and made his way to the pub.

By the time he arrived, things had begun to liven up. The port and sherry had run out, but bottles of whisky and gin had mysteriously appeared. Seeing Nick standing alone, Greengrass smoothed down his hair and went over to stand beside him. He nodded awkwardly in commiseration, and Nick nodded back. Neither said a word, then Greengrass impulsively clapped an arm round Nick's shoulders. He stood a moment longer, to show respect, and then took himself off in search of George and a much-needed double Scotch.

Nick watched impassively. The anger had receded, more or less. From now on, he was simply waiting for it all to be over. He had eaten some ham, because Kate would have wanted him to, and now he found himself storing up details to tell her later on, in the long night that lay ahead, as he saw it, for the rest of his life.

Ventress, awash with a mixture of sherry, Scotch and mawkish emotion, was climbing unsteadily on to a chair. His tie was loose and his collar undone. He had a bottle in one hand, a glass in the other. Clinking one against the other, he said, or rather slurred, 'Ladies and gentlemen!'

Blaketon, trapped behind the ham, looked on, appalled. 'Bellamy! What does he think he's doing?'

Bellamy's eyes swivelled blearily from Blaketon to Ventress and back. The effort of such concentration seemed to have exhausted him; all he could do was shrug.

'A toast,' said Ventress, swaying but determined. 'A toast to the lady who planned this whole do for us. Kate Rowan!'

It took a moment for the surprise to sink in; then there were murmurs of appreciation, even a few cheers. Everyone began to raise their glasses and look at Ventress expectantly for the rest of the speech. He caught Blaketon's eye, and when he saw him warningly closing his eyes and shaking his head, he completely lost his drift, but knew he had to stumble on somehow. 'She were a grand doctor . . .'

'Hear hear!' accompanied by cheers.

'And a lovely girl . . .' More cheers. 'And a damn fine policeman's wife . . . Which is an art given to but a few . . .' The laughter that greeted this left him groping for an appropriate finish. 'And to Nick . . .'

The crowd suddenly fell silent. So did Ventress. Luckily, Bellamy came to the rescue. 'To Kate!'

'Kate!'

'Kate Rowan!'

As everyone raised their glasses and drank to Kate, Ventress clambered off his chair and began to mop his brow, looking distinctly dazed and unsteady. 'Get him out of here!' hissed Blaketon.

'Right, sarge,' replied Bellamy.

Nick glanced at his watch. Five to three. Enough was enough. He made his way to the door. Blaketon, noting his blank-faced expression, decided it was time to have a word with him. As he followed Nick, he heard Gina calling out: 'Masses more grub, everybody! Help yourselves!'

Blaketon took a lungful of fresh air, and quickened his step to catch up with Nick. 'Let's go and see that baby of yours shall we, Rowan?' Nick showed no sign of having heard. They walked across the car park in silence.

The undertaker was trying to start the first funeral car; his chief pallbearer was trying to start the second. Neither was succeeding. Blaketon and Nick walked past without comment.

Blaketon waited in the living-room while Nick showed Rita out. He could tell from the sound of her voice how anxious she was, how uncertain Nick's polite lack of interest made her feel.

'Are you sure you'll be all right now, Mr Rowan?'

'Yes thank you, Rita.'

'She's been fine, bless her.'

'Good.'

'I'll be round in the morning.'

'Thank you, Rita.'

'The made-up bottles are all ready in the fridge.'

'Thank you.'

'I'll be round in the morning then,' said Rita again, unwilling to leave but unable to think of an excuse to stay.

'Thank you.' Nick closed the door on her.

He came back into the living-room and faced Blaketon squarely, willing him to say his piece and get out. 'I want you to know, Rowan,' said Blaketon, undeterred, 'that the Force stands by its men in time of trouble.'

'Thanks,' said Nick coldly.

It wasn't hostility, Blaketon decided, it was just a

wall of blank, bloody-minded indifference. The gates, opened briefly by his outburst to the doctors, had clanged well and truly shut again. Blaketon pressed on, hoping for some kind of reaction. Positive or negative didn't matter; anything was better than this blank wall. 'You'll have big decisions to make, about the baby and so on. The Force knows that, we all do. Just take your time, lad, don't let anybody push you, you're the one that's got to decide what's best for you and the baby, no need to rush into anything . . .'

Blaketon let his voice trail off, conceding defeat. It was hopeless. Nick wasn't even listening. Best leave him in peace, or at least alone with his thoughts. 'I'll be off then.'

Without a word, Nick moved to the door and opened it. Blaketon hesitated at the pram, seeking Nick's permission for a farewell look at the baby. Nick made no move one way or the other. Blaketon peered into the pram. The sight of Sarah, her dark blue eyes wide open and innocently uncomprehending, brought him close to tears. Even he, no great judge of babies, could see a devastating resemblance to Kate.

Nick waited stonily for Blaketon to recover. He moved away from the pram, and nodded his appreciation to Nick. 'Very nice,' he said stiffly. 'Very much like her mother.'

Nick's only reaction was to open the door a couple of inches wider. Blaketon strode over, hesitated, and said in a voice gruff with emotion, 'I'm that sorry, lad. I'm that sorry.'

After he had gone, Nick wandered from room to

room. Rita, as he expected, had left everything immaculately neat and tidy, but it was the tidiness of another hand, and it made the place look dead.

In the bedroom, the bed had been remade flat and tight, with hospital corners. He turned down the counterpane. Clean, starched, fresh-smelling sheets. And one pillow, placed dead centre. He felt burgled by kindness. Even the Valentino 'Son of the Sheikh' poster over the chest of drawers had been dusted and polished. So had Kate's dressing-table.

*Where were her things?*

In a hot, growing panic, he opened and shut one dressing-table drawer after another. No make-up, no perfume, no brush and comb, no books, no writing pad, no clutter of 'Get Well' cards. Not a hairpin or a sixpence in any of the drawers. Kate's life, cleared out.

Frantically heaving open the clothes cupboard door, he found that Kate's clothes were still there. He buried his face in her sheepskin coat and breathed in her smell. At least he still had that . . .

The panicky feeling began to subside. Surely Rita would not have thrown away Kate's things without asking? He looked on the top shelf of the clothes cupboard. Shoeboxes and hatboxes, tidied and piled. Nothing else.

He found them in the top right-hand drawer of the chest under the Valentino poster, neatly set out on a sheet of tissue paper covering Kate's underwear. Nick found himself smiling at Rita's sense of propriety. As he sorted through them, an envelope fell out of the writing pad. It was sealed, and addressed *Dearest Nick.*

248

He stood for a while, holding it to his face, breathing in its faint perfume in the slanting afternoon light, not wanting to open it, dreading the flood of emotion he knew it would unleash.

Come on, Rowan, he told himself, she wouldn't have written it if she thought you weren't going to read it. He unstuck the envelope carefully, trying not to tear it.

*Dearest Nick,*

*I know you'll find this sooner or later. Don't worry, my love, this isn't another boring household list, or another lot of nagging instructions about what to do with Sarah or how to bring her up. I've said all that.*

*This is for you, Nick. To say how happy you've made me, to remind you how much love we've shared, good times and bad, to say how lucky we were, to say 'no regrets'. To tell you how much I love you, how much I've always loved you, and how I'll go on loving you, for as long as you think of me, dream of me, remember me, or go for walks in the places we went together – I'll always be there for you my love—*

Nick stopped reading, unable to see her writing any more.

After helping to clear up after the wake, Maggie and Kate's Aunt Eileen found themselves caught in a blustery March shower. They hurried through the village; nearly all the curtains were drawn, and the streets empty.

'One thing I have to know, Maggie,' said Eileen. 'Did she suffer much?'

'Not physically,' said Maggie tactfully. Even though Eileen was a sensible and kindly woman, there was only so much people could bear. 'But she was terribly sad. Especially about the baby.'

Eileen reached for Maggie's arm, too upset to speak. They crossed the green in front of the Police House and looked up at its drawn curtains.

'How about Nick?' asked Eileen. 'How does he feel about the baby?'

Maggie hesitated. 'I'm not sure.' She knocked on the door of the Police House. There was no answer.

Maggie and Eileen let themselves in and stood in the hall, shaking off the rain. 'Nick?' called Maggie. 'Nick, are you there?'

No reply. They looked at each other, and moved into the living-room. Eileen went straight to the pram. The blankets had been pulled back and the pram was empty.

Maggie ran up the stairs, alarmed. She looked in the nursery, then in the bedroom. The top right-hand drawer of the chest of drawers gaped open, but there was no sign of Nick or the baby anywhere.

In the days that had passed since Nick and Kate had had their picnic at Clouds End bridge, the willow catkins had come out. Nick parked the Triumph Herald and took Sarah out of her carrycot. Wrapped up in blankets, with a white shawl round her sleeping face, she looked so calm, so innocent – and yet –

Nick's thoughts were in turmoil. The shock of Kate's letter had broken through the barrier of indifference and left him full of pain and grief and confusion, desperate to find a way out – any way out.

250

He stepped out of the car, bundled the baby inside his greatcoat and set off for the bridge. Phrases from the letter flitted through the chaos of his mind as he stumbled across the short wet grass.

'How happy you've made me . . . How much love . . . How lucky . . . No regrets . . .'

A fallen branch lay in his path. He kicked it savagely aside. No regrets? For all that love ripped apart, broken, wasted? Kate might have felt that, he couldn't: there was something at fault somewhere, tearing him asunder, filling him full of bitterness and resentment. He walked past the old log where they had sat, having their last picnic.

Why did she have to die? Where was the sense? Who was to blame?

Images of the funeral flickered through his mind. The vicar. The doctors. Maggie. His mother. All thinking they were trying to help. How could they? They were all part of it –

A terrible thought forced its way to the surface of his mind. If Kate had not had the baby, they could still be together. That was what he had wanted, all he still wanted, for him and Kate to be together. He didn't want the baby, he wanted Kate back. It was all the baby's fault.

His footsteps rang out hollow on the small iron bridge. Clutching the baby in his arms, he walked out into the middle and looked down into the dark, fast-flowing stream.

Now –

He felt Sarah shift inside his greatcoat, woken by the sound of the rain-swollen stream. Automatically,

251

he looked down at her – and for the first time, the face he saw was Kate's.

Everybody, from Gina to Blaketon, had said how much she looked like Kate; but Nick, ravaged with grief and anger, had not been able to see it until now. He felt his heart turn over inside him, and shuddered at how close he had come to the madness of grief. He moved back from the rail, back from the abyss.

There, looking up at him, were Kate's eyes. It was like the sun coming out: Kate hadn't gone away altogether. Part of her was still there, with him, not just in his heart, but in his arms. He gazed intently at the small face nestling inside his coat and thought how much she looked like her mother. Smiling, he bent his head, and whispered against her cheek. 'Hello.' Closing his eyes with relief, he nuzzled her soft, sweet-smelling skin. 'Hello, Katie Rowan.'

From now on, that was what she would always be to him.

On his way back to the car, he picked a few catkin-laden willow branches, wanting to take a little of the day back with him. He settled Katie back in her carrycot and took out the letter again, smoothing it out tenderly. Reading it now brought him peace rather than turmoil.

*I'll always be there for you, my love, wherever you are. You're the love of my life, I want you to know that, and I want you to know that, whatever happens, you've made everything worthwhile for me, my love.*

*Kiss our daughter for me.*

*Forever yours,*

*Kate*